AMETHYST & ONYX

THE BINDING STONES #1

KATE ZENIK

F&I

ISBN: 978-1-68046-456-6

Fire & Ice Young Adult Books
An Imprint of Melange Books, LLC
White Bear Lake, MN 55110
www.fireandiceya.com

Published in the United States of America.

Cover Design by Lynsee Lauritsen

BOOK ONE

AMETHYST

CHAPTER 1

HALLOWEEN

"I need to tell you about the Sagestone fire," he says, his voice rasping like each word is being scraped out of him. "I need you to know how this started."

My eyelids are too heavy to open. I try, but it's like two thumbs are resting on top of them, holding them down. I can't do anything but lie there and watch the hallway of the old high school emerge from the fog in my mind's eye. It surrounds me, makes me feel like I'm standing there, two months ago, exactly. I shiver when he tells me Keir chose the place because he knew it'd be empty and he knew how to get in.

"The boy, Matthew Townsend," he goes on, "was dead when I got there."

Every word adds a brushstroke to the scene until his vision is as clear as my own memory. It's the spell that's doing it. I can feel it crouching in the back of my brain like a gargoyle, watching the vision unfold while I'm powerless to do anything to stop it, change it, making it *real*.

I can see the hallway of the old school, everything washed in the grey darkness of nighttime. His feet, *my feet*, send echoes circling off the walls as I follow the faint smell of smoke down the hall. When I stop outside of French room 2B, my hands reach out and open the door.

The fire Keir started is on the floor, singeing the slip-resistant linoleum in the middle of a black casting circle and throwing his long shadow against the wall. Desks sit clustered around it. Matthew's body is slung across the long table in the corner. Seeing him there, so rigid and still, makes my throat close until I almost can't breathe.

The door shuts behind me, drawing Keir's attention away from the embers.

What took you so long? he says, as he snatches a knife off the floor and tosses it at me, hilt first. My hands barely manage to snag the handle.

Get his blood, Keir tells me, sliding a ceramic bowl across the floor until it knocks into my shoe. *We'll do you first.*

My body draws near to Matthew, and I want so badly to open my eyes, break through this nightmare. I watch my hand guide the knife to Matthew's grey-blue skin and split it with a thin line. There are fingerprint-shaped bruises darkening along his neck.

"Keir strangled him before I got there," I hear him say through the vision. "Just before."

He's dead, but Matthew's eyes don't seem vacant yet, like some part of him is digging his nails in, refusing to be torn out.

The ceramic bowl in my hands catches the blood that flows down Matthew's elbow.

His voice shakes when he says, "Lifeblood had to come from an artery. Keir taught me that. The heart was best, but I just couldn't put the knife between Matthew's ribs, dead or not."

My hands hold out the bowl to Keir and he takes it, mixing a fistful of ashes into it, something like pigment powder. He holds the mixture over the fire, speaking in guttural words that don't sound like any language I've heard before. The darkness deepens in the room, as if it's being called, clustering in the corners like silent observers.

Keir digs in his backpack and pulls out a pen, just a regular ball-point that's been emptied of its ink, but it has a needle on its end. I sit in front of him, horrified, as I gather my shirt up to the back of my neck. Keir goes to work, dipping into the rust-colored paste and piercing a stinging pattern into my back.

"I knew how wrong it was," he says. "I knew I was breaking a part of myself that I'd never fix again. It's hard to explain. Each puncture kind of felt like it was filling me. Like all my life I'd been half empty, you know? I couldn't keep going like that. I'd rather be someone else and let this other side take over than deal with being an unfinished person. I never really thought of stopping. Not even once."

In the room, Keir works the makeshift needle down to my lower back.

Almost done, Keir says, his voice strained with the effort of keeping his hand steady. *The last mark is tricky.*

As soon as he's done saying it, the fire in the middle of the room bursts like a mushroom cloud, stretching up in fury up to the speckled white ceiling. The mineral fiber tiles take up the flames like gasoline, and the whole room loses its breath and starts to choke.

"I knew it was Matthew," he says, "driving the fire with all the hatred and anger for us that was too strong to move on, leave the place where his life had been stolen."

The pen drops from Keir's hand, skittering across the floor. We're both on our feet, running for the door. The handle is jammed, swollen with the heat. We try the windows, but the metal burns our hands.

"Matthew trapped us," he says. "His final revenge."

I grab a chair and break it across a window, chipping out a hole in the glass the size of a dime. It takes six more tries to smash a gap big enough to fit us. I scrape my body through as shards tear at my skin. When I'm almost out, still hanging onto the windowsill, I turn back to help Keir, but he's not behind me. He's running to the body, refusing to leave it.

As soon as Keir touches Matthew's skin, the fire retaliates, eating up every molecule of air left in the room before exploding out the windows. Heat surges into my nose and mouth, burning down my throat, as I hurl myself to the grass outside. After that, I drag my body across the parking lot, collapsing behind an electrical box.

"Sagestone High," he tells me, "was gone before the fire trucks even got there. I didn't think there was any way Keir could've gotten out. All the evidence was wiped away by the fire. I thought it was some kind of gift. A second chance, almost. I walked away after that. To this day, I've never once looked at the tattoos on my back."

That's what he says, anyway. I feel the spell losing its hold on me. My vision clears, like a gentle wind sweeping the fog away, and I open my eyes.

It's just me now, in my own body, still stuck in my hospital bed, and him in the chair beside me. He leans forward, pressing the heels of his hands into his eyes like it hurts him too much to see me.

Something's just been lost between us. I can feel our innocence draining from the room, a dark weight settling in its place.

"If you'd told me one day ago," I say to him, "we might have been able to save you."

Two Months Earlier

"I hate this day," my younger sister Charlotte says, slamming the passenger side door. Her green eyes glower at me amidst several layers of eyeliner, flecks of emerald set in coal. The littered floor of my car rattles against our feet as we wait for our brother and sister to come outside.

"You're fantastic in the morning," I say, patting Charlotte on the head.

She swats me hard.

"Everything is going to be different," she huffs. "They didn't ask us if we wanted to mingle with all of Sagestone's rejects."

"They aren't rejects, they're relief students. They had to go to school somewhere." I run my thumbs over the peeling beige leather on the steering wheel, unable to quiet the fluttering of excitement in my chest. "We're all nervous. First day of school is always big."

"I don't care enough to be nervous," she scoffs. She piles her dark chocolate hair into a nondescript bun as if to prove her disinterest.

"This is a good development." Charlotte's twin Callie heaves herself up into the backseat by the seatbelt. She's wearing a dress we bought the day before. We share the idea that new clothes are like blank slates, no previous influence. Thus, any big occasion required new clothes. My father does not agree, but that's men for you.

"Wellsey High needed more guys," Callie goes on. "Our selection did not profit from puberty."

"Wyatt will probably disagree." I roll down the window. "Wyatt! Come on!" I shout toward our house.

Our fourteen-year-old brother slams the front door. His backpack and two duffle bags knock against his legs the whole way down the drive, making him walk like a drunk.

"Dad's taking Abby to school," he says, stuffing his gear into the backseat, much of it directly on top of Callie. "You know, to witness the baby starting eighth grade or something."

"Oh good. We might actually be on time," I say, putting the car in gear. Cutting the drive to the middle school shaves off a good ten minutes. The ancient SUV rocks forward, jostling its passengers.

"Hey! Get down!" Callie bellows, shoving Wyatt's bags to the side. She beats her hand against the window, directing her order toward our house, where her grey and white cat, Ruby, is perched on the roof.

"Jeez, Callie, roll down the freaking window," Wyatt says, doing it for her.

She thrusts her whole top half through the gap, unleashing a tirade at the cat until we turn the corner. Ruby ticks her ears back, but grudgingly starts picking her way down the shingles as we lose sight of the house.

Callie pulls her head back in and leans forward, brushing out my long hair with her fingers.

"You didn't wear the headband I picked out for you," she pouts.

"Nope," I say, recalling the neon red, bow-adorned monstrosity she had cooed over. Our school was absorbing half the students from Sagestone, I didn't need to look like a lobster on our first day.

The overcrowding is evident as soon as we enter the school. The noise of pre-class chatter, usually a gentle hum, is almost deafening now. Charlotte and I look at each other.

"It's a little loud," she practically shouts.

"Something definitely seems different," I jokingly agree.

Wyatt unshackles himself from us, heading for the freshmen

wing. Taylor Fitsch shoves a new girl out of the way to get to me, wrapping me in a hug.

"Hazel!" she says. "It's a madhouse in here. I wonder if there's even going to be seats for everyone. Whoa." Her gaze lands somewhere behind me. Her wide blue eyes look almost hungry. "Check him out."

I snort and glance over my shoulder, expecting to see some hulking jock, Taylor's type. But that's not what I see.

There is an angel in the hallway. He's tall, with jet-black hair and the buttery brown skin half-Hispanic kids come by naturally. I can only see his profile at first, but then he turns to talk to someone else and cracks a smile. My body can't decide if it wants to admit it likes him, or get me out of that walkway. His chin and nose are perfectly proportioned—I can't deny that—but there's a darkness in his face that makes my stomach clench. So serious for someone so young. Taylor's hand closes around my arm.

"I need to meet him," she says, dragging me through the crowd in his direction.

I try to plant my feet.

"Wait, what?" I splutter. The idea of being thrust into conversation with this guy before I've regained my wits is not ideal.

Taylor yanks me forward, her sinewy arms overpowering me. "Come on, he's just a guy."

As we near, Alison Holmes comes into view across from him. She smooths her glossy blonde hair and smiles, working her magic. Now this seems like even less of a good idea.

We stop right beside Alison and the guy, drawing their attention. Alison stabs us with a glare, her grin plastered over her square teeth. The guy regards Taylor good-naturedly, clearly not aware of the awkwardness he's just been thrust into.

"They didn't say we were getting students from Bratton Academy," Taylor says to him.

I groan softly. Bratton is the teen modeling and acting academy in Austin. He chuckles, the tiniest hint of red lacing his cheeks. It softens him just enough to take the sharp edge off his appearance.

"Sorry, no such luck," the guy says. His voice is low, moving fluidly from one word to the next like water over rocks.

I find myself longing to hear him speak again.

"I'm Taylor, by the way," she asserts, sticking her hand out. The guy shakes it, and I think Alison might tackle her right there.

"I'm Luke Caulfield," the guy says.

"And that's Hazel." Taylor turns to me. "Don't stand behind me like a freak, Haze."

She practically shoves me into Luke and I look up at him, my tongue locking onto the roof of my mouth. His eyes are the most vibrant blue I've ever seen, standing out from his tan skin like water in cupped hands. But a strange hardness edges them. They're the kind of eyes that always know something you don't.

He knits his brow just slightly as he studies me. *I know his face*, I realize. I can't think from where, but an overwhelming sense of familiarity hits me as we look at each other. He reaches forward, shaking my hand. I hadn't even realized I'd raised mine.

"Luke," he says again.

"Hazel Sayers," I reply.

We drop our hands, but his eyes keep moving over my face.

"Have we met before?" he asks, voicing my own thoughts.

"I feel like we have," I say slowly.

"Luke and I were just talking about how we went to Mooney Middle School together," Alison says, clawing her way back into the conversation. "Maybe you went there with us, Hazel."

Clever minx, already referring to the two of them like they are together. The bell rings for first period and the spell shatters. Luke and I look in opposite directions and Taylor seizes my arm.

"Well, nice to meet you, Luke," she says. She flashes a shark-like grin at Alison. "See you, Alligator. She looks just like one, doesn't she, Luke?"

Alison's trying so hard to keep her smile on that I swear I see her eye twitch.

"Bye," I manage to say to Luke as Taylor herds me down the hall.

"Bye," he says, his words almost lost in the din of the hallway.

Taylor uses me like a battering ram as we head to our homeroom, shoving me through cracks in the crowd.

"Sparks, much?" she says under her breath as I open the door to our classroom.

I blink, still in a funk. "What?"

"That Luke guy was totally throwing you lines. 'Don't I know you?' I think that's how my dad picked up my mom."

We slip into our seats on the side of the room.

"No, he was right. We definitely know each other from somewhere," I say, desperately racking my brain. Still nothing comes up.

Taylor takes out her books, dropping them on the desk.

"Why did you say your last name was Sayers?" she asks, looking at me sideways.

I smack my forehead. "I did, didn't I? I don't know why I did that. It's my mother's maiden name."

"He got you all flustered, hmm?" Taylor walks her index and middle finger up my arm like a pair of tiny legs. "Ruffled your feathers a bit, *hmm?*"

I brush her off just as our teacher comes in. I bend my head to my book, but can't stop replaying the encounter in my head for the rest of the period.

The day goes by uneventfully, despite the added number of students. In some of my classes, the displaced relief kids have to sit on the floor. I don't see Luke again, which makes me wonder if maybe he's a senior. I could have found out easily enough at our lunch period, which is upperclassmen only, but I have to report to the library in case anyone comes by for English tutoring. Not like it's a hopping pastime on most days. It makes for a good hideout though. One encounter with Luke left me feeling like I'd misplaced my brain. I didn't want a second helping.

———

"Want to go for a run?" Callie asks me on the ride home. I make a face, glancing up at the clouds above us. They look bruised, angry even.

"It might rain," I argue.

"It won't. Those are stratocumulus clouds, not nimbostratus." Callie twists in her seat to see her twin. "Char, how about you?"

Charlotte rolls her eyes. "No thanks."

I get a sudden image of Charlotte running in the rain, in her dark clothes, mascara and eyeliner draining down her face. Running really wouldn't be her thing.

We pull up to the house just as my stepdad and my youngest sister, Abby, are getting out of the other car. His weathered, tan face brightens as he sees us. He's still in his scrubs, straight from the hospital.

"Hey girls," he says as we get out. "Where's Wyatt?"

"Football practice. He's bussing it home," I answer, walking over to hug him. As soon as I turn, Abby rushes me, thrusting a heavy plastic bag into my hands. I almost drop the giant bottles of Mane N' Tail.

"Hazel! Can you please, please make up some of Mom's shampoo for me? I'm almost out," she begs.

"Oh yeah, me too," Callie seconds as she walks past.

I groan. Abby widens her green eyes, the same eyes we all inherited, clasping her hands.

"Please, Haze. I'll make dinner tonight. You're the only one who does it right."

I'm clearly not going to win this. "Yeah, okay."

Abby jumps twice, her blonde hair swinging around her neck.

"Hey," Callie says, poking her head out the door. "Run in twenty. Be ready."

CHAPTER 2

THE CIRCLE

O f course, it starts raining on us halfway through the run. It's only a light sprinkle, but it's enough to make the journey uncomfortable. We take off jogging up the dirt trail along the road, my T-shirt sticking to me in all the wrong places. Our portly black Lab, Prince, weaves between us, lassoing my ankles with his leash. Every time he takes a step, his barrel of a belly swings into my calf. I knee him over to my other side, getting a smear of drool for my trouble.

Fat droplets of water spatter in the dirt. Callie holds up her arm to shield her eyes. "This sucks."

"I *told* you it was going to rain, but you just spouted your useless cloud knowledge at me," I say.

Callie glances at the thick belt of trees to our right.

"I bet we can find a short cut," she says. "We can hop off the trail and head through there."

Generally, we run in a big circle from our house, taking this trail that loops around a patch of forest dividing neighborhoods. I've always imagined creepy homeless guys hanging out in woods like this, waiting to prey on younglings wandering through. The drumming raindrops on my head convince me I'm being irrational. Plus, we have Prince. He's got about sixty pounds on any rapist. More teeth too.

"Okay," I concede. "But let's just go straight through. And Prince should go first."

We step over the curb, tramping into the trees. Callie unwinds the leash from her hand, letting Prince run ahead of us a little. Going "straight" is harder than I thought it would be. With no trail to follow, we're weaving all over the place at the mercy of the trees. Luckily, the wood isn't that large anymore. When we'd first moved in with my stepdad, we'd been surrounded by thick cedar forest on all sides. But over the last seven years, neighborhood developments had cut it down to just this remaining island. Not that that was comforting fifty feet in when nothing but trunks are visible.

"I gotta walk," I wheeze, slowing as a stitch wedges between my ribs.

Callie drops down to a walk too, reining in Prince. We stroll for a while, Callie kicking her legs out to stretch them. Something ahead steals her attention. She squints, pausing.

"Look at that," she says, curving off to our left. I grudgingly follow.

A few feet away, the trees fan out, creating a little clearing. Callie is standing at the center, looking down at a ring of white dust on the ground.

"It looks like a little party spot, or something," she says.

"That was definitely a fire," I say, pointing to the pile of damp ashes she's nudging with her tennis shoe.

The rain, uninhibited by the canopy, leaves pockmarks in the powdery fire pit. I walk around it, noticing the divots spaced evenly in a ring around the center. Like people had been sitting here, often. I step down into one, moving closer to the moldy remains of the last fire.

The next second, I double over, stumbling to my knees. It's like I've been stabbed in the stomach. White-hot agony rips my gut apart, inching deeper and deeper inside me. I can hear Callie saying something, but I can't even open my mouth. I just sit, jaw clenched, trying to breathe through it. Wetness from the ground seeps into my skin, so cold it almost burns. I lift my hand, which has been wrist deep in mud. It comes up red. Dark blood coats my palm, dripping lazily down to my elbow. I rocket back up to my feet, despite the throbbing in my stomach. All down my shins, from knee to ankle, is drenched in crimson. More blood than could possibly be there by accident.

I frantically try to clean my legs, smearing them with my hands. It only spreads the mess. My lungs won't function properly. Between the panic and the relentless pain, they're refusing to hold the breath I need.

"Hazel!" Callie seizes my wrists, forcing me to focus on her face.

"Please get it off me, just get it off!" I beg her.

"What are you talking about? This is mud." She waves my own hand in front of my eyes, raising her eyebrows so I get the point. "It's just mud. Calm down."

I stare at my palm. Raindrops are making quick work of clearing away the brown from my skin. Brown, not red. I look down at my legs. There's no blood.

The stabbing in my stomach ebbs, less intense with each throb, until the only thing I feel is the strong urge to throw up.

"I need to get out of here." I pull my hands away from Callie, sprinting out of the clearing. My legs seem to know where we're going. I can't focus on anything but getting out of these trees, out from under the pressure they're creating.

It's a good twenty feet before I emerge into the sweet, fresh air. I manage to gulp one breath before I face-plant into the ground. Apparently, I've come out right on the precipice of a hill. I slide a few feet down the slope, before I come to rest. Slowly, I raise myself onto my hands, spitting dirt out of my mouth. Callie appears behind me, taking the slope more carefully than I had.

"Oh my God, Haze! Are you okay?"

I sit back on my knees, examining myself. My entire front is soaked in mud, but I'm intact. It's my mind I'm worried about. My heart's still hammering behind my ears, trying to tell me something isn't right. I count the beats, just like my child therapist taught me.

I had seen blood. What piece of my brain was *still* sick enough to do that to me?

Callie seems to be stifling a laugh.

"You totally just ate it," she giggles.

"It's not funny," I grunt, standing up. "How gross do I look, on a scale of one to ten?"

"Eight and a half, but you can shower when we get home." She points down the hill. "There's the road."

From this height, we have a good view of Cody I haven't seen before. The plains are laid out right up to the hill country, sprinkled with clumps of neighborhoods. A red brick house one street over draws my eye. The white window frames tug at my memory. I realize its significance with a sinking feeling.

"What's up?" Callie asks, able to read my mood with that annoying ability she has.

"That's where our old house was," I say. "Where we lived before..."

I can't make myself produce more words, can't say "Before Mom died," but Callie knows. Her face closes down.

"The one that burned down?" she says stiffly.

I nod. She purses her lips, starting off down the hill. She doesn't like talking about our mother, or even being reminded we had one. I follow her after one more look at the bare yard.

We pick up our jog again when we reach the road. Every time a car sails by, I push up behind Callie, trying to hide my mottled T-shirt. She shoves me the third time I trip her.

"Stop running so close to me, Hazel," she huffs.

I open my mouth to shoot something back, but stop. Humming up the road is an old model Honda chopper, the kind my Dad would love. Straddling it is the guy from the hall, his black hair pushed back by the wind. Perfect timing. I seize Callie, making her yelp.

"Ouch, Hazel—"

"Shh, you have to hide me!"

She looks over her shoulder wildly. "Why?"

"I met that guy this morning. He *cannot* see me looking like I just crawled out of a swamp."

"What, you want me to just stand in front of you?"

"Just don't move."

She scoffs, but complies. The motorcycle growls past us, coughing occasionally. When the sound seems far enough around the bend, I break away and start jogging again.

"I hate to tell you," Callie says, catching up to me, "but I'm fairly sure he could see you. Who is he, anyway?"

"Someone from Sagestone. Taylor thought he was cute," I say, brushing it off.

"Obviously, she's not the only one."

I give her a cutting look and we finish the run in silence.

I can't seem to get the shower hot enough to scald away the tingling on my legs. My skin seems to squirm under the water, refusing to shuck off the feeling that there's something on it that doesn't belong. I touch my stomach where the phantom pain had been.

When my whole body is thoroughly bright pink from the steam, I get out and shrug on my baggiest sweatshirt. The whole family collects at the dining room table as Abby assembles fish tacos, depositing them on plates, and sliding them across the gnarled wood. Wyatt trudges in through the front door, still in uniform, shedding bags all the way to the table.

"Hey, Dad," he says, sliding in the seat next to him.

My dad already changed into his favorite T-shirt, the one that says, "I Delivered Life, What Did You Do Today?" When he squeezes Wyatt's shoulder, his laugh lines deepen as he smiles. "Good practice, kiddo?"

Wyatt shovels half a taco into his mouth. "Yep," he grunts.

Dad pans his dark brown eyes around the table. "Girls, how was your first day? Did the relief kids settle in?"

Char, Callie, and I mumble our agreement.

"Did anyone talk about the Sagestone fire?"

"It was a tragedy, Dad. I'm sure they don't really want to talk about it," Callie says.

"I just don't understand how the police didn't raise a finger with all that cult stuff going on at that school. I don't want you guys to get involved with it."

"There was no cult, Dad!" Charlotte says. "The one kid that died in the fire happened to be into Wicca or something. You're way overprotective."

"Did you make my shampoo yet, Hazel?" Abby graciously interrupts, picking at the ends of her hair.

I scoop up my empty plate, heading into the kitchen. "I'll do it now."

Abby has set out the four shampoo bottles on the counter, along with the small wicker basket where Mom kept her ingredients.

She always used to make us this home remedy shampoo. I'd tried others, even the really expensive brands, but nothing worked like this stuff did. Our hair grew at a superhuman rate. We girls just wore it long, it was easier that way. Dad called it the "Parks' family trademark."

Parks, not Sayers, I remind myself. Parks had been my last name since I could remember. Why did it feel so wrong to say it now?

My fingers open the box slowly, reveling in the tiny connection it gives me to Mom. How many times did she touch this exact box? Her fingerprints are still on the tiny glass vials inside. I make sure not to smudge them as I take a pinch from three crushed herb jars, adding it to each shampoo bottle. A few drops of select oils follow. I cap all the bottles and shake them, mixing the ingredients. Finally, I pick up the stiff post-it note tucked between the vials. Seeing her handwriting fills my chest with lead. The day she'd taught me how to do this, she'd just scribbled down the recipe and left this note, which I was supposed to read when everything was done. I thought it was cheesy at first, but now it's my favorite part of making the shampoos. I can almost hear my mother's voice as I read it out loud.

"Long locks will grow strong, not break, or split, or wither.

Beauty within shall grow without. Remember always The Giver."

I slip the note back into the basket. I don't know what the words mean. At one point, I thought she was referencing the book, *The Giver,* since I had been reading it when I was ten and she'd written the note. Now, I think they're more for her, the woman who had given us everything. She wanted us to remember her every time we did something simple, even washing our hair.

The lid comes down with the softest click. I run my fingernail along the engraving right under the lock. *Sayers.*

Maybe it wasn't the worst thing to keep the name alive, even if I was the only one who really remembered using it.

CHAPTER 3

THE MESSAGE

The Tutoring Center actually has customers by week two. Wellsey High is apparently a little more rigorous than Sagestone had been. Most of the kids who come in are people I haven't met before. With no tests on the horizon, not many people ask for an English tutor. Kids generally only come to me when they have essays, tests, or want to bribe me to write their papers. I set up camp at a corner table, trying not to feel like the rejected book nerd as I eat my lunch alone. I'm just starting my Chem worksheet when Mrs. Hall, the proctor, taps my papers.

"Hazel, you have someone," she says.

"No way!" I burst out excitedly, looking up.

Luke is standing next to her, an amused look on his face. I realize my mouth is open and clap it shut.

"This is Luke," Mrs. Hall goes on, gesturing to him. "He's having trouble with senior English."

"Right," I croak, then clear my throat. "Um, why don't you sit down?"

Mrs. Hall moves away, and Luke pulls out the chair next to me.

"Hazel, right?" he asks.

"Yeah," I reply, trying to sound like I don't know *exactly* who he is. "We met the other day."

"I saw you on Skyline Loop last week," he says. "You were with someone else."

Crap. So he *had* seen me running.

"Yeah, that was my sister." I try to laugh breezily. "We were just jogging."

"It was raining," he points out. "Kind of dangerous, don't you think?"

"Says the guy who was riding a motorcycle without a helmet," I retort, then instantly wish I could take it back. Who was I, his mother?

Luke half-smiles, admonished. "It's my uncle's, he lets me ride it. I was bringing it home from the shop."

He glances at the homework I've been doing. A tiny "v" forms between his brows as he runs a finger over the line where I'd scribbled my name. A twinge of uneasiness pulls at my diaphragm.

"My last name is Parks," I say stupidly. "Sayers was my mother's maiden name. I seem to keep saying it lately."

He meets my eyes and the ethereal blue of his stuns me all over again. They almost don't look human.

"I was looking at 'Hazel.' Very Southern."

"Actually, it's very British. My mother was from England. My siblings are named Carolina, Charlotte, Abigail, and Wyatt."

He gives an impressed nod. "Sounds like an English novel."

"Speaking of novel names," I say. "What about Caulfield? Is that your real name?"

He stares at me blankly.

"Holden Caulfield? *Catcher in the Rye?*" I prompt.

Luke dips his head, his lips pulling into a smile again. "I guess that's why I'm here. I'm having a lot of trouble getting what we're doing in English, and I'm not really used to reading in—" he stops, blinking, as if he'd said something he hadn't meant to.

After a second, I cut in. "Well, I can definitely help you. I love English, it's kind of my thing."

Luke reaches into his backpack, setting his notebook on the table. He seems so out of place here in the library. He should be somewhere outside, maybe hiking or rafting, not bent over notes. He hands one of his books to me. "This is what we're working on."

"*The Aeneid*! Such a classic," I sigh.

He gives me that bemused look again, like I'd said something unexpected.

"I can tell you everything you need to know about this book," I promise.

Luke spreads his hands. "Let's do it."

———

Luke is the perfect listener. Usually, people I tutor argue with me, or insist I'm making stuff up. They get frustrated and stop paying attention. Luke stays with me the whole time, locked on my face. He even takes notes! No one has ever thought my ideas were important enough to write down.

When lunch is over, Mrs. Hall circles the tables, reminding us all to get to class. Regretfully, I stand up, sweeping my books into my bag. Luke shoulders his backpack, looking down at me.

"This was surprisingly fun. When do you tutor, usually? Just Wednesdays?" he asks.

I stare at him in shock. No one's ever come back for a repeat session.

"I'm here Monday, Wednesday, and Friday at lunch, so you can kind of pick what day."

"Friday then." He flashes me a disarming smile. "Can't wait."

Luke strides past me. I stay rooted to the spot, trying to decide if I'd actually heard right. I shake my head, smiling at my naïveté. He's just being nice to me, the nerdy tutor girl. Guys like him date girls like Alison. Or they try to date Taylor, but get shot down. Someone like me isn't even on his radar.

I stalk out of the library, twisting the strap of my bag and trying not to let disappointment get the best of me. I'd be stronger next time. Next time, I wouldn't play into his hands so easily.

A few people are clumped around my locker wing, making a very inconvenient barrier. I try to skirt around them politely, then realize no one is talking. The girl closest to me meets my eye, and I can almost see her retreating away from me in her mind. Like smoke dissolving into the air, the group disperses in opposite directions.

When I step up to my locker, my bag slips out of my hands. All six of my books land on top of my foot, but I barely even flinch.

The tattered wing of a bird has been nailed into my locker door.

It hangs there lifelessly, the pale grey feathers contrasting with the yellow paint behind them. It's small enough to be a dove's, or maybe a pigeon's.

Under the gift, someone wrote a message in streaked, red letters...

WE SEE YOU.

CHAPTER 4

GEMMA SAYERS

The nail doesn't come out easily. Whoever left me the heartwarming message meant it to stick. I carry a shifting queasiness in my stomach for the rest of class. Every scrape of my pen against paper reminds me of the pierced sinew of the tissuey wing.

Callie and Charlotte had signed up for track and Anime Club respectively, and with Wyatt at football, I had the car to myself for two hours. The thought of returning to our empty, isolated house seems unbearable, so I decide to go see Gemmie.

The road out to her house had given up on its job of creating safe transport years ago, and my SUV was meant more for puttering at twenty miles an hour than off-roading. It's always worth it, though, to finally turn off and see her little stone cottage. My last living grandparent hadn't brought anything when she came from England, but somehow managed to erect a page from *British Homes* smack in the Texas countryside. The cottage sits like an enchanted scene, an oasis between rough pecan trees, all stone and windows.

I park and hop down from my car. Ducking under some wayward vine tendrils, I reach to knock on the door, but it swings open before I make contact. Gemmie's elegant face pokes through the doorframe, breaking into a smile when she sees me.

"Darling," she says, her crisp accent ringing. "Come in, I made tea."

Gemmie lets me in, herding me into her tiny kitchen. I sit at her tiny round table in the breakfast nook, watching her sweep around the stove, the billowy blue cloth of her dress trailing in her wake. When I was little, I was convinced she was Titania, queen of the faeries. Sometimes I still get glimpses of it, in the way her feet never seem to shuffle, how the air swirls around her as she plucks the kettle off the stove.

Her fat Siamese cat lands heavily on my thigh before heaving himself up my arm to sit backward on my shoulder. His flab hangs over either side of my shoulder, and his thunderous purr vibrates in my throat. Gemmie returns, setting my tea in front of me.

"How are you, my heart?" she says, as she sits in the chair opposite me.

From the nose up, she still reminds me so much of my mother. Were it not for the silver-grey braid and fine lines that touched her eyes and mouth, she could have been Mom's sister. They had the same strong brow and the same way of keeping it completely motionless when they know something is wrong. I don't see the point in hedging, so I say, "Some kid left this on my locker. And I'm seeing things again."

I set the detached wing on the table. Even through four layers of paper towels, I feel like I'm touching the lifeless feathers.

Gemmie gingerly opens the bundle, one layer at a time. "What did you see?"

"Just a lot of blood. We were in the woods behind our neighborhood."

The last layer comes up, and her fingers pause.

"Poor little thing," she says after a moment.

"I thought maybe we could bury it?" I say. It sounds so juvenile, but it feels like the right thing to do.

Gemmie swiftly refolds the bundle. "Yes, I think that's a very good idea."

"I don't understand why people are still doing this to us. I thought it was over."

The real weight of my disappointment settles on top of me like cement. It'd been so long since the spray painting, the whispered insults, the hate that followed the fire. Back then, people hadn't looked at us. Kids weren't allowed to be friends with us. Superstition clung to my family like leprosy, something scarring that everyone could see. I thought we'd finally managed to crawl out from under the Parks' legacy, but this was in a class all its own.

"Hazel," Gemmie says, gathering my hand in both of hers, "this is not about you. It's about fear. Always has been. That is the only power anyone can have over you. You have to be stronger than your fear."

An hour later, after she'd stuffed me with half a loaf of walnut-studded tea bread and the warmth returned to my stomach, I head back out to my car. At the door, Gemmie wraps me in her thin frame.

"Don't let it weigh on you, my pet," she says.

I nod as we break apart.

"And here," she adds, bending to a stringy shrub to the right of the door. She breaks off one of the tendrils and threads it through the strap of my backpack, tying in into a knot. Amazingly, it doesn't break, just hangs there in a tatty ring. "My grandmother used to give me a string of this whenever I needed some extra luck. Maybe it'll help."

"Thanks, Gemmie. Love you," I say, waving as I turn toward the driveway.

As soon as I'm perched in the driver's seat, I pull the plant stem off. It's exactly the kind of thing I shouldn't show up to school with. Something that looked weird and unexplainable. As I reverse out, I see Gemmie slip out the back door into her garden. She's got the wadded paper towels cradled in her elbow.

CHAPTER 5

TATTOO

"**H**azel!"

I spot Taylor's frantically waving arm rising above the mass of students in the cafeteria. I hold my tray over my head and wade through the undulating throng. Lunch has turned into a music festival situation, complete with some kids being forced to sit on each other's laps.

I wedge in next to our friend Gallagher, who's eating from four different bags of chips.

"What up, Hazey?" He flashes me his oversized grin with just a tad too much gum.

"Hey, Gally," I reply.

"Hazel, this is M.C., of the late Sagestone High School," Taylor says, making a grandiose gesture to the pale girl with a blazing red ponytail sitting next to her. M.C. offers me a wave.

"Nice to meet you," I say. "M.C., what's that stand for?"

"Marie-Claire," she answers, pulling a face. "My mom didn't realize she was naming me after the stupidest magazine in the world."

I laugh, liking her already.

"The Alison-beast is on the prowl," Taylor says, glaring over my shoulder.

When I twist around, Alison's sheet of plasticky blonde hair catches my eye from across the room like light on a mirror. She's turned sideways at her table, rambling into Luke's ear. She's practically on his lap.

M.C. groans, tilting her head back. "Ugh, Luke Caulfield is so hot. He's got that 'I love you but I might kill you' thing going on."

Gallagher chokes out a Dorito-powdered laugh. "That's what the girls like these days? Impending death by strangling?"

"Everyone at Sagestone thought he was a creep," M.C. goes on, taking a swipe at Gallagher. "Probably still would, but the fire actually did him some favors. Everyone wants to know if he did it. Something about having an arsonist in your circle seems to entice people."

"Why would they think he did it?" I break in.

"Because he was the only person who talked to Matthew Townsend, the kid who died. *That guy* was a creeper to the tenth degree. He was a Satanist or something, and Luke was into it too, apparently. They hung out like every day up until the fire. The police said it was just a prank gone wrong, but I would bet a hundred bucks Matthew set the fire as, like," she switches to a raspy, ominous voice meant to sway our opinions, "a sacrifice to the Devil and lost his soul in the process."

"In this circle, we don't judge the religious inclinations of others," Taylor asserts heavy handedly, raising her eyes at me. She's probably the only person who relishes in the stigma around my mother.

"Thanks for that," I say flatly.

My mood has just taken a nosedive. If what M.C. said was true, Luke had lost a friend in the fire. I know all too well what it feels like to lose people for no reason, have them just vanish out from under you leaving you falling. I don't have to know him to know the aching emptiness that hangs inside him, follows him everywhere. We have something in common, at least.

When school lets out, I squeeze myself into a stall in the locker room to change. My days of running near my house are dead and gone, thanks to everyone's afterschool activities. I've resigned myself to running along the track in full view of many, many people.

As I pull out the shorts I packed, I groan. I'd accidentally grabbed

Callie's tiny spandex shorts instead of my longer ones. They look great on Callie, who is seventy percent leg, but they are a little daring for me.

Halfway down to the track, there's a wolf whistle from behind me. I wheel around and spot Taylor walking with M.C. and Gallagher toward the parking lot.

"Work those tiny shorts, Haze," Taylor jeers, winding her arm like she was about to make a softball pitch.

I yank the shorts down as best I can. "They're Callie's," I yell back at her.

She makes some whooping noises, drawing everyone's attention within twenty feet.

"I hate you," I shout, half-jokingly.

She blows a kiss at me. I turn around and manage to stop myself right before I collide with Luke's back. He's leaning on the fence that borders the track, looking out at the sprinters preparing for warm up. He spots me, a confused look taking over his face.

"Oh, hey," he says. "I thought that was you out there."

He gestures to the other side of the track, where Callie is stretching with her back to us. She does look slightly like me from behind, I notice. If I were the type to wear blindingly pink jogging shorts.

"Ah, stalking me, are you?" I say.

Luke laughs softly. It's a strange laugh, without any sound. Just a grin accompanied by a breath out.

"Thanks for calling me out," he says.

Alison, clad in spandex and not much else, stares at me from amidst the mass of cross country runners, looking like she wants to set me on fire. So that's who Luke was really watching.

"Are you thinking of joining track?" I ask, holding Alison's stare until she turns around and bends over, presumably stretching her hamstrings.

"No, just on my way to the pool," Luke answers. "I was on the swim team at Sagestone. I'm hoping they'll let me jump on here."

I blow out a low whistle. "I could never do that. The thought of swimming in the winter makes me want to cry."

Luke shrugs. "Never bothered me. I'm a water guy."

He rakes his fingers along his scalp, and as his hand falls back down, I notice a blotch of color on his forearm. The sleeve of his jacket is bunched up in the crook of his elbow, and a half circle of red ink is poking out.

"Is that a tattoo?" I blurt.

His smile disappears like it's been whisked away by a fishing line. He tugs his sleeve down to the wrist.

"Yes."

"Is it a pentagram?" I'm mildly impressed at my power of recall.

He swallows, shifting to his left foot, away from me. "Sort of. My parents practiced this certain tradition of Wicca; it has to do with that. But I'm not like...completely into it."

"Hey, no judgment," I say weakly.

His gaze flicks back to me, almost guiltily. "I've freaked you out."

"No, no. If anyone understands weird parents, it's me," I say, glancing in Alison's direction. "A lot of people don't like my family just because of some stupid rumors about my mother."

Luke tilts his head. "What rumors?"

I hit a mental block, the wall my brain always throws up when I start talking about Mom. But something in me needs to tell him, if only to keep Alison from poisoning one more person against me.

"My mother made herbal remedies, like holistic medicines and stuff. She worked as a midwife for a while with my dad: he's an obstetrician. She was really good, but she lost one baby, and then everyone said she was a witch who killed children."

I blink. Had that all really just come out of my mouth? I had known this guy two weeks, and I'm already spilling family secrets.

Luke presses his lips together. "Hmm. It's interesting hearing your side of it."

So he's heard already.

He shoulders his duffle bag, offering me a slight wave. "See you around."

As he heads down toward the lap pool, I give myself an internal slap on the hand. I shouldn't be digging up stories about my mother, especially with someone already trying to stir something up. I step back onto the track and set off at a jog, counterclockwise to what the track team is doing. As I near the group, Callie gives me an up and down scan.

"I want my shorts back," she hisses when she's in earshot.

"Gladly. And maybe tomorrow you can buy some that aren't from Babies 'R' Us," I shoot back.

CHAPTER 6

OGGUN

After dinner, I creep into my dad's office to set up my laptop. It was one of the few places our ancient house allowed WiFi to pass through with anything close to speed. My fingers type "Wicca" into the search browser seemingly without my direction. Eleven million results answer my query. Most are trying to sell me "Authentic Sacrificial Daggers," but a few offer histories or guidelines. There are too many sects to even count, it seems.

Some have the sinister, threatening feel that had given witchcraft such a bad rap, but others seemed…benign. Most of what I find is for herbal healing, or spells to gain courage, or change your luck. No more freaky than any other religion with their little superstitions. As I flick through the websites, I wonder which one Luke's family is involved with.

"What are you looking at?" Callie's voice says over my shoulder. My stomach takes a flying leap into my ribcage.

"Jeez, Cal," I say, blowing out a breath.

She leans forward, studying the screen. Her eyes slide to me. "Okay, freak."

I roll the chair closer to the desk, blocking her out.

"There's a kid at school who's Wiccan or something. I was just curious," I say.

She arches an eyebrow at me, popping a piece of chocolate in her mouth. "You really think you should be digging this stuff up? With that display someone left on your locker? You're just giving people a reason to hate you."

"It's my life, thanks," I say.

She shrugs, padding out of the study. I tap my finger on the track pad, thinking, then search: "metaphysical, Cody TX." One address in Austin comes up, so I quickly scribble it down on a sticky note.

"Cat bomb!"

I whirl in the chair just in time to see Wyatt toss Ruby at me. She's not happy, and she lands on my legs with all twenty claws out.

I let out a sound like *"gyah!"*

"Wyatt, you stupid idiot!" I shout, prying Ruby off my jeans.

He laughs hysterically, running back into the hall. I set Ruby on the ground and peel the note off the stack. Tomorrow is Saturday; I'd have a chance to explore a little.

———

Austin is only about half an hour south of Cody, but the expanse of flatlands in between makes you feel like you're making a trek across the desert. Every time I get to come into town, it's a bit like rounding the corner to see The Emerald City clustered in front of you. There are actual businesses and buildings higher than one story, and the dusty brown quality of Cody's streets doesn't seem to hold sway here.

The address I have is in the numbered streets downtown, east of the highway. When I get close enough, I ease off I-35 onto the frontage road. When I stop at a light, I have the briefest twinge of second thoughts. My dad wasn't strict, we had few rules—we called it "stepdad syndrome"—but the one thing he insisted on was never venturing east of the highway. That rule was meant for nighttime excursions, but part of me knew he wouldn't be happy if he found out what I was doing. But then, the whole purpose of the trip would probably make him rethink my car privileges. I was in this now, better to go for broke.

When I start to think I've gone too deep into the warehouse

district, I see it. It isn't the earthy, hippie-infused hutch I thought it would be. It's just one in a line of brick squares, set apart only by the sprawling murals painted across the front. The symbol of a huge bird takes up most of the wall, its wings stretching from one side to the other. Its claws clutch a scythe.

Oggun, the store's name, is spray painted over the doors like a black halo.

I park a few blocks down, noting that I'm the only car on the street. *It is Texas*, I reassure myself. Even in Austin, which is by far the most open city in the state, there would never be a line out the door for a place like this.

I'm about to go in when writing on right side of the wall draws my eye. Someone's done this by hand, not a spray can. It reads, *"Muerte Se Lleve Ninguno De Nosotros."* I try to piece a meaning together. Death, something. Death carries no one? That can't be right.

I pull open the door. For such a large building, the shop is surprisingly small. The back wall seems to be a construct, a thick wall of curtains from ceiling to floor that halves the room. Rows and rows of aged wooden shelves rib the center, all laden with baskets and jars. I wander to the nearest shelf, leaning down to peer at twine-wrapped bundles of dried leaves. A hand-written sign in front of the wicker basket labels them "white sage."

I'd been to a place like this before, but it hadn't been nearly as well stocked. My mother had brought us to a *curandera* a few times, a healer. Someone who used herbs to make medicines, just like she did. But the woman she went to had lived in a tiny shack out in the country and her stock had been stuffed into clay pots. Nothing on this scale.

A man ducks out from between the curtains, moving lazily like I've interrupted his day. He clearly fights the urge to roll his eyes when he sees me.

"Just curious?" he asks. I can't help feeling a bit sorry for the guy. He probably deals with ten people a day wandering through just to get a thrill of doing something edgy. I'm filled with a desire to prove to him how sincere I am.

"I'd actually really like any information you can give me. Do you have any books?"

He's such a gangly thing, maybe just out of college. When he moves to the checkout counter, he looks almost like a grasshopper that just found out it can walk on two legs. He produces a clipboard, smudging his fist across his forehead wearily as he holds it out to me.

"We offer subscriptions to *Witches Monthly*. That's the best I got."

I take the clipboard and outstretched pen defiantly. "Perfect. I just put my name and address?"

"We only take cash," he adds. With his country accent, it takes him a painfully long time to get the four words out.

"That's fine," I say, writing my name across the top line.

I'm halfway through my street name when he says, "Pay first."

"Okay." I try not to get irked, I just set the clipboard on the counter and fish out my wallet. I want to punch myself when I see only nine dollars in the pocket.

"Sorry, how much is it?" I ask, looking up. The guy is locked onto the subscription form, his eyes refusing to blink. When he snaps his head back to me, his face has changed. His jaw is clenched, and his irises bob in the whites of his eyes like pool floats. I take a step back.

"This is your name?" he asks. I glance briefly at it, realizing I made the mistake of writing Sayers instead of Parks again. Annoying misstep, but it doesn't deserve the twitchy reaction I'm getting.

"Yeah. But listen, I don't have enough cash right now. I'm going to have to come back."

"No," he says quickly. "It's free. Just… can you wait here for a second?"

His upper lip is getting slick. My stomach retracts, and I hitch at the uncomfortable pressure that wells up inside me. It's like someone has a hand around my diaphragm and is squeezing, squeezing.

"I need to go now," I rasp, fighting down a drift of nausea.

Fingers grip my forearm, like snakes wrapping around prey. The guy looks just as surprised as me by his action, but doesn't loosen the hold.

"Let me go," I say, remarkably evenly.

"Just stay for a second," he says desperately.

I pull myself backward, dragging him along for the first few steps until he gets his feet under him.

"Let go!" I yell, twisting my arm to pry his fingers off.

He swings me to the left, knocking me into one of the shelves. When I trip, I take him down with me. We both sprawl out on the floor, dried herbs raining down on us. His elbow digs into my thigh as he works for a better hold, and I keep shoving him off with my knees, blood pounding in my ears. His hand makes it to the back of my neck, index finger digging into the base of my skull. Words start pouring out of his mouth, hushed and hurried, and heat starts to blossom under his fingertip. His left arm is right in front of my mouth, so I take my only option and bite down on it as hard as I can. He lets out a catlike yowl, and all the pressure disappears.

I throw myself onto my feet, sprinting out of the store. My knees feel every slam of my feet against pavement as I run up the street, internally kicking myself for parking so far away.

When I finally reach the SUV, I throw my bag on the hood to dig for my keys. It doesn't look like he's following, but I need to be as far away from this place as possible. Movement to my left makes me jump a foot, a short yelp tearing from my mouth.

A very small Mexican woman puts a warm hand on my shoulder. Despite the hammering in my ears, I manage to not burst into tears at the sight of her.

"This man just attacked me, can you call the police?" I say. She shakes her grey-streaked head, the lines in her forehead folding over each other.

"*La lechuza,*" she says. Her dark eyes search my face for confirmation.

"*Lo siento, no hablo bien Español,*" I ramble in my badly halting version of Spanish. "*Neccesito ayuda.*"

Her other hand catches my right arm. "*La lechuza te esta buscando.*"

I open my door, backing away from her. "*No comprende, lo siento.*"

This was the culmination of my three years of Spanish classes, not even being able to tell a woman to call the police. I pull the SUV back, skirting around her. She stares after me, those black eyes never leaving my face.

CHAPTER 7

GYPSY

There's a storm over Cody as I drive home, thunderheads pushing out of the mass like cobras. The woman on the police line I talk to seems less than impressed by my complaint, and suggests that if I want to avoid that kind of situation I shouldn't go to "those places." She doesn't even promise a follow-up.

I throw my phone down into the cup holder, irritation rattling around in my stomach like coins in a can. My fingers go to the back of my neck. The nerves in the little bowl of my skull feel raw and tender. In fact, none of me feels quite right. Every shadow across the passenger seat makes my heart seize, preparing to launch me into survival mode. When the sticky note flutters in the AC, I almost slam into the bumper of the car in front of me, I twitch so badly.

I pull off the road at the next cluster of buildings. I'm in south Cody, where the town square is, but from here, home seems hours away. I can't trust myself to drive even that far, with the way my hands are twitching every time I see movement. If I can just sit, just get my head around it, my body will catch up. I pull into a parking lot tucked between two cafés, both too polished to have been in town long. Gypsy, the building to the left, I've actually heard of from Taylor. They serve entirely organic food, farmed locally. That was more of an Austin fad, but even Cody isn't immune to the influence. The sapphire blue walls of the exterior alone make it look like a gemstone tossed in the washed out, sun-leached scenery of Cody.

I get out. I'm not hungry, completely the opposite, but a cup of tea sounds like it could save my life. Even at such an awkward time of day, patrons are still scattered around the patio. I pull open the doors and cold air brushes across my cheeks. I pick a two-person booth, nestle against the wall, and tuck my feet under me. It feels slightly better to be around people. I look around the café, awed by the artistry of it. Every inch of the walls is painted by hand, scenes of dancing gypsies and white birds, caravans and palm readers.

"Hazel?"

My feet come down, ready to propel myself out of the booth. Luke is standing on the other side of my table.

"Who's stalking who now?" He smiles, those aquamarine eyes dancing against his skin.

"I was just on my way home," I say quickly. "Do you work here?"

There's the tiniest crack of disappointment in his face. "This is my aunt and uncle's place. I help them out when I can. You really didn't know I work here?"

I notice the Gypsy logo on his white shirt, right over his heart, and the towel tucked into his jeans. "I didn't know that."

"You okay?" That little V engraves itself between his eyebrows.

I take a breath, about to recount the episode at Oggun, but I catch myself. The only reason I'd gone was to learn more about him and what he did. I'd driven all the way into Austin to do it. Not the kind of thing I wanted to admit right after showing up randomly at his aunt and uncle's restaurant.

"I'm having a weird day," I finish carefully.

An idea lights up behind his eyes. "Wait right here. I got your back." He turns away, rounding the corner into the kitchen.

A moment later, he returns, balancing a squat green teapot in his left hand and a plate in the other. He spreads out tea and cups and a four-inch thick slice of cinnamon-sugar cake in front of me.

"On the house. If it doesn't make you feel better, I'll bring you lunch for a week. Promise."

"You're not a very good salesman," I say, carving out a forkful of cake. It dissolves on my tongue into warm, buttery softness, trailing a comforting heat all the way down to my stomach when I swallow. I do my best not to sigh. It's exactly what I need, good old-fashioned fat and sugar.

"If you want to share, that's totally an option," Luke says, picking up his own fork and digging in.

"Is it allowed for waiters to steal from customers?" I tease.

"I'm not a waiter, I'm a busboy. And I just got off." When he reaches out for another bite, I catch the trace of reddish brown at his elbow again. He's not wearing long sleeves today, but his T-shirt still covers the entirety of his biceps.

"Do you always wear sleeves so people won't see your tattoos?" It's out of my mouth before I realize how rude a question that is.

He chews roughly, obviously uncomfortable. "Yeah. People kind of judge you if you don't."

"How does that work with the swim team? Don't they see?"

"Swim tees." He itches at his left arm, where the half-moon of pentagram rests in his elbow.

"How far up do they go?" I ask.

He swallows heavily. With his index, he points to the pentagram, then drags his finger up his arm, across his chest in a downward "v," then up to his right shoulder and down to the other elbow.

"Wow," I say. I can't picture him with those harsh red symbols scattered across his body. They seem too hard for him.

He puts both of his elbows on the table, leaning closer. "Why are you so interested in them?"

I shrug, answering honestly. "It's all interesting. I never grew up with *one* religion, but because of my mom, we never touched anything remotely witchy. Even with the scary parts, I still think it could be cool, you know, having something you believe in."

"There doesn't have to be scary parts," he says. "It's the people that make it scary, not the craft."

I press my mouth into a line.

"For real," he insists. "Look at my aunt and uncle. Everyone in my family grew up as *brujas*. My mom and her two sisters were from a tiny town in Mexico, and they all got taught the same thing. My mom took it to a bad place. My Aunt Idra, even worse. But Iona, she took the good parts. About loving the earth, and using what it gives us to heal people. About using your energy to make good things happen. That's what it's about."

"She sounds great," I say genuinely.

His face warms. "She is. She and Finn, they're more parents to me than my mother and father ever were. I ran away when I was thirteen and they took me in. They showed me that religion shouldn't be a weapon. Which, now, I'm going to show you."

He digs a pen out of his pocket, pulling my paper napkin in front of him. His hand moves over the square quickly, filling it up with his boyish, scrawling handwriting. "I'm writing you a spell to try. Worst case, it won't do anything for you. Best case, maybe it'll give you a clear mind. Try burning a candle when you say the words."

He gives it to me, his hand hovering in the air as he says, "Actually, come with me."

Luke slips out of the booth, taking my wrist in his long fingers. I scoot out after him, letting him lead me down the aisles of tables into the back of the café. We squeeze down a hallway, Luke opening a door to the right.

The tiny room we go into shimmers like a diamond mine. All along the walls hang strands of beads and necklaces with pendants ranging from pea-sized to bigger than lemons. Against the far wall, a rugged wooden desk is barely visible beneath spools of twine and jars of whole gemstones, still rough and uncut.

Luke wanders to the left wall, scanning the dangling pendants.

"Iona makes these," he says, pausing to delicately pluck a thin silver chain off its nail. "Stones have energies and each one is different. When you have the stone, it gives its energy to you. This one is amethyst."

He rests the chain with a tiny purple stone in twisted silver in my palm.

"It's beautiful," I say, holding it up so glows violet in the light. "So all these stones do something different?"

Luke nods, glancing around.

"Some make you open to love, or heal you, or give you strength.

But this will do for now. It'll help open your mind." He takes the necklace, unfastening the hook. "Lift up your hair."

"I can't take it," I say quickly. "I'll buy it. I'd love to."

"She doesn't sell them. She gives them away."

I watch the perfect tiny orb sway from the silver chain. "It's too beautiful. Give me an ugly one."

"Shut up and take your gift," he grins.

I relinquish, gathering my hair off my neck. He leans over my shoulder to fasten it. He's so close. I can feel the warmth from his skin, smell chlorine mixed with laundry sheets in his T-shirt. He steps back to survey me, taking the warmth and leaving me chilled.

"Looks good," he says.

———

We walk out together, Luke waving goodbyes to every staff member he passes. Outside, wet wind sweeps through the street, buffeting us as we head toward my car.

"What are your plans for today?" Luke asks.

"I have to do chores at home," I say, touching the tiny gem where it hangs in the hollow of my throat. "What about you?"

"I think I'll go swimming in the lake before it rains," he answers with a grin. "You're welcome to join."

I look up at the clouds. They've turned gangrenous, laden with the kind of heavy heat that births ground lightning.

"No thanks. I like living," I say.

Luke laughs that quiet laugh. It's the second time I've heard it and I already know it by heart. The wind snatches my hair up, twisting it across my eyes. Before I can move it, Luke's brushing it away, letting it thread through his fingers. He seems to realize what he's doing, and drops his hand like it's made of lead.

"It's long," he says.

"Yeah. Kind of a family thing." I wrap my arms around my chest, suddenly feeling like I'm not wearing enough. My fingers brush the tender skin on my left arm where the shopkeeper's vise of a grip had landed.

"I guess I'll see you Monday for tutoring," he says. "Let me know how the incantation works."

I nod. "Yup, I'll let you know if I turn into a goat."

He snorts, turning toward the far end of the parking lot where the old chopper waits like a lopsided black horse.

"There are worse things than cute goats," he says, waving over his shoulder.

CHAPTER 8

THE ELEVEN-YEAR SPELL

I have to wait until Sunday night to try the incantation, when there's a lull in the house after dinner. Everyone's retreated to their rooms, leaving the halls in a sort of suspended silence. If there's a time to try Luke's meditation, it's now. I hunt around our pantry for some unscented candles, eventually locating the dust-caked cardboard box Mom had kept them in. I choose a thick white pillar candle with whorls in the creamy wax, clearly homemade.

When I've scrounged some matches, I retreat to my room. Folding my legs under me, I set the candle on the floor. The wick takes up the flame with a tiny *pfftt!*

I take Luke's note out, reading it over until the words stick in my mind. Eyes closed, I take a series of deep breaths, as per Luke's instructions. The words leave my lips in a hushed stream.

> *"Open my third eye,*
> *Open my mind's eye,*
> *Help me to see the unseen.*
> *Let me Be as I have never been,*
> *Let me See as I have never seen.*
> *Release my soul within."*

At the exact moment, I'm done saying it, an unseen force slams into my shoulders, pitching me backward and smacking me into the floorboards. It feels like a railroad spike is being shoved between my eyes, breaking open my head as it goes. I want to scream, or throw up, but nothing comes from my mouth. I try to roll, to move my arms, but my body has been cut off. My vision is flooded with a sheet of white. The nerves behind my eyes are trembling in agony, trying to get a hold on what's happening.

Just as quickly as it came, the pain is gone. My ceiling materializes above me, as plain and grey as before. The candle lies in a charred lump, the wick buried under bulbous layers of melted wax. I wonder vaguely how long I've been out though I know it would take days for the pillar to burn down on its own.

I force myself to sit up, running a check on my body. I feel...okay. Shaky, disturbed, but physically I'm alright. I stretch my hands out in front of me, trying to feel any speck of difference.

My door drifts open and Charlotte walks in. I scream.

Charlotte reels back against the wall, pressing her hand over her heart, wide-eyed.

"Jesus, Hazel, what?" she gasps.

"You're on fire!" I shout, jumping to my feet. I grab the blanket off my bed, remembering you're supposed to smother clothes fires.

Crackling, orange-red flames engulf Charlotte's whole body as she spins, looking at herself. Seeming to see nothing, she raises her eyes to me.

"Is that supposed to be funny? You freaking scared the crap out of me."

I freeze, halfway through throwing my blanket at her. She can't see it. *How* can she not see it? The air around her whips with the orange tongues of it, so fierce it's a wonder the walls don't catch fire. *It's not real*, my rational mind tells me harshly. *You know it's not real.*

"No, uh," I stammer, "I just, I thought I saw it."

Charlotte narrows her eyes at me. "Okay. Well, do you want to come downstairs? We were going to have ice cream. Maybe you should be with people for a bit."

"No thanks, I feel kind of sick," I lie. Each word sounds like a kick to a piece of sheet metal as I say it, rattling in my head. "I think I need to go to bed."

Concern crosses Charlotte's face. "You want some ginger?"

I shake my head. "Just sleep, probably."

Charlotte nods and shuts the door softly. I collapse onto my bed feeling like I've run a marathon. My brain spins in circles, trying to process what I've just seen. I'm too tired to get a hold on it all. I can't even try. My head sinks into my pillow, and I'm asleep in seconds.

In my dream, I'm lying against the old wood floorboards of our house in Louisiana when I was two, my back pressed against the underside of my mom's bed. There are voices outside our room.

Then it's blackness, and I'm paralyzed, a huge weight lying across my body. I feel eyes, someone's gaze on me, sending an itch skittering across my skin. I know he's smiling. He's watching me squirm like a butterfly being pinned to paper.

"There you are," his voice says. "Hazel."

———

My eyes snap open. It's morning, and I'm alone. The walls of my room are brushed with watery blue light, reassuring me that the night is over. My clothes are soaked, hanging to me in clammy wrinkles. They feel like wet hands on my body as I sit up.

Ruby is at the foot of my bed. Occasionally, she did creepy things like this, staring at us while we're sleeping. But Ruby is just sitting, eyes closed. I nudge her gently with my toe.

Her head cracks to the side with a muffled snap. It hangs there, bent at an angle, and her eyelids retract. Underneath are not the eyes of a living thing. They're cold and moldered, covered by a thick blue-grey film.

I shoot backward in bed. Before I can scream, she's vanished. Flickered out of existence in a second. *It's not real,* I tell my pulsing heart. *Be stronger than the fear.*

I head straight to the bathroom to douse my face with icy water. When I catch my reflection, my toothbrush clatters out of my hand.

"What the hell?" I say aloud, leaning forward to look at myself.

I'm surrounded by a roiling, gold-flecked cloud. It moves almost like a storm in fast forward, growing, collapsing, and growing again.

I don't even bother with a morning routine, just tug on a T-shirt and go downstairs. In the kitchen, I pull out a tub of cookie dough from the fridge, digging into it with a spoon. The sugar granules and melting chocolate on my tongue make me feel mildly better.

"Eww," Callie says, coming into the kitchen for her cereal. "Salmonella for breakfast?"

I stare at her for a second before answering. She has a rosy, glowing circle around her that reminds me of early sunset. I dig out another spoonful.

"I'm having a bad day," I say.

Callie sips her apple juice. "Already?"

CHAPTER 9

CONFRONTATION

I t gets worse. As soon as I walk into school, the tumult begins. Colors and temperature shifts batter me, coming from a thousand different sources. I dip my head, focusing only on the floor, and power through the crowd. My only thought is to find the person responsible for this.

I reach the senior locker wall, stopping when I see a pair of black sneakers that could only belong to Luke. I raise my eyes, but Luke's upper half is shielded by his locker door.

"Luke."

The door shuts and he turns to me. His eyes widen several centimeters.

"Whoa," he says.

That's when I know he can see it too.

"Yeah, whoa," I snap. "I can't stop seeing these *things*," I lower my voice to a hiss, gesturing to the cloud, "around my siblings. Around everyone. I feel like I'm going crazy. I just want it to stop!"

To my horror, my eyes sting, threatening tears. I fill my lungs, steeling myself. The color around Luke draws my attention, a deep sapphire blue that ripples like water.

Luke takes my arm in his hand. "Look, let's go outside."

Fabulous idea. I stare at the ground again as Luke steers me towards the doors. We burst outside into the fresh air. I close my eyes, letting the silence surround me. Luke wheels me around to face him, bending at the waist a little so he can look directly into my eyes.

"Tell me exactly what you're seeing," he orders.

Over Luke's shoulder, a tree draws my attention. The rough brown of the trunk is turning black, as if it's burning without fire. It's dying right in front of me, caving in. The leaves drop off, and the dead tree crumbles to the ground, twisting back up into the air as dust. My mouth hangs open in shock.

"What's up, what do you see?" Luke asks, his brow creasing.

"That tree just died."

Luke glances over his shoulder, but apparently sees nothing.

"Did you see an omen?" he asks.

"What does that even mean, 'an omen?' I have no idea what I'm seeing! What did that spell do? Why didn't you tell me this would happen?" I clamp my jaw so my lip won't twitch.

Luke pulls back, holding his hands up. "Hazel, I had no clue this would happen. I'm sorry. Just sit down here for a second. I promise this'll help."

He sinks down to the grass, cross-legged. After a pause, I follow suit.

"Lean back on the ground," he commands, stripping off his jacket and handing it to me. "Use that as a pillow."

I want to comment on his bossy tone, but I'm running on fumes as it is. I slip the jacket under my head, feeling the cool grass pressing against my back. The open, blue sky extends above me, and it's a relief not to see anything weird for just a moment.

"Are you going to explain what's going on?" I ask.

Luke twists something off his index finger. He hands me a thin, silver ring with a tiny, striped orange stone set in it. I hadn't even noticed him wearing it.

"Put that on," he says. I slip the ring onto my middle finger, the only one it even remotely fits. It hangs loosely enough that I can spin it slowly.

"That's carnelian," Luke says, tapping the stone. "It focuses your mind, keeps out unwanted distractions."

Glancing up at Luke, I notice the dark blue has disappeared.

"Thank you," I say before sighing.

Luke nods.

"Just keep that on until you learn to focus your thoughts a little more. And maybe take this off." He points to the amethyst necklace at my throat.

My fingers grasp the thin chain, and I'm strangely distressed at the thought of losing it. Still, if it's going to help. I unclasp it and hand it to him.

"Okay, first of all," Luke starts, folding his hands. "That incantation I gave you isn't supposed to do that much. It's just meant to remove mental barriers, like prejudices. The only thing I can think of that happened is that you pulled too much energy. Did you do the spell exactly the way I wrote it down?"

"*Yes*," I snap defensively.

"That still wouldn't explain this," he says to himself, gesturing to where the golden cloud had surrounded me. "What you're seeing, people's auras and omens, those are things that only witches see."

"Okay, but I'm not a witch. I only did the one spell, and obviously, I messed that up."

"That's not what I mean. There are people who practice witchcraft, and there are actual, full-blooded *witches*. People who are born to it."

I prop up on my elbow, looking at him. "So?"

"So." Luke looks at the ground. "You said people thought your mother might have been a witch, right?"

I feel fury and hurt rising up in my chest. "She wasn't."

"Look, Hazel." His fingers rest on my collarbone. "You need to consider the possibility that she was."

Before he's even finished, I bat his hand off me and struggle to my feet, brushing the grass off my jeans in violent swats. My mind scrambles for something to grasp onto, something that makes sense. Is this some sort of elaborate prank? Could he have drugged me somehow?

"She *wasn't*," I say. "And if this is something Alison put you up to, it's not funny. Screw you both."

I turn away, not even looking at his reaction. After two steps, his hands grab my shoulders, spinning me around to face him.

"Hazel, please. I'm not trying to freak you out. But if you are actually seeing what you say you are, that's the only explanation. It's not something you can turn on and off, it's just something you *are*. You don't have to be afraid of it."

"I'm a witch, like my evil witch mother?" I snap. "Then why am I seeing this stuff now? Why not my whole life?"

Luke frowns. "It has to be a spell. You had a spell on you that made it so you wouldn't see what you're supposed to see. In that case, the incantation I gave you would have taken it off. Your mom must have done it, that would explain—"

"My mother was not a witch!" I yell. "Stay away from me!"

I throw up my hand to him, palm forward. It's a motion I've made a thousand times at my siblings, but something about this time feels different. "Don't ever talk to me again."

I turn, and this time Luke doesn't stop me. I don't even bother going back into school; I just storm around the building to the parking lot. By some miracle, no one is outside to see me, but somehow, I had the feeling they wouldn't be. I drive right through town, and I don't stop until I'm grinding the SUV up Gemmie's driveway.

CHAPTER 10

THE SAYERS CLAN

Gemmie's waiting at the door when I slide the SUV to a stop. I yank my keys out, trying to get a handle on the spinning images that flood my mind: when I was sick my mother made us tea from plants she got in the garden, candles she always kept burning in the windows during storms, the way she always could tell when someone was going to call us or show up at our house, how she always knew *exactly* when one of us was going to get hurt...

A memory comes back to me, something that has to be pulled up by the roots, I've pushed it so far down: The night of the fire at my old house. The arsonists running around outside. I hear their shouts, their muffled footsteps as they drench our lawn with gasoline. I remember my mom, pregnant with Abby, standing in the living room, arms spread wide, muttering something. I was so small, probably only three, sitting at her feet as Charlotte and Callie clung to my arms. We weren't even able to open our eyes, much less believe it was happening. The fire ate away the front of our house, but not that room. Somehow, she held it back. Outside, they shouted, *Burn, witch, burn!*

I get out of the car, walking on weak legs toward the cottage. Gemmie looks older than I've ever seen her before. Dark circles discolor the delicate skin under her eyes.

"Come inside, my heart," she says when I reach her, her voice drawn.

"I want to know about Mom," I say, planting my feet. "I want to know about the things I see. They're not hallucinations, are they." I say it as a statement.

"Tea first, darling." She reaches down to pick up the massive cat that's bumping around her ankles, holding him close as she leads me inside.

I follow, sitting tensely at her kitchen table. She places a teacup in front of me, settling into her chair.

"Yes," she says finally. "Your mother was a witch. I am a witch. *You* are a witch."

She watches my face, waiting for me to fall apart.

I swallow, going to touch the amethyst drop and finding it gone. "Are we evil?"

The question sets her back. She lets out a short, falsetto laugh. "What a question. No, my heart. It's choices that make people evil, not how they're born."

"Why didn't I know? Why did you keep it from us?"

"After the fire, your mother and I decided it was the best decision. She wanted you to have normal lives, to be able to choose paths for yourselves the way a Sayers witch was never able to before." Gemmie runs her hand over the cat's broad head, more to comfort herself than him. "We spelled you and your siblings, to protect you."

"*Spelled*? You put a spell on us?"

She sighs, dipping her head.

"To protect you," she says again.

"The things I see, is that because I'm a witch?" It seemed a cruel joke for a child to have to deal with the visions I'd had my whole life —the stress-induced hallucinations stemming from childhood trauma that I'd been counseled for years about—just because I was born into my family.

"You see omens, just as your mother did. They were something not even our spell could keep from affecting you. They're meant to warn you of things to come. But you must be careful, letting them steer you around. Emily struggled with them her whole life. I think it may have been the reason she joined Stolam."

"What's that?"

A sharpness knifes through her expression. "This will be hard. You must remember how much you meant to your mother. She loved you more than you can know."

She's quiet for so long, I'm afraid she's deciding against telling me.

"Is it bad?" I prompt.

"Yes, my darling. It's very bad." She pushes back from the table, winding her way through the kitchen and into her bedroom. When she returns, she has a book under one arm, and a tarnished grey dagger clutched in the other. I barely have time to blink at the strangeness of seeing her with a weapon. When she reaches the table, she circles her hand high, then stabs the blade into the thick wood with such force that it sinks in two inches.

I rocket backward, my chair skittering out from under me. Gemmie says a string of words I can't understand and slowly peels her hand away. The marbled silver hilt begins to ooze a black, smoky substance that globs across the table. A portion rounds out into the shape of a tiny head, as big as an orange. Black, stick-like appendages flail on either side.

It looks like a skeleton, I think numbly, unable to take my eyes off it.

"This is the man your mother killed."

Frigid confusion grips my chest. I watch the infant sized pitch-creature drag itself an inch at a time across the table, heading toward me. Its spindly little arms keep dissolving and reforming from the tar-like smoke.

I take a step back, still trying to process what she said. *"What?"*

"The Sayers clan lived on Inis Mór, one of the Irish Isles, when Emily was a young girl. We come from a very old family, Hazel, which was once very powerful. Very few of us are left now."

Tiny black fingers extend from the creature, reaching for me. I press closer to the wall. At my feet, Gemmie's cat bristles and whines. This can't be real.

"Emily never took to life on the island. It was too small for her. When she was sixteen, she ran away to America. I didn't find her until she was twenty-three and pregnant with Abigail. In the mean-time, she'd fallen in love with a man who had convinced her to join

Stolam, a witch cult. To earn her place, she had to kill this man." Gemmie's gaze ticks over the turbulent black figure. "Another blood witch. This dagger is spelled to trap her victim's essence, keeping him bound to earth forever. It's a brutal fate, even if he deserved it."

She leans forward, grabbing the hilt. As she works it back and forth, loosening it from the table, the black creature is pulled back, further and further, until it's absorbed into the metal. When the last of him disappears, Gemmie pulls the dagger free and pushes it into its sheath.

"We're capable of very dark things, Hazel. You have to be stronger than the part of you that wants to give in to them."

Stronger than the fear.

"Why would Mom want to be a part of that? How could she ever *kill* an innocent person?" My mind rejects the idea. It can't be possible, therefore it doesn't exist.

"This man was not innocent. But Stolam doesn't care about that. They care about power, and power is in blood. Emily thought that with enough power, she could change things. She could change the world." Gemmie lays down the dagger, coming around the table to where I'm still shaking against the wall. "She wanted you and your siblings to have power she never had. You have lineage from the two oldest families in our histories. Each of you was birthed on a solstice or equinox. And five is the most powerful number in the craft."

"So what, we're tools?" I swipe the back of my fist over my nose. "That's the only reason she had us?"

"You changed her life, my darling," Gemmie says, taking my chin in her hand so I look at the sincerity in her eyes. "She left the cult for you—to *protect* you."

"What about our father?" Never in my life had I given him a second thought before now. It seemed odd, but Jack Parks, my stepdad, had always been my father. I hadn't needed another one. Gemmie turns away, but not before I see the expression of hate that pulls at her mouth.

"Faolan," she says. It takes me a moment to realize that's his name. "He was from the Sicario family, descendants of the Crowthers. Your parents first met in Louisiana and joined the cult together. Emily left him when she was pregnant with Abigail. She wanted a life for you, away from him and the cult."

"Where is he now?" I ask.

"Dead," she answers stiffly. "Dead and bound. We made sure of that."

I sit back in the chair, my bones hollow. "You didn't tell us so you could protect us."

Gemmie lowers into her seat, resting her hand on the table. "We did. Though I wonder now if it was a mistake."

We sit in silence for a while, both processing the gravity of Gemmie's admission. The cat is the only one that seems to have brushed off the encounter entirely. He settles across my thighs, kneading his pads into my jeans.

Eventually, Gemmie picks up the book she'd brought from her room. I'd forgotten about it in the commotion. She places it in front of me. At some point, it had been bound in leather, though now it's so badly flaked it's hard to tell.

Delicately, I open the cover. On the first page of thick yellow parchment paper, someone's handwritten the name *Emily S. Sayers*. My heart folds in on itself. I clutch the book closer, turning its pages with painstaking care. It's her handwriting.

"This is your mother's diary," Gemmie says. "Starting the day she ran away. She always planned to give it to you one day. She hoped it would explain…"

She doesn't finish.

I come across a blank page halfway through. There are three more in another section. Flipping quickly, I notice whole chunks are missing, some cut off midsentence.

"Why are these blank?" I ask.

"They're not. I spelled them so you can only read them after your eighteenth birthday."

"Why?" I can't keep the crossness from my tone. They're my mother's words, and I want them all.

"Some things are not meant for children." The way she says it leaves no room for negotiation. "Now I must ask you a question. Why did you lift our spell?"

"I didn't know I was." I pick at the gritty dried cover of the journal. "It was just an incantation to open my mind."

"The spell was meant to lift when you wanted it to," Gemmie says, resting a tired elbow on the table. "When you wanted to see."

"I guess I can't take it back now," I say ruefully.

A glance at my phone tells me it's time to pick up my brother and sisters from school. I stand, feeling like my blood has turned to sand. Gemmie walks me to the door. I hug her, breathing in her scent of lavender and honey. I turn to leave, but stop.

"Should I tell them?" I'm thinking of my siblings. The discovery had come at the cost of my safe, stable world. But if it was part of me, it was part of them.

Gemmie draws in a long breath. "You must. You're most powerful together. I'm afraid something is coming and they will need to be as prepared as they can be."

CHAPTER 11

REVELATIONS

"Smells great, sister H," Wyatt says when I set a big bowl of pasta on the table. I tried to make the most comforting meal I could manage for dinner.

He sticks his fork in it, peering at the noodles closely. "What did you do different?"

"I used some herbs from the garden," I say, spooning some salad onto my plate. Mom had meticulously crafted her herb garden over the years, something we'd neglected to care for once she was gone. It had slowly burgeoned into a shaggy outgrowth, the stronger herbs overtaking the weak, and everything refusing to die.

Abby glances at Dad's empty chair. "Should we wait for Dad?"

"He's running late. Someone had a miscarriage," I answer.

Everyone turns to me, and I blink, wondering where that had come from.

"Did he call?" Abby asks, scrunching her brow.

"He can't call because his phone is dead," I go on slowly.

"Did someone else call?" Abby prompts.

"No, I just know," I say honestly. The answer seems so clear to me. I feel the truth of it, but I can't voice the reason. They all look at me for a second before returning to their food.

"Hazel's being weird," Callie whispers to Charlotte.

"Seriously?" I say loudly. "I'm like a foot away from you."

Callie turns to me, her eyes defiant. "Well, you are. You've never skipped school before, and you acted like it wasn't even a big deal."

"I'm going through some stuff," I say, my voice faltering.

I chug down apple juice to keep myself from breaking down. When the secret comes out, it has to sound real. It can't sound like I'm having one of my "episodes."

"Do you want to tell us about it?" Abby asks sweetly, and I adore her for caring.

"I do. Look, I found out something about Mom. She—"

A shrill ringing cracks out from the house phone in the kitchen. Charlotte slips out of her chair to answer it. Callie watches me through narrowed eyes and I glare back at her. After a minute of garbled conversation, Charlotte returns, her arms wrapped around her stomach.

"Dad's nurse said he's going to be another few hours. His patient had a miscarriage, and his phone died."

Four faces turn to me.

"Okay, what's going on?" Callie asks stonily.

"What did you find out about Mom?" Charlotte says, as if she hadn't even heard her twin. The way she looks at me, the steady knowledge in her eyes, I can tell she's already guessed it. Out of all of us, Charlotte's always the one who unravels the puzzle first.

"Mom…was a witch."

Not even one muscle moves on anyone's face. "Gemmie's a witch. We're all witches."

A precarious silence paralyzes the air in the house. Callie breaks it first, scraping her chair back in a restricted rush.

"I'm calling Dr. Hoffsteter," she says. "While I'm at it, should I tell him you're hearing voices again, Wyatt? Hazel's breaking out the crazy train, everyone on."

Wyatt puts his fork down and stares at the table. I wish he was closer, I want to touch his shoulder, to tell him we weren't crazy our whole lives.

"Callie, I'm serious," I say, hoping my words will break through to Wyatt. "The things I've been seeing all my life are omens, they're something only witches see."

Callie clenches her jaw, crossing her arms. "This is so stupid, Hazel."

"*Listen* to me," I say, my voice rising. "It's not something to be scared of, we just *are* witches. We can see and do things. All the medicines Mom made, and what happened with the fire, it's all because she—"

"Stop saying she was a witch!" Callie shouts across the table.

"Callie, shut up," Charlotte says, silencing her twin. "You're only scared because you know it's true."

The two lock eyes, a silent conversation passing between them.

"What does that mean?" Abby's young voice sobers us all. I decide to take a less aggressive approach.

"Mom and Gemmie put a spell on us when we were really little to keep us from knowing we were witches. She wanted us to live normal lives. There's...a lot of crap that comes along with it."

"So we have a spell on us that keeps us from seeing and feeling things we should be able to?" Charlotte asks.

"Yes. I lifted mine by accident, and everything is different."

"You did *witchcraft*?" Callie uncrosses her arms. "Do you have any idea what Dad would do if he found out?"

"This is more important than house rules, Callie!" I snap, anger pounding in my throat like hot water.

"You're always so reckless, Hazel," she goes on. "You never know when to just butt out and leave things alone."

"Let me freaking *talk!*"

As I shout the last word, the light above the table bursts, showering down on us in shards and powder. Abby squeals and covers her head, cowering against the back of her chair. Everyone jolts in their seats, then freeze, as if waiting for more.

The rest of the lights are still on, but for some reason, the house feels as wrong and eerie as if we were plunged into pitch darkness. No one knows what to say.

Charlotte finally turns to me.

"Take my spell off too," she says.

CHAPTER 12

FAMILY TIES

W e decide to do it in my room. It's a toss-up as to when Dad gets home and we can't risk being caught. Thinking about him, with his tired face and deep worry lines, I'm struck with the realization that he must not know. Maybe he was just part of the fabric Gemmie and my mother wove around us to keep us safe. Make us normal. Maybe she never loved him at all, he was just a tool like we were meant to be.

As soon as I think it, my mind rejects the idea. His stability, his trust in the world as it is, must have been one of the things my mother loved most about him.

What would he think, coming home to find us huddled around a candle, speaking in hushed chants? He'd taken responsibility of all of us without even blinking. We were his children, no question. But this was something different, something he could never accept. He might even hate us for it. Or fear us. It had obviously been on my mother's mind, or she wouldn't have worked so hard to conceal it from him. Somehow, I can't bear the thought of shattering the world he'd worked so hard to create for us. It had to be our secret, my siblings and mine.

I fish out the napkin with Luke's incantation, which I'd tucked into mom's journal in my nightstand. The candle is still where I left it on the floor, cemented to the wood with dried wax.

"Right, so, you should probably sit down," I say to Charlotte. Everyone else has chosen a corner of wall to watch us warily.

"What about casting a circle?" she asks.

"Casting a what?" Suddenly, I feel horribly inadequate to be doing this.

"It's what you do before you cast a spell. So you're in a protected space and nothing outside can influence you? You draw it with chalk."

I shake my head in wonderment. "Where did you learn that?"

"She reads all those teen witch books," Callie drawls from the corner.

"Well, I didn't use one, but if you want to we can," I tell Charlotte.

"I have some," Abby pipes up. "In my—"

"Backpack, I know," Charlotte finishes, ducking out of the room. She returns with a pack, pulling out a worn white stick. Kneeling on the floor, she spins in a slow circle, dragging the chunk along the floorboards. When it's closed, she sits back Indian-style.

"You have to read this," I say handing her the napkin.

While she reads it over to herself, I light the candle. I sit next to her, my knee just outside the line she's drawn.

"I'm right here," I say. Charlotte nods, closing her eyes and taking a breath through her nose. She's got a better memory than I do. The words come tumbling out of her in perfect order, no hitches. When she gets to "release my soul within," the tiny flame pops, then leaps a foot higher, jerking and quivering in a thick blaze. Charlotte is flung backward as if invisible hands shove her. I wince at her twisted face, remembering the pain I'd felt and wishing I had warned her.

The flame sucks back down to the wick and smolders out. Charlotte sits up, her brow glossed with sweat.

"That sucked," she bursts. "Thanks for telling me—"

Her eyes widen. "Whoa," she says. "You have this cloud around you."

"I know," I say and grin. The feeling that I'm not in this alone anymore is enough to make me smile for the first time all day. "Apparently, it's an aura."

"I feel..." Charlotte presses her palm to her chest, struggling to articulate something. "I feel..."

"I know," I say. "It's like that at first. But eventually the pieces fit right."

"I knew we were different," she says, raising her smoky-lidded eyes to mine. "I felt it. Things always happen to us, you know? Like Melanie Carver, after she left the broom in my locker and told everyone our father was the Devil. I used to sit and just think about her skin drying out and shriveling, and that year she got Ichthyosis and had to leave school."

"Charlotte," Abby breathes, her eyes huge and horrified.

"I want mine off too." Callie steps forward, twisting her hands together. "Sometimes... sometimes I have dreams that come true. I'll see something so vividly, and it always happens. Last night I dreamed you talked to Gemmie, and a ghost came out of a table. She gave you a journal that was Mom's."

I get to my feet, walking to my nightstand. My fingers have trouble gripping the journal as I take it out. When I turn to Callie, her brow collapses, acceptance finally caving her resolve. She takes the journal when I hold it out to her, tears rolling out of her eyes.

"Mom," she says.

"The ghost did come out of a dagger," I tell her. She nods, her gaze locked to the pages as she turns each one as delicately as if they were tissue.

"I want to take my spell off too," Abby says. Her little chin is unwavering in her determination.

We all turn to Wyatt. He shifts under the sudden attention. It dawns on me that he hasn't said a word since I told them the truth. I take a step toward him. "Wyatt. We're in this together now. You're not alone."

"I want to go last," he says flatly.

I blink. We all seem to be coming apart at the seams like old stuffed animals, but he's not even chinked. *Must be a boy thing*, I tell myself. I turn back to Callie, who's already taken her sister's place in the circle.

Callie takes it better than I did, barely letting herself wince at the pain. Abby is the hardest to watch. She squirms and cries when the spell leaves her, her face twisting under the torture of it. When she's finished, she retreats to my bed, hugging my pillow to her chest.

Wyatt still hasn't moved an inch. His hands are hiked up under his arms, and a strange scowl has taken over his expression.

"Just try it, Wyatt," I say gently, holding the incantation out to him. He takes it between two fingers, his back still flush against the wall.

"Get in the circle," Charlotte says.

"I don't want to. Hazel didn't," he snaps.

I haven't seen him this petulant since he was ten and Dad took away his Playstation.

"I didn't," I say. "You don't have to if you don't want to."

He scans over the words a few times, shoving the napkin into his pocket when he's done. He closes his eyes, speaking them in a sloppy, hurried stream. Everyone winces, waiting for the pain to hit him.

He opens his eyes and shrugs. "Sorry. Don't feel anything."

He turns sharply, skirting around the bedframe, and a twitch of movement in his hand draws my eye.

"What were you doing with your fingers?" I say.

His neck goes rigid, like someone jerked his puppet string. He pivots slowly, raising his hands, spreading his fingers wide. "Nothing."

"Let's try it again. One more time." I can hear my big-sister voice coming out, the tone that used to be the only thing he'd listen to. But I know I'd seen it. He was crossing his fingers.

He stays still but something moves in his eyes, like shuffling embers.

"No. It's a waste of time," Wyatt says. His voice is low, not the voice of a fourteen-year-old anymore. In fact, looking at him now, I don't see Wyatt at all. All the smooth innocence in his face has turned to jagged anger and distrust. Something about him is off, and I want so badly to put it right again.

"Let's just try it," I say. I don't wait for him to answer. I'm already striding across the room and grabbing both his hands. The minute my skin touches his, cold spasms grip my muscles. I know I can't hold onto him for long, he's a foot taller than me, so out of desperation I yank him forward. He's just off-balance enough to stagger into the circle.

The sound that comes from him tears my heart to shreds. I'd heard him cry before, when he got shots or when he'd broken his arm, but nothing like this. It was the wailing scream of someone in more pain than I'd ever experienced. His shoulder blades pull together, and his spine curves backward, as if someone is dragging a rake down his back.

Abby covers her ears and screams over him, "Hazel, stop it! Let him go!"

My knees finally bend and I rush toward my baby brother. The toe of my sneaker crosses the circle first. Before I get my body past the line, my feet are ripped out from under me. The back of my head smacks floorboards, shooting a white flash across my vision. Blackness creeps in quickly from the corners of my eyes as the lights in the room surge angrily. The last thing I see is Abby and the twins hurl against the far wall like leaves in the wind, and Wyatt, still screaming on his knees in the circle.

CHAPTER 13

IONA

"Where is he now?" Luke asks, pressing the towel-wrapped icepack to my head.

Its coldness seeps through my hair, cradling my throbbing skull. Luckily, I had gotten the worst knock out of all of us. My sisters are jammed on the loveseat across from me, nursing minor bruised elbows and tailbones.

"We don't know," I say. "We were all knocked out, and he was gone when we woke up. He won't answer our calls. I can't believe I forced him into the circle like that."

Luke sits on the coffee table in front of me. It's not the living room I would have imagined him in. It's too colorful, almost whimsical. His aunt and uncle seem to be from much different stock.

"Why did you?" Luke asks.

The silent judgment in his voice makes me feel like I've made another misstep, a serious one this time. Why was I so bad at this? It was supposed to be in my blood.

The ice nips at my brain stem, and I'm almost glad of the pain. It's a fraction of what I deserve. "I don't know why. I just couldn't believe it worked on all of us and not him."

"He was crossing his fingers," Abby says. Her usually musical voice has gone hoarse. In fact, we all seem a bit dampened.

"He was, wasn't he? You saw it too?" I ask her. "What does that mean?"

I turn to Luke. For once, he looks taken aback.

"Are you sure?" he says. "You saw him crossing his fingers?"

I say I did, and my sisters back me up with nods.

"Because that's something only a witch would know how to do."

"Okay, I'm pretty sure every four-year-old can do *this*." I hold up my own intertwined index and middle fingers.

He looks like he desperately wants to sigh at me, but manages to restrain himself. "Yeah, but guess where it comes from? It's a way to ward off spells. If you know someone's aiming a spell at you, cross your fingers. Nine out of ten times that spell won't work."

"But how would Wyatt know that?" I say slowly, rolling the implications around in my mind.

Luke shakes his head. "Sorry, but I'm done pretending I can tell you anything about your family."

I swallow, taken aback by his tone. Then I remember the last time I'd seen him, I'd screamed at him for trying to tell me exactly what Gemmie had. I open my mouth to apologize, but there's a jangle of noise outside. The wind chimes are tapping together in the breeze. Luke stands up. "My aunt and uncle are home. I'm going to tell them you guys are here."

His long stride carries him into the hall, leaving the four of us alone. Six pairs of identical green eyes stare at me with mixed degrees of distrust. The sibling camaraderie that just an hour ago, had been thick as tar seems to have evaporated.

"I didn't mean to hurt him," I say.

"How do you know this guy?" Charlotte asks, tipping her head in the direction Luke went.

"It's complicated." I resituate the icepack. "I tutor him. His family has a background in Wicca and *Brujeria*. He was the one who gave me the incantation."

"He knows about us?" Callie asks. She says it like I've just handed over state documents to a North Korean spy.

"He does now. He didn't at first. It was all kind of a big accident."

"I don't think we get to believe in accidents anymore," Abby says, closing her arms around her thin frame.

The front door shuts, and voices banter back and forth in the hall. A woman bustles into the living room, tossing her jacket blindly onto the floor as she makes a beeline for us. Several strings of gemstone pendants click together as she hustles around the coffee table, pausing directly in front of my sisters. Her momentum keeps her thick black hair swinging even after she's stopped.

"You poor things," she says, touching Abby and Callie on the tops of their heads. "You must be so scared. I'm Iona, Luke's aunt. We'll get you some tea and some bread pudding, everything will seem better. Finn!" she barks at the doorway, where Luke is trailing back in with a middle-aged man, who's watching his wife with knowing amusement, "get the babies some tea, they're shaking. Which one is Hazel?"

Guiltily, I raise my hand. The woman steps toward me, a warm smile melting across her mouth. "Of course you are. I'd know you anywhere, Luke's spent hours talking about you."

"*Iona*," Luke and Finn say at the same time.

"Let's get them that tea, angel," Finn goes on, extending a hand to her. His patient expression reminds me of my father. Iona swishes off, her long dress hovering just above the floor. Now I know where the style in the house comes from. When they've gone, Luke shoves his hands deep into his pockets.

"Hazel, can we talk?" he asks, his voice low. I nod and stand, handing off my icepack to Abby. Luke silently leads me to the back of the house, past the kitchen where Iona is spooning out an entire pan of bread pudding onto plates. We stop at the last door on the left, Luke stepping back to let me inside.

This room suits him. The Caulfield house isn't big by any accounts, and Luke's room reflects that, but the calmness and simplicity has his touch all over it. Almost everything is white, and his floor puts mine to shame. Not a single dirty shirt or wayward sneaker.

"I hate to tell you, but I think you're a hoarder," I say, noting his lack of possessions.

Besides two books and a lamp, nothing else is on display.

Luke breathes out, and when I look at him, he's smiling.

"Thank you for letting us come here," I say. "I know it was weird for me to ask you, but all the power went out after the circle. And my dad still hasn't come home."

Luke moves over to his bed, leaning against the aged brass frame.

"I'm sorry," I say at last. "You were right. You were trying to help me, and I was horrible to you."

He taps his fingers against his knee, his face somber. "It wasn't just you. I grew up knowing I was a witch, like my parents and my aunts and uncles did. I can't imagine what it would be like to just wake up one day and find out."

"It's not the best day of my life," I say.

"You cursed me, you know." He finally turns those pale eyes to me, and my lungs forget how to function. "When you told me never to speak to you again. Not a strong one, but still. You said it and you meant it, put all your energy into it. I wanted to stop you, but I couldn't talk."

The knowledge is more than I can process. I don't know where to begin deciphering how that works. But I remember how it had felt when I said it, like something had drained from me, chipped off.

"I can't believe I did that." I touch my throat again, wanting to feel the firm stability of the amethyst stone, but it's still gone. Luke pushes off the bed, pulling the silver strand out of his back pocket.

"You need to learn to control your spells," he says, walking toward me. "You can't just be throwing curses around when you're angry or scared."

He clasps the necklace at the back of my neck, and the drop settles comfortably between my collarbones. His finger lingers for just a moment under my ear, grazing the soft skin and making my breath catch.

"Will you teach us?" It comes out unbidden. I'm glad some part of my brain was lucid enough to say "us" and not "me."

Luke makes a sound like half a laugh. "Uh—"

"Nothing complicated. Just show us what we're supposed to know. So we're not so..." I twist the carnelian ring, trying to think of the right word. "Behind."

He glances at the ceiling, weighing things in his mind. "Are you going to get frustrated and curse me again?" He says it teasingly.

I press my hand over my heart. "I won't, I promise."

He chucks me under the chin. "Got you already. Promises for witches are binding. Don't throw those around either."

"Good thing you're here then, *sensei*." I glance at my phone, noticing how late it's getting. "We should probably go home. We all have to act sane enough that my dad doesn't think anything's going on."

As we walk back down the hall, his aunt swings her head out of the kitchen. I can see the resemblance in their facial shape and coloring, though Luke is fairer. But Iona lacks any of the sharp lines that Luke has.

"Hazel, love," Iona says. "Your sisters just left. Callie took your car."

"She did not," I say, before I can stop myself. Callie had missed out on getting her license by a full ten points. She knew better than to get behind the wheel of my car. Luckily the SUV was more boat than vehicle, it could handle a couple of knocks.

"I can take you home," Luke says.

Iona curves an eyebrow up to her hairline. "Helmets," she says.

"Always," Luke answers, bending to give her a kiss on the cheek. "G'night."

She opens her arms to me, and I step into them. When she hugs me, it reminds me so much of my mother that for a moment, my lungs freeze. Iona seems to sense that I'm tottering on the edge of an emotional breakdown, and brushes a hand over my hair. "You're always welcome here, sweetheart. Anything you need."

———

Luke pulls his motorcycle up to the curb, leaning its weight onto his left foot. I unwrap myself from his back, my legs instantly missing the contact. I unstrap my helmet, fastening it to the back.

"I'll see you for tutoring tomorrow," Luke says, only his eyes showing from under his helmet. "We'll try Friday night for our first circle. Supposed to be a full moon, so we might get some cool stuff going."

"Sounds good," I say, clasping my hands behind my back. "Thank you again. I don't know what I would have done without you tonight."

"You would've been fine. You're a strong one." He nudges me with the toe of his sneaker before rolling the chopper into motion. He waves as he disappears down the street.

I open the front door, gearing up to ream Callie for car theft. The lights are back on, but the house is silent. I pad through the living room, listening for a telltale creak or rustle to let me know where everyone is.

"Hello?" I call. "Callie, I think we need to talk about crime and punishment!"

Bang! Every door on the bottom floor slams shut at once. I jump so hard, it sends a lightning bolt through the bruised part of my head.

I'm about to give my sisters an earful, to tell them tonight of all nights isn't the time to pull pranks, when the kitchen, bathroom, closet, front, and back doors all fly open at the same time, revealing that no one is behind any of them.

Bang, bang, bang. They open and close, smashing the air with such noise that I can only cover my ears until it's over.

When they finally stop, settling back into lifelessness, my heart-beat fills my ears with almost as much noise. Was this some kind of omen? If it was, I didn't know how long I was going to last at this witch thing before I had a heart attack.

Movement on the stairs snatches my attention. Callie is crouching on the fourth step, clutching her comforter over her like a parka.

"Um, yeah," she says acidly. "We have a ghost now. This is going really great so far. Yay."

CHAPTER 14

CIRCLE CASTING 101

Monday morning, I'm practically catatonic. None of us slept well between waiting for Dad and Wyatt and the incessant moaning of the pipes and wood. Whatever had slammed the doors seemed to have been satisfied with its message and crept into the walls.

In the kitchen, I drag myself between the fridge and counter, assembling cereal for myself. I'm too tired to even care about the creaking anymore. Dad weaves around me, pouring coffee.

"I need to get the plumbing checked out," he says when a particularly loud whine comes from the ceiling above us.

I grunt an assent. He gives me a hug around the shoulders and heads out, grabbing toast off the counter. The front door opens a few minutes after he's gone, and I go rigid.

"Wyatt?"

After a painful moment, my brother slumps around the corner into the kitchen. As tired and ragged as I feel, he looks ten times worse. The way he moves, it's like his back is barely strong enough to keep him upright. He leans over the counter, wearily pulling the plate of toast closer.

"I don't want to talk about it," he says coarsely.

"I just want to say I'm sorry. I shouldn't have forced you into something you weren't ready for."

He chews, expressionless. I watch him for the slightest hint of what's wrong. Of all my siblings, he and I have always been on the same wavelength. Maybe it was the hours of child therapy we had to go through together growing up, me for "hallucinating" and him for "hearing voices", but I could always read him perfectly. Now, it's like staring at a house with no lights on inside. I keep trying to convince myself his reaction to the circle was out of fear, but the feeling keeps gnawing at me. Something still isn't right.

"Where were you last night?" I say, leaning onto my elbows. "We covered for you with Dad, but still. We were really worried."

"Went to a friend's."

I'm about to press him for details, but a mass the size of a basket-ball plummets from the ceiling, landing right between us on the counter and smashing into pieces. Wyatt and I reel back, just missing being clipped by flying chunks of pottery. It's one of the fancy serving bowls we keep on the high shelves that line the kitchen wall. Something pushed it off.

Wyatt looks about four years old, with his wide eyes and gaping mouth. His chest pumps in and out as he tries to catch his breath. In this light, I can't see a trace of what I saw last night. He's just my brother, same round cheeks, same cleft chin.

"What the hell was that?" he splutters.

"This stuff started happening last night when we got home. We think it's a poltergeist."

He throws up his hands. "Perfect. You couldn't just leave it alone, Hazel."

He marches out of the kitchen and I wilt a bit as the refrigerator starts rattling against the wall. With one eye on the ceiling, I sweep up the shattered fragments on the bowl, trying not to think of it as my life.

———

"I have some ideas," Luke says, laying his backpack on the ground. Callie, Charlotte, and Abby sit on the floor of the living room like three little ducks in a row. All week we'd been planning for Friday, our first real circle. We'd gotten Dad out of the house with bowling coupons for him and his friends, which gives us a few hours of freedom.

Wyatt still wants nothing to do with it. When Charlotte told him what we were doing, he was gone within an hour. I'd stopped trying to make up for the circle. Whenever I reached out to him, all I got was venom and sulking.

Luke starts unloading apple-sized chunks of rough quartz from his backpack, setting them in a pile.

"I figured I'd teach you basic circle casting, then we can get fancy." He waggles his eyebrows at me.

"Are you a *brujo*?" Abby pipes up.

From his expression, she may as well have asked him where babies come from.

"Uh. Yeah, I guess so. That's how I was raised, anyway."

"*Brujos* use animals in rituals, right? Do you kill animals for sacrifices?"

"*Abby!*" I hiss at her.

"It's fine." Luke clears his throat. "No, I don't do that. But my parents did. And my Aunt Idra did, before she went nuts. They did a lot of stuff you don't really want to know about," he finishes heavily, and Abby's smart enough not to press him. He claps his hands, shaking off the somberness. "Right. So before you know anything else, you gotta understand energy. We're powered by energy. We give it off and take it in constantly. So does the earth, but on a much bigger scale. Spell casting is a manipulation of your—or something else's—energy for a specific purpose."

He hands me four chunks of quartz.

"Kindly pass those around, assistant," he says with the voice of a talk show host.

I make a face at him, but dole them out as he picks up a quarter-thick roll of chalk.

"As a witch, you can use certain things to help focus your energy. The quartz is going to help you call up power. I want to see what I'm working with." He rises to a half crouch, dragging the chalk along the ground in an arc behind us.

"Circles are spaces that you create. Negative energy can't cross chalk, same with salt, so it's safer inside the circle."

Wyatt. I can't help the thought, and instantly I'm ashamed all over again.

"When you get really good, you can create circles for different purposes, like if you don't want a particular person to cross it. But if you do it wrong, it can hurt someone."

Everyone turns to me. I chew my lip, trying not to remind them all that the first circle wasn't even my idea.

Luke goes on, cutting between us to draw a star. "Alright, now you say something like 'I cast the circle for blah-da-blah,' whatever you want to do. We're going to use this one to get your spirit to manifest. When we know what it is, we can work on getting rid of it."

I meet my sisters' eyes, my apprehension mirrored on their faces. Luke holds out his hands, closes his eyes in concentration. A hushed flow of Spanish tumbles out of his mouth, deep and alluring. I have to hide the smile that fights its way across my lips. When he's done, he directs us to each take a point of the pentagram, setting our crystals at our feet. He places the chalk stick in the center. He has us join hands, taking Abby's and mine. The rough underside of his palm feels warm against my fingers, and a shiver slips between my shoulder blades.

"Since I know the most spells, I'll say the words. Everyone else just focus on what I'm saying and try to imagine calling energy into yourself. And don't be scared. It can't hurt you in the circle."

"I'm not so sure," I grumble.

Luke squeezes my hand. "It'll be okay."

He closes his eyes, and we all do the same. His voice breaks the stillness of the room.

"Spirit, friend or foe,
Cross our circle and speak to us.
We call you across the spirit world.
Reveal your name to us."

Silence falls over the room like a heavy veil. I feel Luke's hand in

78

my left, Charlotte's in my right, both growing warmer and warmer. With no sight to anchor myself, my body seems to float, like I'm suspended in water. Excitement, or maybe fear, spirals up in my chest, rising into my shoulders and lifting me. Curious, I open my eyes to peek.

The crystals are floating. They form a ring in front of us, all quivering in the air at chest level. My head snaps to Luke, but he's looking at me with equal bewilderment. His lips part, about to speak, but then the chalk twitches. It rolls back and forth, then jerks upright. Painfully slow, like a child learning to write, it scrawls a line, then another.

Abby breathes in sharply, hearing the scratching against the wood. I can't look away until the chalk drops back into lifelessness.

In jagged, mismatched letters, the ghost has written MATTHEW TOWNSEND.

CHAPTER 15

LETTERS

I can't help it. I try to be stronger than the fear, but it flattens me like a wave, throwing me back against the sand. I'm ripped backward, my hands torn from Luke and Charlotte's as the crystals clatter to the ground.

A shattering sound crashes down on us. Everyone ducks as one by one, the glass picture frames on the wall explode into splinters. Luke shakes my shoulders, cupping my face in his hands, blocking out everything but him.

"Hazel, you're fine. Calm down. Breathe."

I nod, trying to suck in a breath that doesn't make it to my lungs.

"You pulled too much energy," he says, "and it's trying to find an outlet. Just let it go. Breathe and let it go."

I exhale, my body deflating. My heart stops drumming as insistently, slowly accepting that we aren't in danger. The last picture frame swings on its nail, cracked, but intact. Luke helps me stand up.

"Jesus, Hazel," Charlotte says, her cheeks still red with breathlessness.

"Um." Callie points to the writing on the floor. "Did we talk to the ghost?"

Luke walks back into the circle, peering down at the message for the first time. I can almost feel the weight pressing down at him as he stares at the name, his face clouding.

"Matthew?" he says, barely a mutter. "Matthew, is that you?"

We all wait for a sound, a creak, anything, but the house is lifeless again.

"I'm sorry." Luke grinds his fist into his chest, over his heart, his voice twisted with such pain it makes my throat close. "I'm sorry I didn't protect you."

At the corner of the room, the metal vent in the ceiling clatters to the ground. Out of the hole, a rectangular box plummets down, landing squarely on the floor. Charlotte wastes no time marching up to it, while the rest of us stay motionless, as if we're afraid it might charge us.

Charlotte lifts up a faded shoebox, barely held together by leather strings wrapped around it. She brings it over to the circle, setting it on the floor and gingerly removing the ties like a surgeon.

"If there's a skull in there, I'm out of here," Callie states.

The lid comes off, and Charlotte pulls out a handful of cream envelopes.

"Letters," she says. She paws through the box, setting out two more bundles.

"Are they Mom's?" I ask.

"Got to be," Charlotte says, opening one and unfolding the paper inside. "But it's not her handwriting."

I take the sheet from her. It's stiff and thick, old paper that's done its time with dust. I peer at the wide, curvy handwriting, coming to the same conclusion. Mom's handwriting was a constricted, almost Edwardian cursive, a product of her British upbringing.

"Why would she hide these?" I wonder aloud.

"Why did the ghost want us to find them?" Charlotte adds.

"Not a ghost. Matthew Townsend," Abby says, her voice uncharacteristically serious. She looks at Luke, who doesn't seem to be fully with us anymore. "Did you know him?"

"Yeah, I knew him. He died in the fire at Sagestone High. He's," he stops, correcting himself, "he *was* my friend."

"Why's he in our house?" Callie demands.

Luke shakes his head, swallowing hard. "I don't know. But it's not a good thing. If he hasn't moved on, there's a reason for it. Sorry, guys. This took a lot out of me. I'm going to head home. We'll do this again next Friday." He slings his backpack over his shoulder. "I'll be more… prepared."

He stalks past us, veering to the left, down the hall. My chest constricts as soon as I hear the front door close, and I know I can't leave it like this.

I catch him in the front yard as he's strapping his backpack to his bike. "Luke!"

He turns to me, and I almost don't recognize him. He's carrying such a burden, it's drawing down the corners of his face.

"I'm so sorry," I say. "I know what it's like to lose someone."

"Do you know what it's like when it's your fault?" he says bitterly, like each breath is tearing into him. "When you could have stopped it, and you didn't because you were too stupid to see it coming? I knew what he was getting into, and I thought I could save him by myself, but I couldn't. It's my *fault*." His voice cracks on the last word. "Mine."

I wrap my arms around his shoulders without even thinking. I can't just stand there and watch him break apart on the sidewalk. He rests his head against my neck, his hands crossing over my back, holding onto me like the world is spinning and I'm the only stable thing in it.

"I do know," I say quietly into his shirt. "My mom killed herself."

He stiffens, his arms tightening around me. "Jesus. I'm sorry."

I pull away, feeling the abhorrent sting in my eyes that preludes tears. "It's okay. We're all fine now. I just wanted you to know, we're a bit damaged too."

Luke nods, forcing his mouth into a tiny smile. It's a feat, given the night we've had.

"It gets better than this," he promises. "We're going to find a way to help him, then I'm going to show you the beautiful parts of the craft."

"Good, because I'm not really sold on it yet," I say heavily.

Luke throws a leg over his chopper. With his first finger, he taps me under the chin.

"See ya, kid."

He pulls away from the curb, rumbling down the street. I wait another moment in the warm darkness of the night. Somehow, it's soothing to be outside, away from the cold starkness of the house and the dead boy's spirit creeping around in our walls. I steady my breathing, counting heartbeats, when something lands in the mesquite tree above me, beating strong wings against the air. I look up, hoping maybe it's one of the barn owls we get in the fall.

A white face looks down, vast eyes like black glass fixed on me. I take a step back. It's by far the creepiest bird I've ever seen. It's the size of a vulture, with the same unforgiving beak, but its face is flat like an owl's. The rest of its body could be beautiful, with feathers the color of milky tea cloaking its chest, growing darker as they reach its wingtips. But the eyes throw me.

It stares at me, motionless and without even a trace of fear. It's almost human, the way it's sizing me up.

"Hazel." Abby's voice comes from the front door. "Is everything okay?"

"I think I'm seeing an omen," I say. I don't dare break the staring contest having spotted her claws, four thick curved daggers that are meant for tearing things apart in record time.

"The bird?" Abby says, coming out onto the porch. "I see it too. What is it?"

"I don't know."

She spreads her wings and I almost duck. They take up at least three feet on either side of her. She sweeps them twice, and she's gone. I shake it off, walking back toward the house.

Charlotte's emptied the box, sorting letters and envelopes into three piles. Callie sits cross-legged next to her, peering at a page full of scrawling, spiky script.

"Do we know what they are yet?" I say.

"It's letters between these two people 'Salem' and 'Isolda,' if those are their real names. Honestly, I'm not convinced," Charlotte says. "They're talking about some kind of spell, I think. They call it *Veri Segno*. There's this entire letter on directions for making ink."

She holds out a page to me. I read through it, my skin turning cold.

"Not ink," I say. "Blood. This is how to make ink out of blood."

The twins put on the exact same expression of distaste.

"Why?" Callie says.

The antique lamp in the living room trembles violently, the ceramic clattering against the table underneath. Before any of us can react, Abby marches into the center of the living room, fists clenched.

"Matthew, *enough!*" she bellows with all the might she can muster. "Stop breaking our stuff! If you want to communicate with us, do it with the lights like a civilized ghost."

Immediately, the shaking stops.

"Thank you," Abby says.

The twins and I share impressed glances, not daring to interrupt Abby's roll.

"Obviously, he knows something important is in those letters," Abby says, turning to us. "He wanted us to find them. Is that right, Matthew? Blink the lights once for yes, twice for no."

We wait on our toes for a moment. The lamp flickers once.

"Do you know what this ritual is?" I hazard, holding up the page.

The lamp blinks *yes*.

"Does it have something to do with our mother?" I go on.

Nothing.

"Maybe he doesn't know?" Abby guesses.

"He was friends with Luke. Does it have something to do with Luke?"

Yes.

I sink to the floor, peering at the letter closely. It's from Salem to Isolda, dated 1992.

"*I know the Veri Segno will work, it's just a matter of finding the right binding symbols,*" Salem writes. "*Without being bound to the body, the blood will be useless.*"

I turn the paper over. Isolda has written back with half a page of drawn symbols, each connected to the other in a continuous line. It's as beautiful as it is frightening. They seem to swim under my sight, moving with their own energy. I may know nothing else, but I know these drawings are powerful. They're meant for a purpose so far over my head I can't begin to guess at it.

Across the room, Callie lets out a strangled breath. Her hand covers her mouth as she reads the letter she's holding.

"I know what the *Veri Segno* is," she says.

"The ritual?" Charlotte asks, leaning over to look at her page. "What is it?"

"It's meant to steal a blood witch's power. You kill them and drain their blood. Then you mix it with ashes from Yew bark and tattoo it into your body. This guy Salem invented it."

She tosses the paper down, pressing her hand against her forehead.

"I feel sick," she says.

"Why would Mom have these letters?" Abby asks.

Their voices echo around my head hollowly. I can only think of one thing: Luke's tattoos. They can't be. But the strange color, the symbols...

"Matthew," I say, "did Luke do the *Veri Segno*?"

Shock buffets the air in the room.

"What?" Callie says.

"Hazel, what are you saying?" Charlotte seconds her twin.

"I'm asking Matthew."

For so long, I stare at the light, willing him to say no.

Finally, Matthew blinks *yes*. My ribs collapse on themselves, crushing my lungs. All this time, he had looked at me and lied to my face. He'd carried the death of an innocent person in the back of his mind, and still been able to laugh, to smile, to make jokes. Was he really a monster? A murderer?

I stare down at the letter in my hands, the lines muddling together. I move my thumb, noticing a stamp in the left corner. The paper is charred under it, like it has been branded. The mark consists of a tiny bird with outstretched wings. Holding a scythe.

"I know this symbol," I breathe. It's the same one that had been splashed over the front of Oggun.

———

"This has to be some sort of sick cult," Charlotte says, sifting through the stack. The symbol is burned into every single one. I run to my backpack, pulling out Mom's journal. The pages flip roughly in my fingers as I pray to find nothing. But there it is. The mark has been burned into the back cover. I slowly turn to my sisters.

"Not just any cult," I say. "Stolam."

It's all slotting together in a horrible, nightmarish truth: Luke's parents, my parents, the man at Oggun, why Luke had seemed so familiar, all tied together by the same evil. Abby was right. We weren't allowed to believe in accidents anymore.

My sisters all look up, waiting for an explanation. I swallow, scraping moisture down my dry throat.

I say, "I think it's time I told you the truth about Mom."

CHAPTER 16

BEGINNER'S CURSE

I catch a glimpse of myself in the warped mirror hanging in my locker. The weekend wasn't kind to me, and it shows. Luke called every day, each time its own torture session, seeing his name and experiencing the devastation all over again. My body was reflecting the slow mental deterioration I'd been going through since the day I'd accidentally lifted my spell.

"Hazel."

I've been preparing internally for days, but Luke's voice still slithers down my lower back. When I turn, he's standing behind me in a dark blue sweatshirt, sleeves pushed up to his elbows, his hair still wet from swim practice.

"I called you all weekend. I was worried about you guys. Is everything okay?"

There's actual concern in his eyes, which only makes the betrayal more vicious. The entire speech I had prepared evaporates in my mind.

I say the only thing I can think of. *"Veri Segno."*

If there was a small part of me holding onto the hope that he didn't know anything, it dies when he drops his arms, his eyes widening. "Where'd you hear that?"

"So that's it then. Your tattoos. You killed a blood witch and stole her power."

He shifts his eyes to the crowded hallway, shuffling from foot to foot.

"Hazel, we can't talk about this now," he whispers. "Please let me come over and I'll explain it. It's not what you think."

There's only one thing I need to hear him say.

"Are those tattoos *Veri Segno?*" It's a miracle I can keep my voice steady.

He swallows. "Yes."

"Then there's nothing to explain." I reach out and grab his forearm. Studying Mom's journal had taught me that this was the one and only way to make sure a curse got to the person it was meant for. "I may not know what I'm doing, but I want you to look in my eyes and see how much I mean this. *Never talk to me at school again. Do not ever come to my house. Stay away from my sisters and my brother.*"

His face goes slack. Something stuck, even if it was just a beginner curse. My hands shake with the gravity of what I've just done. I slam my locker, shoving my way through the crowd. No sound follows me, but I feel his eyes on my back until I turn the corner.

———

"Why aren't you at tutoring?" Taylor asks me at lunch. Her baby blue eyes narrow as she looks up at me.

I set my tray down next to M.C.

"I just didn't want to go today," I say stiffly. "Why, is it a problem?"

"Yes," Taylor answers with convincing sincerity, "this is when Gallagher, M.C., and I have our threesomes, and now you've messed it up."

I laugh, relaxing a bit. I couldn't risk Luke showing up and trying to talk to me during our usual period. I wasn't sure how long my spell would last, since the last one only stuck for a couple of hours. I don't know how strong I am, but I'm pretty sure Luke's stronger.

I take his ring off my finger and the world instantly jumps into a riot of colors. I close my eyes for a moment, telling myself I'm not going to be afraid of it anymore. This is who I am. I'm going to live with it.

When I open my eyes again, everything has dulled to a gentle glow. I let the ring rest in my palm. I'd worn it since the day he gave it to me, even when it burned my heart to look at it. The only way to get it back to him was Taylor. She didn't know what an awkward situation was.

"Could you do me a huge favor?" I ask her, holding out the ring to her.

She takes it, studying it inquisitively.

"Can you give that to Luke? He forgot it," I say, "and I don't want to see him right now."

Taylor nods, slipping it into her shorts pocket.

"So he proposed then?" she says with a grin.

"We actually kind of had a fight," I say.

It strikes me this is the first time I've lied to her in our years of friendship. But *I* can hardly get my head around what's happened with my family. I'm not even sure I could explain it to her.

"Really? Like a lovers' spat?" Taylor cranes her neck around the lunchroom until she spots where he's sitting. "Ugh, Alison is after your man. Like, *all* after your man."

Everyone glances to their table, but I keep my eyes forward. Seeing Luke with Alison is the last thing I can handle right now. I scratch my neck as a tingle runs up it, like fingers softly dragging along the nape.

"He's looking at you," Taylor says, looking directly behind me at Luke's table. "He's full on staring at you."

I shift my shoulders, feeling invisible fingers brush across them.

"He looks miserable," M.C. says.

"Good."

Taylor raises her eyebrows. "Wow, I've never seen bitter Hazel before. What a tiger. I have something to cheer you up though! Guess what we're doing for Halloween?"

"Halloween? That's in like three weeks," I say.

"Yeah, but the awesomeness cannot be contained. We're all

driving down to Austin to go to a Full Moon Party at Barton Springs! Excitement is now acceptable."

"Ehh," I say.

"*Ehh?* Okay, your lack of excitement is excused based on your boy issues. But by Halloween, you better have some enthusiasm."

I tear off a piece of sandwich, wondering if I'll ever feel enthusiastic about anything again.

CHAPTER 17

THE DEAD-BLOOD CURSE

When I get home, I go straight upstairs to my bed and pull out Mom's journal. It's been my only comfort the past few days. It's mainly a collection of spells she'd either created or come across, but occasionally she'd add a note for context. I lived for those. Seeing what she was doing, where she was.

I trace her name on the first page, feeling the loops as if I'm writing it myself. *Emily S. Sayers.* She wasn't that much older than me when she started this journal. I let the book fall open to where I stopped, a recipe for spelled hazelnut tea, meant to keep omens from coming at night.

I turn the page and freeze. It's the first time I've seen my father's name on a page.

Faolan taught me this. I've never seen such intricate circle casting. He's clearly next in line to be leader.

I turn the page. There it is again, that name.

Faolan taught me to spell a dagger. I have to use it for initiation. I worry that I'm not strong enough to do this, but I have no choice. I'll die if I can't be with him.

The spells that follow grow darker, stranger. One calls for the head of a coyote in order to call a storm over a specific location. A curse to make someone's feet grow sores *"for the bastards that killed my little cat, Penny."*

The next mention of Faolan is under a new-house cleansing ritual. *Faolan and I moved into a little cottage on Fisher St. There's a room to put the baby when she comes.*

The baby. That's me. Tears leap to my eyes as I look at the word. Hungrily, I turn the next page and almost throw the book in frustration. Blank. It wasn't fair for Gemmie to keep parts of my life from me, things I needed to know to be whole.

The next entry I can read is far at the back. It's just an herbal blend for tea.

Helps with paranoia, my mother's written. *Calms nerves. Tasteless. F. doesn't notice when I brew it with his Earl Grey.*

There's a drawing on the next page, something that looks like a slab of rock balanced on two pillars. The entirety of its face is covered with symbols.

F. is making a Cutter Stone.

I put my fingertip over the letter. Somewhere along the way, my father became just "F."

He thinks I don't know about it, but I've seen him carving the marble in the barn. Even if he's powerful enough to craft one, it won't be finished for years. I want to ask him whom he's planning to sacrifice, since the blood must come from a member of your family. And his has died out, besides the children and me. How can he want immortality if it means we can't be together?

Immortality. Could that even be possible? A cold chill climbs down my back. Had Faolan been planning to sacrifice one of us to get it?

They found me, the top of the next page reads. *They find me no matter where I go. F. has them so wrapped up in his lies, they'd throw themselves on a fire if he asked them to. I can't keep running anymore. They'll keep coming for the children if I can't find a way to hide them. There has to be a way to stop all this.*

With heavy fingers, I turn the last page. It's a curse.

The Dead-Blood Curse. There's a list of ingredients, horrible things like hearts of doves and a snake's stomach, that make up some sort of brew. *Once drunk, only an hour of life remains. There won't be any going back. The Cutter Stone will be a good one, with his skill. It'll only take the blood of a family member. He's stupid to forget I'm his family too, bound to him by the laws of his own religion. The stone will work once, and F. will take the curse along with my life. One sacrificed soul buys eternity from his god. What kind of god is that, who takes immortality so lightly? Maybe his soul can live forever, but his body will die with me. There is no better end for us, none more deserving of the things we've done. I can die for my children. He can die for his greed.*

"No!" The scream rips out of me before I can stop it, and I fling the book away from me. I already feel it again—the way the universe tore in two when we heard she was dead—and I don't want to. I *can't.*

"Your mother killed herself," the worst police officer in the history of police officers had said, "slit her wrists in a backyard in Louisiana. Probably a mental breakdown, due to her history."

Who even *says* that to a kid, much less four kids? Even then, even at ten, I knew it couldn't be true. Whatever a Cutter Stone was, it needed the death of a family member to work, and apparently Faolan was depraved enough to try to kill one of his own children. The only thing that had saved us was Mom. She'd *sacrificed* herself for us. The knowledge feels like concrete in my stomach.

My door swings open and Charlotte runs in. Right away she knows something's wrong.

"What?" She sinks onto the bed in front of me. "What happened?"

"She died for us. Mom did." The words tumble out of me. I can't hold the hurt in anymore. "Faolan, our father, he was going to kill one of us, and Mom took our place. She cursed her blood and sacrificed herself to kill him."

"I don't understand. Who wanted to kill us?"

I push the journal into her hands. Sobs pummel my insides, too strong to speak through. I watch her face as she reads, follows the same threads until the last page.

"Mom," she whispers when she finishes. "She *saved* us."

"Why would she fall in love with someone like that?" I say, dragging my knuckles over my eyes to stop the flow. "How could she be so blind about him?"

"You don't think you did the same thing with Luke?" Charlotte says, not even looking at me. Her face is stone, closed off. I open and close my mouth, her statement lodged in my heart. It's true. I didn't see because I didn't want to see.

"Where do you think he is now?" Charlotte asks. "Immortal soul with no body. What happened to him? You think he's stuck somewhere, like Matthew?"

All I can do is shake my head. This world we've opened is too big for me. There are a million things I don't understand, and all of them can hurt me.

"Gemmie said they bound him. Maybe he's trapped somewhere, like the soul in Mom's dagger," I say.

Charlotte gathers the journal to her chest. "We have to tell the others. They deserve to know why she left us."

When she leaves, I fall back on my pillows. The one person who might understand this pain, who might be able to explain the chaos we've been thrown into, is the one person I can never speak to again.

CHAPTER 18

WATCHERS

The bird is back. She's watching as I take the trash out one Sunday, perched in the same u-shaped branch. That strange, pale face tracks my progress down the sidewalk, the two coal orbs of her eyes never blinking. I glare back, replacing the lid of the trashcan.

"Go away," I say.

Her head ticks right, then left, almost mockingly. I turn my back on her, heading inside.

Sundays became our circle nights. Using Mom's journal, we've been casting simple spells, things with no chance of backfiring. We spelled a protection sachet for Dad's car using herbs from the garden. We tried to get more answers out of Matthew, but it was hard when the only possible responses were *yes* or *no*.

Today, we're using one of Mom's oldest spells to try to get Abby's crush to ask her out. It's one of the most benign, since we still don't know how far we can stretch our abilities, and Gemmie had warned us not to push too hard too fast.

We spread our supplies out on the floor of my room, since it's the furthest from Dad's room, on the opposite corner of the first floor. Abby's tongue pokes out of her mouth as she cuts out a picture of her crush of the month.

"This feels a little stalker-y, Abby," I say, unwrapping a brand new red wax candle.

"What's the point of being witches if we can't make our lives a little better," she says, laying the photo on the ground proudly.

The peal of the doorbell echoes through the house.

I blow out a breath, standing. "I'll get it."

"Be fast!" Abby calls after me.

I open the door on a kid about Wyatt's age, but half as tall and twice as wide. He looks like someone squashed him down with the bottom of a shoe.

"Hi." He grins at me, showing two rows of pointy teeth where not a single one is in the right place. "Is Wyatt home?"

"Who are you?" I say. I can't explain it, but my insides were set squirming the second I saw him.

"I'm his best friend," the kid says, "Keir."

His coloring is agonizingly similar to Luke's, but his eyes are so dark and black, I can't tell where the iris ends and the pupil begins. It's like looking down into two tiny, never-ending wells.

"His best friend is Bradley Smith," I say coldly.

"Things change," the kid says as he chews the inside of his cheek. "Can you just get him?"

I'm about to tell the kid to come back later, but Wyatt's hand grasps the door, pulling it open.

"Come inside," he says to Keir.

"Dad doesn't want company on school nights," I mumble to Wyatt.

"It's fine," he snaps.

"Do you even know this kid?"

For the first time, Wyatt peers right into my eyes, and I step away from him. His gaze is icy, so unlike Wyatt at all that I don't even recognize him for a moment.

The door slips out of my hand before I even realize it. Keir takes the opportunity to shuffle in, but I can't look away from my brother. I'm afraid to even blink until he turns away from me.

The pair trudges up the stairs, not even talking to each other. Keir turns his head over his shoulder, giving me a salute and another toothy grin. I press my hand to my chest, trying to tell myself how irrational I was being. Maybe he was spiraling into something I couldn't touch, but he was still my brother.

"Who was it?" Charlotte asks when I close the door to my room.

I join them in the circle they've drawn, closing it with the chalk and sitting down. "Some creepy friend of Wyatt's."

The mood plummets, making the air in the circle cold. Wyatt had been shunning us since we broke our mother's spell, slinking around the house in silence, disappearing after school for hours. He'd even quit football. It wasn't like him. But then, nothing these days really seemed like him.

We all hold hands, casting the circle like Luke had taught us to, stating our purpose outright. We assemble the parts of the spell, Abby writing her name over the boy's picture, Callie filling a mason jar with honey, and Charlotte lighting the candle. Everything's handed to me, and I submerge the picture in the jar, twisting the lid and sealing it with wax. I place it in the center. I still haven't gotten over the shudder of fear in my chest every time we call energy. Our voices blending together when we speak the spell sounds like a scene from a movie when people are calling up the Devil.

I feel a familiar tingle working up my spine, the sensation of waves gently floating under me. I open my eyes just to peek.

The jar is spinning slowly on its rim, but that's not what grabs my attention. Keir is standing in my open doorway, watching us with the expression of a cougar stumbling upon a hurt deer.

I suck in a breath, startled, and the jar explodes. A shard rockets across the circle, burying itself in Abby's shin. She lets out a cry, breaking hands with Callie and Charlotte. The room turns into a vacuum, like someone's blown a hole in an airborne plane, dragging us all toward Abby. She's pulling too much power.

Before I can reach her, the windows burst open, smacking against their sills. Wind pours in, so strong it's as if we're in the middle of a tornado. Papers and books fly off my shelves, ripped from the shelves in the tumult.

"Abby!" Callie throws her arms around our little sister, rubbing her shoulders to calm her down. As she catches her breath, the wind peters out, everything settling across my floor. Abby whimpers softly, examining her injury.

I whip around to look at Keir.

He's unflinching, as if he's seen it a hundred times. The light in his eyes gives me the sick feeling we've just done something very wrong.

"Cool," he says.

The door slams shut on him, taking his leering face away. My bed scrapes across the floor, screeching in protest, and hurls into the wall, blocking the doorway.

"Matthew, stop!" Callie orders. "You know you can't do that when Dad's in the house!"

The ceiling begins to groan and wail, pipes beating against pipes in a loud percussion.

"We get it, you don't like Keir," I hiss. "I don't either."

The whining of the house slowly falls off as Matthew loosens his grip. I leave my bed where it is, thankful for the barrier it makes between the unsettling boy and us.

"He *saw* us," Charlotte says. "What do we do?"

"I don't know," I say, "but I definitely don't think it was the first time he's seen magic."

100

CHAPTER 19

HALLOWEEN

"Okay, so I know you've been driving me a lot lately," Callie says to me over her pizza.

"Quite a lot," I second.

She rolls her eyes. "Fine, but as it *is* Halloween, and you're the best big sister in the world... so please take me to Shannon's!"

Dad bustles into the kitchen, rifling under papers for his keys.

I take a huge bite, trying to hurry through my meal.

"I'm still mad about when you took my car," I say, swallowing way too quickly. "Remember, when you left me at Luke's? Besides, I'm going to Austin to meet Taylor and Gallagher. I have to take it."

Callie turns her pout on Dad. "Dad, please take me to Shannon's. None of my friends can drive yet. It's my only chance to do something fun tonight."

"Sorry, honey, I'm headed to the hospital. One of my patients went into premature labor, we're having to do an emergency C-section." He digs his keys out from under Abby's lunchbox.

"That's horrible," I say.

He shakes his head. "Totally healthy mother, never had any problems. Must just be a Halloween curse."

Callie and I look at each other, not sure whether to count that as a joke or not. Dad gives me a kiss on the forehead.

"Be back at eleven. I'm not sure when I'll be home, but it's still a school night."

As he hurries out the front door, Callie sighs exasperatedly. "*Fine,* I guess I'll be a loser and stay home all night."

"Everyone else is home," I say, tucking a slice of pizza up in a paper towel. I'm late meeting Taylor at Barton Springs already. "Have a fun circle with Matthew. Tonight's supposed to be the night the veil between our world and the spirit world is thinnest." I raise my eyebrows suggestively. "Maybe we can finally see what he looks like."

"I know what he looks like. His picture was on the news," Callie grumbles. "Über dork."

The blender turns on furiously.

"She didn't mean it, Matthew," I say, punching the off button. "I gotta go. See you in a few hours. Happy Halloween!"

"Yeah, yeah." Callie slumps into a chair while I rush out the door.

———

Barton Springs is a strange construct, half nature and half manmade. Apparently, M.C. had given Taylor the idea to throw the party at a natural spring the size of three Olympic pools, one with a huge concrete square laid down around it. The sloping hills on either side of it are crawling with people in swimsuits. They all seem to be Sage-stone kids.

I sit on the side of the spring, dangling my feet in the frigid water. Taylor joins me, passing me a purple plastic cup filled with grape juice.

"Blood of the ancestors." She bares her teeth in a lion's grin.

I try not to give away the weighty, sick feeling the idea gives me. Gallagher drops down on my other side, letting out a long howl. Everyone around us picks up the call, and soon the entire park rings with the forlorn sound.

"It's tradition," he says to me. "I did my homework."

"We should dance!" Taylor insists. "We need to distract Hazel from the horribleness in her life."

I snort. "Thanks."

"I concur," Gallagher says, standing and heaving me up by my elbow. "'When all else fails, we dance.' Stephen Hawking said that."

"I'm not sure you have the right Stephen Hawking," I say, but the pair is already pulling me toward the circle of bouncing dancers. Gallagher launches into his shockingly-accurate-yet-still-out-of-place-80's-moves, while Taylor reenacts some sort of kickboxing routine. I do my best to smile and bob along, even joining in the next howl when the clouds part and moonlight washes over the grass.

I sway a bit as my mind fills with a light fog. I peek at my drink, wondering if I could possibly have gotten a spiked cup by accident. My body seems to get heavier by the second. Prickling warmth scurries up my limbs, like getting into a hot bath after being very cold. Taylor claps her hands in front of my face, giving me a sharp slap of clarity. I stare at her blearily, her face swimming in and out of focus.

"You okay?" she asks.

"Totally," I answer, sounding much louder in my own head. "I'm going to go to the bathroom."

I push away and weave through the crowd. Somewhere along the way, my drink slips out of my hand. The crowd thins as I trudge along the fence line, until the thumping beat of music has almost faded. My eyes land on a pair of shoes, attached to legs, connected to a body that's blocking my path.

Luke stares down at me, his blue eyes almost glowing in the hazy light.

"Hi," I say hesitantly. I should be angry at seeing him. I should scream and run away. All I can feel is a slightly pulsing numbness.

Slowly, my muffled mind puts the pieces together. "Did you spell me?"

I'm proud of the shred of anger I manage to conjure, despite my body feeling like it's stuffed with cotton.

Luke cracks a very small, apologetic smile. "You didn't really leave me a choice. You won't talk to me. I knew if you saw me, you'd run away."

"You're not supposed to be able to talk to me," I protest. It'd been three weeks since I'd heard his voice. I'd almost forgotten what it sounded like.

"Not at school or your house," he says. "Right now, we're at neither. The problem with curses is you have to be specific."

"How did you know I'd be here?"

"Taylor told me. I asked her if there was any place I might catch you outside of school." I remind myself to give Taylor a lesson in loyalty later.

"This isn't fair," I say.

Luke drops his smile, backing off instantly. "I know. I'm sorry. I really came here to explain."

He takes my hand, tugging me inside the stone building that houses the bathrooms. We slip into the unisex room, the only thing remotely private, wedged in the corner. He closes the door and I maneuver myself onto the sink, pressing my cheek against the cool mirror.

"This is romantic," I say coldly.

"I know you're afraid of me," Luke says.

"You're a murderer." I start flipping through recollections of every spell I've seen, trying to think of some way to break his curse. I focus on the feeling of glass against my skin, staring at the tiles in the wall until the fuzziness fades slightly.

Luke cups my face in his hands, shaking it roughly so the clouds clear out of my eyes.

"I'm not," he says. "I never killed anyone. You can't know what it was like, growing up knowing that no matter what you do, someone else had just been given more power than you'd ever have."

"Totally. So it was justified. Let me out of here." I try to get my legs under me, but end up crashing sideways into the wall.

Luke hooks my arm, setting me onto the toilet. When he leans down, his eyes are even with mine. That sad face makes a reappearance, begging me to believe that it's seen more horrors than I could ever imagine.

"I told you my parents were evil. They *are* evil. They've been obsessed with power since way before I was born, it's like an addiction to them. My mother is the leader of a cult called Stolam. They search out blood witches and perform the *Veri Segno* to steal their abilities. When I was thirteen, they made me go through it. I didn't kill the witch, but I didn't stop it either. I couldn't. You have to understand, I'd lived my whole life with the cult, I didn't know how to say no. My mother is very powerful. She can make it so you can't fight back."

The muscles in his jaw tighten and shift. *He's afraid of her*, I realize.

"That's the reason I ran away. I didn't *want* the *Veri Segno*. I would give anything to undo it. Her blood is in me now, I can't change that. But I'm not evil, and being tattooed against my will doesn't make me that way."

My mind is fighting, pushing the murkiness back. The room becomes more distinct with every passing second. I feel the twisting hurt in my stomach again as I look at him, so thoroughly beaten by the sheer memory of what had happened to him.

"Show me," I say softly.

His hands tighten against his chest. "Show you...?"

"The tattoo. I want to see it."

A battle takes place in his eyes. He wants to say no, to hold his ground, but sadness and defeat tug at his strength until finally he gives in. His fingers grip his shirt, peeling it upward as slowly as if it were his own skin. The dark red whorls and lines begin to poke out at the divot between his ribs. By the time he tugs the shirt over his head, the tattoos have taken over his entire upper body. They cling to his chest with spiny symbols, reaching over his shoulders and twisting down to his elbows. They look almost alive to me. They seem to tremble with fury, as if the blood that made them is still yearning to break free, leave its prison. Luke's face doesn't belong to that thieving body.

"This is what Stolam does," he says. "I have to live with it now. I didn't know who you were when I met you, please believe me. I would never hurt you, or your family. But there're other people that will if they find out who you are. That's what happened to Matthew."

I try to swallow and can't. It's like a hand tightens around my throat. "What do you mean?"

"Stolam tracks down blood witches. There's not many left anymore, and even fewer people who can detect them. Stolam has one Seer, someone like you and me who can see auras. They move constantly. It's impossible to know where they are. I didn't know they were here until they'd already killed Matthew."

The load of guilt presses down on him, pushing his shoulders forward under the weight. I want to do something to fix him, to put the pieces back together.

"My parents were in Stolam too." The words are out before I can think.

He freezes. "What?"

"My mother and father. Emily Sayers and Faolan Sicario. My mom left when my dad went crazy. She ran away with us because she was afraid of what he'd do to us."

"That means we know each other. Or did." His fingers rest on my knee as the recognition spreads across his face. "We must have been kids together. Thousands of places we could have gone, and we ended up in the same city by accident."

"Abby thinks we can't believe in accidents anymore."

He smiles. Something sticks in his brain, drawing his eyebrows together. "Emily. There was never an Emily in the cult. Are you sure she went by that name?"

I shake my head, rubbing the stiffness in my neck.

"I don't think so." But just then, it hits me like a sheet of ice. "My mother. The 'S' is for Salem. Emily *Salem* Sayers." As soon as I say it, I know it's true. "She invented the *Veri Segno*."

Luke's hands grasp my arms, but the world tilts sideways. "Hazel. She left the cult because she didn't want to keep doing it. She wanted a new life for you." His voice trails off. "We have to find a way to keep Keir from seeing you. If he enrolls at the school, we won't be able to hide you."

"Keir, the little troll guy?" I ask.

"You've *met* him?" Alarm crackles in his tone, though he's trying hard to keep his voice level.

"He's a friend of Wyatt's."

"No, no, Hazel." Luke shakes his head, pressing his fingers into his closed eyes. "Keir's my cousin, the son of my Aunt Idra. Keir is the Seer for Stolam. Has he seen your powers?"

"He saw one of our circles." A scalding panic rises in my chest, and I almost miss the numbness. "He's been in our house."

Luke yanks me to my feet. "Go home. Cast a circle around your house and get your sisters inside. I'm going to get Iona and meet you there."

"My sisters," I say, choking on the lump that congeals in my throat.

"They'll be fine. You're going to be fine, just be careful." He yanks the necklace off his neck, black cord with a circle of blacker stone dangling from it, and ties it roughly around my wrist. "Onyx. If there's anything that'll help you..."

Before he can finish, I clasp my hands around his neck and pull him toward me until our mouths close around each other. A weight seems to leave him, just for a second, and he presses me closer. It's the briefest moment of happiness I've had in weeks, but I know it can't last. I push back, and he lets me go.

"I take back my curse," I say, hoping it's enough of an apology.

"You have a lot of time to make it up to me," he says, pressing his thumb between my eyes, before dropping his hand, and blinking in confusion. "My spell's gone. Did you do that?"

I smile as I whip past him, desperate to get home.

As the door closes behind me, I hear him say, "You might give them a run for their money after all."

CHAPTER 20

TRAPS

The SUV can't move fast enough. The tires fly over the rocky asphalt, turning the scenery outside into a rushing river of grey. I get home in record time, but it still feels too late as I pull my car right up to the house, jump out, and nearly trip in my haste to get up the stairs. I slam the door behind me only to find Wyatt standing in the hall.

"You scared me. Where is everyone?" I keep some calm in my voice, not sure which Wyatt I'll get this time, my brother or the dark stranger that sometimes talks with his mouth.

"They're upstairs," he says. "What's wrong?"

I know I can't tell him, even though when I look at him now, he seems like the innocent, playful brother I'd known his whole life. For whatever reason, he knew Keir. He'd invited him to our house. Maybe he was just as oblivious as we were, maybe Keir was using him to get close to our family, but maybe it was something else.

"Will you just start locking up the house?" I say to him. "A huge storm is coming. And tell Abby and the twins to meet me down here."

I brush past him to the kitchen, pulling Mom's box down from the pantry shelf. I toss fistfuls of rock salt and dried rosemary into the mortar and grind it, hoping it'll be enough to cover the yard. I dump the mixture into a bowl and head for the front door.

When I pass the stairs, I shout, "Everyone start locking doors and windows!" My big-sister voice is back. Should be enough to get them moving.

I cast the circle from the left side of the yard to right, trying not to move too fast. It's too dark to see cars down the road, but there seems to be no one around. We just have to make it until Luke and Iona come. That's it.

Outside, a shriek splits the constant sound of cicadas. It sounds like something halfway between animal and human. I spot the owl-bird resting on the branch over my head then, her claws curving into the bark. Her eyes watch me with mild amusement before I hurl a handful of salt in her direction, making her push back from the branch with a great swat of her wings.

Back inside, our dog is having a conniption. Prince throws himself at the door to the porch, scrabbling his claws against the half-pane of glass. Wyatt appears on the stair landing, looking uneasily toward the commotion.

"Is everything locked?"

"Not the backdoor," he says.

I get to it quickly, yanking Prince back by the collar and twisting the lock. A head and shoulders step up to the glass on the other side. I reel back, nearly tripping over the dog.

Keir smiles at me through the window.

"Happy Halloween," he says.

His eyes lock on me like I'm already trapped. No way out.

"Stay away from my family, you little shark-mouthed hobbit," I spit at him.

His lips close over his teeth like curtains.

"I just came by to see Wyatt. Is the hostility really necessary?"

"We know who you are, Keir." His name comes out of my mouth as a shout. I can't hold it inside me. "Get off my porch and I won't call the police."

"Ooh, police, ooh," he mocks, leaning his hands against the glass.

I whip my head around to Wyatt, who's still frozen on the stairs.

"He can't get in, right?" I hiss at Wyatt, but he says nothing.

"Sure I can," Keir says. "Like this."

He winds up and slams the pane with a flowerpot. It sails at me in a shower of crystalline shards. I duck before it catches me in the temple.

"It's not all smoke and mirrors, you know. I can hurt you with my hands just as easily as with magic." Keir's hand snakes through the shattered hole, fingers fumbling at the lock. I throw my whole weight against the door, prying his grip off the knob.

"Wyatt, get Dad's gun!" I yell toward the stairs just as my head is ripped backward. Wyatt has a handful of my hair and is peeling me away from the door.

"What are you *doing*?" I shout, but I see them.

The dark, glassy eyes of the brother I don't know. The stranger.

"Quiet now," he says, in a voice much older than Wyatt's.

Keir steps in, and immediately a pan flies at him, followed by all the dishes in the sink. Matthew chose an excellent time to make an appearance. Keir bats them away, sucking in a breath each time they clip him.

"Come on, Matthew," he says snidely. "No hard feelings. You'll have company soon enough."

He digs in his pockets, pulling out a vial that he empties into his hands. He rubs them together and places his palms on the wall, closing his eyes to say a garbled spell before stepping back. A satisfied smile twists up the corners of his mouth.

The pipes above our heads begin to moan and creak so fiercely that I think the ceiling might collapse, but whatever Keir's done has trapped Matthew.

Wyatt drags me backward, making sure not to give me an inch of room to struggle. We stumble into the living room as Keir pushes furniture back, exposing the wooden floor beneath.

"Who are you?" I demand of the stranger wearing Wyatt's face. "What do you want?"

His sigh blows cold across the top of my head. "I did hope something in you would know me. I remember you best of all. You were my favorite."

Paralysis grips my body. It's like I'm trapped under ice, too cold to move. I do know that voice. It's been a lifetime, but I feel it in my bones.

"You're Faolan," I say. "You're my father."

Before he can answer, there's commotion on the stairs. Someone's dropped something big. Thinking my sisters are still in their rooms, I twist in Wyatt's grasp and yell to them.

"Get out of the house! Go get Gemmie!"

From under Wyatt's arm, I see a woman descend the stairs. She's tugging Abby by the wrists. My sister's limp body bumps over each step like a dragged doll. The woman heaves her the short distance into the living room, letting Abby's head smack the ground when she drops her. The woman turns to me then, and I know exactly where I've seen that same sharp nose, those penetrating blue eyes set in caramel skin. It couldn't be anyone else. Luke's mother smiles at me the way a tiger might smile and it's so familiar it makes me shiver.

"We've waited a long time," she says to my father.

"Death takes none of us, Isolda," he says, an old fondness in his voice.

She smiles, her mouth so like Luke's it stirs up bile in my stomach.

"Death takes none of us," she repeats. Her gaze ticks to me. "Hazel. All grown up."

She runs a long finger down my cheek as she speaks. I kick out at her, and get a punch to the skull from Faolan that rattles my brain.

She doesn't even blink at my outburst. "I wondered when I'd see you again. Your mother and I had such plans for you and Luke. It's only fitting you spent your last months together."

"What'd you do to my sister?" I demand through clenched teeth.

Isolda doesn't even look at her, just purses her lips. "Don't worry, she's rather simply spelled. We need her alive for now."

As soon as she says it, two men emerge from upstairs. They're hauling Callie and Charlotte down behind them. On the stairs, my sisters put up more of a fight than I did. Callie tears at the shoulder of her captor with her long nails. He's got a greasy ponytail and a vacant face, someone I wouldn't look twice at out on the street. But when he looks at Isolda, a sickening light fills his eyes, like he'd do anything for her.

Charlotte has an open cut in the middle of her forehead, but she's still clamping her teeth down on any exposed skin she can find. I recognize her kidnapper as the scrawny shopkeeper from Oggun. When they reach the living room, the twins are dropped heavily on the floor. It's then that I see what Keir's been working on. The living room floor is one huge casting circle, symbols layered over symbols with thick white chalk.

Isolda gathers her glossy black hair into a braid like a runner before a race. "Come now, sweet thing," she says to me. "We have a long night ahead of us."

CHAPTER 21

SACRIFICE

There are five of them, including Wyatt and his puppet master. Each member takes a point of the gigantic pentagram, the outlying mark on the floor. When they close the circle, the house moans and the floorboards seem to rock like a boat in a storm, making me sick. I curl forward on the floor, locking my head against my knees. The shopkeeper stands directly behind me, and by the way Charlotte stares daggers at him, he's responsible for the gash on her forehead. Abby is still unconscious, her head in Callie's lap.

One thought presses down on my whole body: Luke, his aunt, his uncle—*they're not going to get here in time.*

I fix my eyes on Wyatt's, trying to pull my baby brother out with my stare. It's useless. But Faolan hadn't had him this whole time. But at some point, Wyatt had wrestled his own mind back, had forced Faolan out. He was strong enough to do it again. I knew it.

But only Faolan's eyes stare back at me, cold and glazed. It strikes me that Wyatt must look like him. I feel stupid for not noticing before. He never had Mom's heart-shaped face, or the thin nose we all shared. Faolan ticks his head to the side, trying to puzzle out what I'm thinking.

"What kind of man kills his own children for power?" I growl. It doesn't even sound like my voice.

The armor cracks. He drops his half-sneer, paling a bit.

"You were never my children," he says breezily. "You were tools."

"Liar. You were afraid of us." Fury boils in my chest, roiling up into my throat. "You knew we'd be more powerful than you. And you knew she loved us more than you. You're a coward."

Movement flashes across my vision as Isolda's hand smashes me across the cheek.

"Do not speak to the Prophet like that!" She spits when she says it.

"Prophet?" I press my hand against my stinging face. "He's a psychopath. You're *all* psychopaths. We're children!" I yell at her, the sound raking my throat.

From her pocket, she pulls out a smoothed red stone the size of her palm. She whispers words in Spanish, breathing on it, then presses it over my heart.

My skin ripples under the burn that spreads from the stone as pain punches into my chest, setting my heart on fire. I scream, trying to pry her hands away, but she pushes me backward onto the floor, holding me down with her left hand. With her right, she raises a dagger over my head, the point hovering between my eyes. My limbs seize up one joint at a time, elbows, knees, hips, until I can do nothing but let the pain split my ribs apart.

As Isolda begins to chant, the room stands still.

> *"Our God of fire, we call you.*
> *Take this body, this blood, these bones,*
> *And return to us the soul of our Prophet to the body we choose.*
> *Take our payment and make him whole—"*

"No!" Callie throws herself on Isolda's arm, snatching at the dagger. The two pitch backward, and Isolda's hand comes off the stone in my chest. Cool air rushes into my lungs, extinguishing the fire. Even without the stone, the circle still makes me feel like I'm in an over-pressurized container, anchoring me to the ground. It's a wonder Callie can move.

I force myself to sit up, roll onto my knees so I can help her, but it's too late. Keir wrestles her off his aunt, pinning her arms behind her. Callie goes limp, and I know she's spent all of her energy saving me.

I try to pull myself over to her just as the front door slams open, breathing air into the house. Luke and Iona sprint into the living room, pulling up just before the circle.

"Sister," Iona says, her jaw set in pure hatred, "let the children go. The police are on their way."

Still recovering from the tussle with Callie, Isolda lifts herself to one knee and the animal smile returns to her face as she bares sharp white teeth. "Oh, I think they'll have some trouble getting here. Perhaps a little water on the road."

"Oh, we saw that," Iona says with the tiniest hint of a smirk. "You really should know better than to use water magic against your son."

That sets Isolda back a tick. Behind her, I see the bony shop-keeper from Oggun sweating, trying to gauge how much of a shot he has against Luke. He decides to make a run for it, darting for the open door. Luke intercepts him there and downs him with a left hook before spinning on his heel, reaching deep into his pocket, and bringing up a closed fist. He holds his hand to his mouth, like his mother had done, and speaks a fast string of Spanish into it. Without warning, he flings his hand forward, scattering white powder over the heart of the circle.

Right then the pressure lifts, freeing us.

"Get out of the circle!" he shouts at me.

Charlotte and I snap to it, flipping Abby over and grabbing her shirt on either side to pull her away. Greasy Ponytail cuts right past us, heading for Luke. He has a look of righteous fury on his face. It's obvious that, son or not, Luke has gotten in Isolda's way, and Pony-tail figures he's going to put a stop to it. When he reaches Luke, he doesn't bother with punches. He goes straight for the throat.

Charlotte and I have almost got Abby to the far side of the room. As soon as we're out of the circle, I set her down as gently as I can and turn back, heading for Luke.

"Isolda!" Faolan bellows over the commotion, "I'm not losing this body!"

Isolda brings her arm back, then whips it forward, fingers aimed at me. I don't even see the dagger, I just feel a punch in my gut. It's only when I look down that I see it buried up to its hilt in my stomach.

CHAPTER 22

PURGE

I'm lying on my side, watching the spreading red puddle overtake the white symbols on the floor. My thoughts come slower now, like my brain is lagging behind my breathing. I try to run through the list of spells I've read, but not one of them can help me. Outside the circle, Callie cries and Charlotte's eyes lock on me as she positions herself protectively over Abby. She only flinches a little as Iona rushes past her, taking four quick strides to Wyatt and throwing a handful of salt directly into his eyes.

It wouldn't have hurt a normal person much, but Wyatt's possessed body lets out a wail that breaks my heart. He paws at his face while something like smoke curls up from his skin. He sinks to his knees, and Iona kicks him to the ground. Quick as a cat, she pulls a pair of silver scissors from her pocket and splits his shirt so his back shines in the light. Every inch of skin is tattooed over with a net of symbols.

Iona holds a cross to her forehead, speaking in a rush of Spanish. She leans forward, pressing the cross against Wyatt's back. He writhes under it, every muscle tensing and twitching and the tattoos *move*. They squirm and twist like snakes, turning black as if they're dying in his skin.

That's when the police bust in. They pour through the front door, fanning out through the room. What's left of Stolam bolts in two opposite directions. Isolda runs right past me, and I glare at her with all the hatred I've ever felt, imagining my hands closing around her ankles.

She trips. It's only for a moment, but she whips back to me, her eyes wide. I blink, just as surprised as she is. As an officer moves for her, she turns from me, her black hair flying behind her as she tears past the policemen and out the front door. They're after her in a flash, swarming like bees.

Faolan meets my eyes, still prone across the floor, his face is pink with fresh burns. He's so pale. His head jerks from side to side, but whatever Iona did has taken any power he had.

"She's ruined it," he says. "She ruined the seal."

The prickling beginnings of numbness take over my left arm. When I lift it out of the wetness, the black stone on my wrist bumps against my palm, like a cat wanting to be petted. I hold it up, peering at the dark beauty of it.

If he hadn't been a foot from my face, I would have missed it. But I see the stab of fear in Faolan's eyes when he sees the onyx. I can't explain why, but my hand closes around the amulet. I summon the last strand of strength in my body and rise onto my elbow.

"Give me back my brother," I say, and push the stone against his forehead.

CHAPTER 23

ONYX

It smells like Lysol. I open my eyes, wondering who's cleaning my room so early in the morning, but instead of seeing my ceiling, I'm staring at white industrial tiles and rectangular fluorescent lights.

It's a hospital. I try to sit up, but my stomach gives me a sharp warning not to.

"Hazel?" Luke leans into my sightline, his hand on my shoulder.

"I got stabbed," I tell him blearily.

He laughs his breathy laugh. "I know. You got a lot of stitches, but you're okay. I'm going to call your family."

"I'm going to go back to sleep," I say, but my eyelids have already made the decision for me. His lips press against my cheek. It's the last feeling I get before I spiral down into blackness.

———

I don't see her, but I feel her. Gemmie's hand rests on mine, her touch cool on my burning skin. The rim of something hard and ceramic bumps against my lower lip.

"Darling, drink this. It's going to help you get through this more quickly."

I take a gulp of the tepid liquid, tasting faint chamomile and something sweet.

"Is it going to heal me?" I ask. My voice sounds so low and gritty, it could be coming from a different body.

There's a heavy pause. Gemmie smooths the hair off my face, tucking it behind my ears.

"Even I can't do that, my heart. I can just give you a little comfort to pass the time. It makes your mind very open, so try to be aware who's around you."

Two of her fingers settle between my eyes, and she whispers a quick chant. The weight that's been pressing me into the sheets leaves me. My mind whirls with color and images, and I sink into them.

Our old house stands in front of me, still towering in its Victorian height, not a single singed board. I walk toward it, feeling the lush grass under my feet. The front door opens and she steps out to meet me.

My mother, exactly as I remember her. Her feet are bare and her red hair is pulled to the side of her neck in a thick braid. She stops in front of me, tipping my chin up with her cool fingers. Her jade eyes are warm when they meet mine, filling with that laughing light like they always did.

"Mom?" I say.

Dark clouds move across her face, the corners of her mouth falling just slightly. She opens her mouth to say something.

———

"Hazel?" It's not my mom's voice.

The world swims into focus again. Wyatt's sitting in the chair beside my hospital bed. Despite my bandages and the doctor's orders not to move, I almost shy away. But when he looks at me, I see my brother. I see only hurt and sadness. The lingering evil and the hardness it brought with it is gone. Now he's a sickly yellow color, with circles under his eyes so dark he looks like he has two black eyes.

"You look as bad as I feel," I croak.

He smiles sadly before saying, "Iona said you saved me."

"Iona saved you."

"You took him out though." Wyatt's voice cracks. "You drew his soul out."

I touch my wrist, remembering the onyx stone. It's gone, along with the cord that held it.

"I guess I did," I say slowly. "Wyatt. Why didn't you tell us? How could you keep it from me?"

He lets his face fall into his hands. "It was the voices again. I was hearing them everywhere, telling me someone was looking for me, that we were all in danger. You and I are the only ones that get omens, you know what it can be like. I felt like I was losing my mind. Then Keir just showed up out of nowhere and said he knew what was going on. That I wasn't crazy. That he could help me. It was just small stuff at first. We practiced in the woods by our house; he knew so much."

"The circle," I say. "I've been there. That was you and Keir?"

He nods. "But I wanted to do what he could do. He could *move* things, make people do what he wanted. He said he could make it so I could do it too."

My head dips under an impossible weight, suddenly too heavy to keep upright. I relent under the pressure, letting it fall back onto the cloud of pillow beneath it.

"Hazel," Wyatt says, his voice coarse. "I need to tell you about the Sagestone fire. I need you to know how this started."

He tells me the story the remnants of Gemmie's spell painting the picture in my mind.

"Keir tricked me," he finishes. "He told me we were doing the *Veri Segno* to make me stronger, but he was just using Matthew as an offering. He sealed Faolan's soul in me." He swallows roughly. "Doesn't feel right calling him Dad, does it?"

"You should have told us," I say, my voice rasping under the strain of holding myself together.

"Told you what? That I helped *kill* a person? Matthew was my age. Just a guy. When you pushed me into the circle, we raised something from his blood. I'm responsible for that, for the fact that he's still not moved on."

"Wyatt, I know you. And you are a *good* person. We'll find a way to make it right."

He leans over, resting his head on the bed next to me. I run my fingers over his hair, the way Mom used to do.

"What happened to the cult members?" I ask. "Did the police catch them all?"

The thought of them doing prison time gives me just enough satisfaction that I don't think about the ache in my stomach for a moment.

"They got the two guys. Keir and Isolda got away."

"That's not possible. I *saw* them chase Isolda, they had her."

He shrugs, looking exhausted. "They said they lost her. She just vanished."

"There's just no way she could've gotten away," I say, massaging my forehead. She was right *there*.

The image of her face, those merciless watching eyes, burns behind my eyelids. My head snaps up. All this time, I thought the familiarity I saw was because of Luke, but I had been seeing that face for a month. It had been staring down at me from trees.

Lechuza. The word the old woman outside of Oggun had hissed into my memory. Finally, I remember what the name means. *Lechuza*, the witch-bird. It was one of the stories Mom used to tell us when we first moved to Texas. The *brujas* in West Texas who turn themselves into giant birds. But it hadn't been real. It couldn't be real.

———

"I can't believe you get to miss school," Abby says, sinking down onto my bed.

I shove a corner of grilled cheese into my mouth.

"I'm traumatized," I say happily.

"So am I! I went through it too."

"You were spelled. You slept through the whole thing," I say, closing Mom's journal and setting it on my dresser. "Don't get too jealous, though. After the attack, it's not like Dad's ever going to let me out of his sight again."

"Small price." Abby stands up, fluffing out her skirt. "Do you want to watch a movie tonight?"

"Sure," I say, touching soreness in my stomach. It's almost healed, just feels like a pulled muscle most of the time. "Luke's coming over after school, we can all hang out together."

She wrinkles her nose. "No, y'all are weird with your PDA."

She flounces out of the room, waving as she closes the door. I open my Chem book, wanting to start the horrible process of catching up. A soft knock interrupts me.

Wyatt is standing in my doorway.

"Oh," I stammer. "Hey."

"I have something that I think belongs to you," he says.

The onyx stone dangles from his finger.

"Wyatt, you found it." I get up, taking it from him.

"I didn't lose it. I just didn't know what to do with it." He breathes out. "I think a part of me liked having him around. Like he'd kind of become part of me. I can't explain it."

"What do you mean?"

He taps the stone. "Look into it."

I hold it closer, peering into the dark heart of it. Only it isn't dark anymore. What had once been a dead reflection now roils with an angry red glow.

"What is it?" I say.

Wyatt cocks his head. He says, "You can't feel it?"

I shrug.

Wyatt takes the stone, resting it in his palm so the red light dances against his skin.

"It's him," he says. "This is Faolan Sicario's *soul*."

BOOK TWO

ONYX

CHAPTER 1

OMENS

It comes in under the doorway. It's cloudy, like dishwater, gray and gritty, spreading hungrily across the floor. Water slaps into the corners of my room, seeping under the door with such force that the wood rattles. It overtakes everything in its path, pooling around the legs of my bed.

All warmth drains from the air. Cold prickles over my skin. I try to sit up, clenching the muscles in my stomach, willing myself to move, but I can't. The water tugs at my blankets, sloshing my bed from side to side until it peeks over the edge, creeping toward my legs and outstretched arms. It rises so fast that the next breath I take isn't air, but silty wetness scraping down my esophagus.

The water closes over my face, flooding into my eyes. I shake my head from side to side, pressure pushing against my forehead, holding me down.

Hazel!

My shoulders yank upward, almost tearing from their sockets. Someone's pulling me up. I can feel Luke's long fingers wrapped around my arms, the familiar roughness of his palms.

My eyes finally spring open and the water vanishes along with his grip. I'm staring at the ceiling of my room, everything glowing a soft gray from the moonlight. Spiderwebs of shadows cast by the tree outside my window shift across the smooth walls, but nothing else moves.

I press my head into my pillow, squeezing my eyes shut and trying not to convince myself of the one thing I know is true. That it's not just a dream.

It's an omen.

A sharp pain digs into my forearm, and I suck in a breath. I pull the covers down to my elbow, sitting up enough to unwrap the silk cord from my wrist. The onyx stone sticks as it comes away from my skin, revealing a puckered red abscess beneath it. I ball the yolk-sized gem in my fist and hurl it across the room. It cracks against the wall and falls to the floor, not even rolling over once, like it weighs ten pounds.

"*Stop it*, Faolan," I hiss at it through gritted teeth.

As soon as I say his name aloud, I wish I hadn't. It almost feels like he might answer. I hate thinking about him: my insane, evil father, or what's left of him in the onyx. How much of a burden he's become.

In the first weeks after I'd managed to pull his parasitic soul out of my younger brother and trap him in the stone, my siblings and I had shared the responsibility of watching it. We didn't dare put it down. Stolam, the cult Faolan started, would come for it eventually, and we had to be ready to keep it from them when they did.

We used to be afraid of breaking it. We held it as if it were made of thin glass, cradling it close to our bodies, under our clothes, or wrapping it tightly around our wrists. We witnessed its true tenacity when Abby, my youngest sister, dropped it down the stairs as she was hurrying to catch the bus to middle school. It hit every step on its way down, each hollow smack hitting us like a slap. But it didn't break.

I won't say we tried to break it after that. We were slightly less careful though, just barely reckless with it. We'd let it knock against tables or countertops, sometimes dropping it a little more roughly than necessary. Just to make life a little more miserable for Faolan, if he could feel it. That's when he started to fight back.

It started with Abby, as an outbreak of hives across her chest where she wore the pendant. Generally, we took turns keeping it, equally fascinated by it and scared it might grow legs and run off. Then Callie said it felt like it pinched her randomly throughout the day, leaving red marks on her arm. Charlotte folded after that because she said it got so cold against her skin that it made her shiver all day. We never made Wyatt wear it. He'd carried that black weight around too long already.

The first night I slept with it on, I woke up with a throbbing blister the size of a quarter on my forearm. Two weeks later, I set it down to wash my face, and when I picked it up again it was as hot as an iron, burning my fingertips.

It wasn't until a month later that I realized it'd planned the whole thing. Saving its energy, causing just enough pain to my siblings that I would take it, then brutalizing me because it knew I wouldn't ever put the burden back on them. That's when I knew.

Even if he was just a flickering red facet trapped inside the glassy face of the onyx stone, Faolan Sicario was still alive, still in there, and still thinking.

CHAPTER 2

CROSSINGS

I can hear Luke's motorcycle from two blocks away. It's like hearing muted thunder and knowing the rain is close.

I throw my phone into my bag, hurrying past my Dad in the living room. He's looking out the window, his crow's feet pulling down at the corners of his lips.

"You know how many motorcycle victims we get at the hospital every month?" he grumbles as I hustle by.

"What was that?" I stall, opening the door.

"Fifteen, that's how many."

"Sorry, Dad, I can't hear you. Love you!"

I close the door, cutting off his last protest.

Luke looks up from his motorcycle at the curb, tugging off his helmet to reveal tousled black hair underneath.

"You ready?" he asks.

I skip down the front steps to meet him, taking a practiced swing up onto the back of the motorcycle.

"Always," I say, snagging the spare helmet he hands to me.

"Uncle Finn got someone interested in buying this hog." He taps the rusty black body of the chopper. "I might finally get a real car."

"But then I don't get to pretend I'm dating the bad boy in a nineties movie," I tease, tightening my knee-grip on the seat. Every time Luke drives us anywhere, I spend the whole trip devising an exit strategy if the chopper rolls. Can't say I'll miss that.

"What do you want to do? Something normal or something *witchy*?"

He waves his fingers, trying to look intimidating. He almost pulls it off for a moment, but then the light comes back into those bright blue eyes making my heart clench. I can't believe I was ever afraid of that face.

"Could we do something witchy *combined* with something normal?"

He nods decisively, sliding the motorcycle away from the curb. "You got it."

Luke takes the curving road out of my neighborhood, passing the woods where just three months ago, my little brother had been secretly calling up black magic.

The street narrows, trees and grass encroaching over the asphalt. Suddenly, I know where we're going. Luke has a fondness for free-swimming in the lakes that pepper the landscape around Cody, and I'd bet ten bucks some frigid water is in my immediate future. The memory of the nightmare claws its way into my mind, sending a cold sweat down my back, but I push it away.

We pull down the pocked road, the motorcycle cutting over the choppy asphalt. Even above the engine's sputtering roar, I hear the river before we get to it. Usually, it just pops and burbles along the rocks about four feet under the low-water bridge, but now the sound has risen to a velvety roar, its water lapping over the concrete. The sight of it makes my breath catch.

"Stop!" I call to Luke over the noise.

He brakes to a halt, propping us up on his right foot. "What?"

"We shouldn't go over the bridge. There's water on it."

Luke swivels his head to the river, then back to me. "Barely."

"Let's just be safe," I say. Already my stomach is quivering, being so close to the fast-moving water. From here it almost looks like a living thing, each rising wave like a hand reaching for purchase on the concrete.

Luke lets out a slightly peeved sigh. "It's like another five miles to go back around."

Annoyance snaps like a rubber band against my diaphragm. I can't explain it, but it's almost like a malevolent cloud is hanging over the bridge.

"Alright then," I say, swinging my leg over the bike to the ground. "I'll just walk."

"Come on, don't be like that," Luke says, tugging off his helmet.

"Look, you haven't been here that long. People die on these roads."

It's a bit of an exaggeration. One person had died on the low-water bridge—and it was during a flash flood—but still.

Luke's eyes narrow, fixing on my face like he's trying to dig something out of my expression. "Do you feel something?"

I loop my finger around the edge of the onyx dangling on its cord at my wrist.

"Yeah. I had this nightmare last night about water. Drowning."

His mouth makes an almost perfect straight line, devoid of reaction. He runs his thumb over the slick surface of his helmet. "Drowning, huh?"

I cross my arms. "Yeah. From what I remember, witches and drowning go hand-in-hand."

After a moment, he tugs the helmet back down over his head. "Long way it is. Hop on."

"Just like that?" I say, taking a step toward him.

He walks the bike back until it's even with me, balancing on the balls of his feet. "Yeah, just like that."

CHAPTER 3

WATER MAGIC

Twenty minutes later, Luke steers the bike off the road, slowing the roar to just a grumble as the tires roll over the soft grass. He pushes out the kickstand, tipping the bike to the side so hard that I slip halfway off, nearly taking him with me when I grab his jacket.

He pulls me upright, hiding a snicker. My abs clench as I try to steady myself and a sharp pain twists its way into my stomach. I massage the clump of scar tissue just above my hipbone where a few months ago, Isolda, Luke's mother and the new leader of Stolam, had stabbed me with a ritual dagger. It had healed remarkably well with Gemmie's help, but it still pinched if I moved too quickly.

I look around, shading my eyes against the sun, as tough blades of grass poke through the fabric of my flats.

We've made it into the outskirts of Cody, past the last standing house. There are only plains of pale yellow grass on either side of us. It's so quiet and still, it's like being adrift in a calm golden sea.

"So now I have to ask," I say, turning to Luke with a mocking smile. "Did you bring me here to kill me?"

Luke rolls his eyes, swinging his leg over the bike.

"Totally. I just wanted to wait until *after* I'd saved your life from my mother and your father."

"Where are we then?"

"My favorite spot."

He reaches for my hand, twining his fingers into mine. His skin is always so warm, even in the sterile January cold of Cody winter. We crunch over the knee-high grass, me following in Luke's wake.

"Ow," I say as a particularly tough stalk stabs through my shoe. "I wish you'd warned me we were going on a cross-country hike."

"It must be so hard to be you," Luke says, his lips tugging into a smirk, "being swept off on a romantic date by a dark and handsome witch."

I detangle my skirt from the clutches of a sapling. "Don't get carried away."

"I'll carry *you* away."

Before I can stop him, he scoops me off the ground, one arm under my knees, the other behind my back. I grip his shoulder with my fingers, trying not to let out a yelp of surprise.

"Too much," I say, trying to wiggle down. "It's too much romance!"

"Just let it happen," he retorts, hiking me up higher.

We tramp over the grass for several yards with me nestled in the folds of Luke's hoodie. I'm just starting to get comfy when he steps over the last barrier of shrubs onto flat land.

He sets me on my feet and I nearly step off the ledge he's put me on. We're at a natural spring, the kind that pops up all over the land surrounding Cody. The earth here is perforated with underground caves that collect water and spurt it back up to the surface in rivers and pools. This one is healthy, the water so clear it looks like it's being poured from a tap.

Rocky limestone funnels the spring into a pool backed by small cliff, only twelve feet high, like the back of an armchair. It's such a perfectly contained little oasis in the middle of the bland countryside that I can't help smiling. It's like our own mini resort.

"This is so cute," I say, looking over at Luke. He's already yanking off his shoes, the ones made by his aunt and adopted mother, Iona, that look like something they'd wear in the African Congo.

"Maybe it seems cute, but that pool over there goes down thirty feet. I practice my diving out here."

"Hidden depths." I raise my eyebrows at him.

"Seriously."

He holds out his hand to me, and I slip off my flats and join him. He walks us down into the shallow water and I suck in air through my teeth as the cold bites through my skin.

"Yeah, I know, it's bad," he says, wincing too, "but the water here is completely natural. It sits in the earth and gets purified by layers of rocks, then gets brought back up here. In terms of elemental magic, you can't get better."

"I don't know what that means," I say, trying not to sound irked.

Sometimes Luke forgets I didn't grow up with this stuff, launching into lectures I have no way of understanding. It's the most frustrating thing in the world, knowing how much my magic can do, but having so small an idea of how to use it.

"Okay, so, you know how the Earth gives off more energy than we ever could hold in a lifetime?" Luke asks. "As a witch, you can communicate with that energy, use it to strengthen you, or alter it. Each witch is drawn to a different element. It's just a personal thing. For me, I handle water better than anything else. We'll have to see what speaks to you most."

He turns himself so we face each other squarely, rolling up his jeans so they don't dip into the water. When he straightens, he shakes out his arms.

"So just close your eyes and focus on the water. Try to feel the energy in it."

He closes his eyes and I follow suit, letting my arms hang at my sides. The water licks at my calves, like it's trying to climb my legs, and I swallow the faint panic the feeling brings. I feel cold, that's for sure, but the more I send my focus to my feet, feeling the movement and life in the water, the more I can feel the familiar tingle of power rising in me. It's like a warm prickle, a faint push-and-pull in the center of my chest. I hold it between my ribs, letting it swell and ebb with the moving water. My lips pull into a smile. Nothing feels better than tapping into that glow, feeling a sliver of the power that keeps the world going.

There's a spot of humming, cool air a few feet in front of me, like standing next to an open fridge. I push my focus out to it, trying to feel what it is. I try to imagine pulling some of it into me, tearing off a piece, and bringing it into my chest.

"Aah!" I feel Luke flinch, and the cool spot quivers, pulling into a ball. I open my eyes. Luke's face is confused, slightly twisted in pain.

"What did you do?" His voice is so fierce that I step back.

"Nothing," I say indignantly. "I—I was feeling the energy, like you said."

"I felt…" He presses his fingers into the space between his ribs. "It's like you took something."

Anger boils up in my lungs. I can't even put my finger on what's upsetting me, but I turn away anyway, sloshing out of the water onto dry rock.

"You can't just throw me into this stuff and then be mad when I do it wrong," I growl over my shoulder.

"Whoa, Hazel—"

He snags my wrist, his fingers pressing the onyx into my skin. There's a white-hot surge from it, like I've accidentally touched a stovetop. A high-pitched yelp escapes me and I rip my arm out of his grasp, curling it to my chest.

Luke's open hand hangs in the air, like he's afraid just moving might hurt me. His face pales, then his eyes fall on the black cord wrapped around my wrist. It has been content to sit under the cuff of my jacket until just this moment, when Faolan knows it will get me into the most trouble.

"You're still wearing that?" Luke demands, his dark eyebrows in a straight line.

"Yes, okay?" I snap. "It's not like I can just leave it at home. We have no idea where Isolda is. For all we know she could just be waiting for me to set it down."

He walks toward me, his feet dragging in the water roughly.

"I've told you a hundred times, it's about energy. Being around something with bad energy, it's going to seep into you. And *that*,"— he won't even look at it, he just points—"is entirely bad energy."

His lips pull together the way they do whenever he talks about Faolan. It took him almost a month to realize *who* Faolan was. Growing up in Stolam he'd been taught to call him "The Prophet" and had rarely even been allowed to see him except during rituals.

I still see the reverence the thought of Faolan instills in Luke. For a week, he could barely look at me after he realized whose blood I had in me, after he realized who was responsible for half of what makes me...*me.*

"I can handle it," I say, making sure my voice stays even. Between the dreams and the burns though, I'm starting to question how true that is.

"We don't even know how it works." He scowls at the ground. "Why would you not tell me you had that on? Why would you hide that from me?"

And just from his body language, the reason why is screaming in my face. He's already taken a step back, his chest turned away from me. The hand that touched the onyx is spread out, and he's holding it away from his body like it's diseased. He's repulsed by the stone. And when I'm wearing it, he's repulsed by me too.

"Because..." I tug at the cord, wishing it didn't feel so tight. "Because you're afraid of it."

His dark eyebrows twitch, but he keeps the rest of his expression still. With a few drags of his feet, he steps out of the water, scooping his shoes up roughly.

"You should be, too," he mutters.

CHAPTER 4

OLD FRIENDS

I can't think of a single thing to say on the way back. I keep my wrist tucked against my stomach, avoiding any contact with Luke's back. When he slows at the front of my house, I swing my legs off and turn away, wanting to slink off in shame. I only make it a step before a tug on the hood of my jacket stops me.

"No, c'mon," Luke says, pulling me back toward him, "don't be like that. I'm sorry. It's just, you don't know what it was like in Stolam. Having Faolan around again, even like that... it doesn't bring up good things for me."

I turn to face him, letting my body lean into his torso. His arm circles around my waist.

"I don't know what it was like because you won't tell me anything," I say.

He blows a warm sigh into my shoulder. "You don't want to know."

"I do want to know."

"If I tell you, you'll just wish I hadn't."

I bite the inside of my cheek. No matter how many times I ask him about Stolam, he always bats it down. I know it's sick, but I'm fascinated with it. The cult that nearly swallowed my mother, that hunts and murders people, that found a way to steal magic from witches by draining their blood. Stolam, as deranged as they are, is part of my history. Even if I was too young to remember my childhood in the cult, it's still inside me.

Luke drops his arm, his gaze falling on the house.

"Who's here?" he asks.

I swivel to look through the bay windows in our living room. I can see Callie, in her favorite white dress with the corset top, swishing around the room as she talks to a very tan, sandy-haired guy perched on the couch.

"That's Jacob," I say.

Jacob is the result of Callie's overly optimistic stint in a church youth group. She went for one day and came out with a new respect for the collective cruelty of kids and a borderline stalker in the full throes of puppy love.

Callie is pretty blasé about the whole thing. She decided in middle school that she was meant to marry into the royal family, which Jacob falls short of, but I've always liked him. Not that he's completely on my good list, but anyone who treats my sisters like they're the only girls in the world is at least halfway decent in my book.

Luke narrows his eyes at me, tilting his sharp nose upwards. "Do I need to come inside for some routine intimidation?"

"No, not for this one. He's a good kid," I say, leaning down to punctuate the sentence with a kiss.

"If you say so." He zips up his jacket. "Think about what I said. About the onyx."

He lets me step back onto the curb before twisting the handle on the hog and gliding off down the street. I watch him go before I head inside.

The TV is on when I pull open the front door. As I walk into the living room to say hello, Callie pivots toward me with the most pleading, desperate eyes I've ever seen. It snaps me into big-sister mode so fast that I'm rounding on Jacob before my brain can even work out why I'm mad.

Then I see what they're watching. Under the bold white heading "Manhunt in Louisiana" is Isolda's face, staring back at me with frigid, black eyes. The newscaster is recounting the break-in, every detail except our names, and my skin starts to burn. He rattles off the planned massacre of five siblings in Texas, the cult ritual, the stabbing, like it's some kind of history report on people who died too long ago to care that you're slobbering their story all over TV.

Callie grips my elbow.

"He saw this on the news and wanted to come over to 'keep me safe', or whatever," she whispers, adding air quotations.

"How does he know it's us?" I hiss back to her. For what it was worth, the police had never released our names to the news. It was the shred of sanity our family still had left.

Callie rolls her deep green eyes. "*Everyone* knows it was us."

Jacob looks over his shoulder, spotting me for the first time.

"Hey, Hazel," he says, his face crinkling up in a grin. He has a pretty sizeable gap between his front teeth, but he wears it like he earned it.

"Hey, Jake," I say, adding an unconvincing smile.

"Have you heard about this?" He jabs his thumb at Isolda's picture like he's jabbing it directly into her real eye. "That psychopath was spotted in Louisiana trying to buy something from an herb store. I'm sure they'll get her."

"I don't think it'll be that easy," I mumble to myself. Isolda has a talent for slipping through fingers. Whether or not that was due to something magical, I had a pretty good idea.

The news flips over to an oversized image of a hamburger, and Callie snatches the remote off the coffee table, powering the TV off. As the screen goes black, Callie's twin, Charlotte, swings around the corner, crunching loudly on an apple in her hand.

"What's up?" she drawls at Callie and me. Then her eyes land on Jacob and she stops like she's hit a wall.

"Hey," she says to him, disengaging her teeth from the fruit. "I haven't seen you since last summer."

"Yeah, well, since I see Callie at school now, I don't have to hang around here to get her attention," Jacob answers, turning to pinch Callie teasingly.

He had been at Sagestone, I realize. After it had burned down, all of its students were transferred to our school, the only other option in the county. Wellsey is so packed now, it's hard to pick out any face unless you're looking for it.

Charlotte twists the pink stone on her necklace, her face picking up a hint of red.

Is she nervous? I find myself wondering.

"That's pretty," Jacob says, unable to ignore the obvious fidgeting. "What kind of necklace is that?"

"This?" Charlotte stops long enough to hold out the teardrop stone. "It's rose quartz. It brings you happiness and love." She gulps after the last word, realizing how strange that sounds.

Jacob tilts his head questioningly. "Is that Chinese mythology or something?"

"It's nothing. She's superstitious." Callie shoots Charlotte a look I can only interpret as *shut up*, before angling her body toward Jacob, resting one fist on her hip.

"I have homework," she says. "Don't you have to, like, go?"

Jacob stands, shaking his head to himself. "Sure. I'll see you at school."

He leans in to give her a hug, which she dodges, then waves at Charlotte and me.

"Good to see you guys."

"Bye, Jacob," Charlotte and I respond at the same time.

Once the door is closed, Charlotte practically bolts out of the room. I turn to Callie.

"You are so mean to him and he just likes you," I say.

She makes a coughing noise, tossing the remote onto the couch. "I didn't ask him to come over. He just assumes we can't take care of ourselves. And if he's over here all the time, how long will it be before one of you does something weird, or Matthew decides to move a chair? It's too big a risk."

As if to prove her point, the chair next to her flips over, the wooden back cracking against the floor. Matthew Townsend, the accused arsonist—or at least what's left of his spirit—had been bound to our house after Wyatt had been tattooed with his blood in order to gain his power. It had been a Stolam trick, allowing Faolan to possess his body, and Wyatt had paid dearly for it. Unfortunately, it meant Matthew was stuck here, communicating through flickering lights and moving furniture.

"Even witches need social lives," I say, righting the chair and turning back to Callie.

"Yeah? How'd that work out for Mom?" She turns so quickly her skirt whooshes out behind her as she stomps out of the room.

I sink down on the couch, turning on the TV again. But there's nothing more about Isolda. I wish I could let it go, but every day since I got back from the hospital, the thought of her has been circling my mind.

I know she's coming for the onyx. I just don't know when.

CHAPTER 5

SLEEPWALKING

A warm, purring pressure on my chest prods at my sleep until I open my eyes. Ruby, Callie's cat, is curled up on top of me again, her gray face inches from mine, her eyelids pressed together. I must have forgotten to close my door.

I pick Ruby up gently and place her on the floor.

"Go back to Callie's room," I croak, giving her a pat to show I mean no ill will. I hear her soft feet padding out of the room, but it's so dark that there's not even the usual glow from the window to see by.

I sit up, rubbing my eyes. Shifting my weight off the bed, I stand up. Might as well go to the bathroom while I'm awake.

I've made the journey from my room across the hall to the bathroom so many times that I don't even hold my hands out for guidance in the dark. Six steps to the door, turn left, five down the hall, turn right. I set out, stepping quietly across the wood floor.

The house is so still, I can hear my own joints moving. I make it to my door, turn left down the hall, then turn right.

My foot doesn't meet wood on the next step. My whole body pitches forward, hurtling down with nothing to stop it.

I fling my arms out, my stomach leaping into my chest as the floor drops out from under me. I try to seize something—anything—

149

as I fall. My hand hits hard metal just as my heel cracks against something wooden underneath me. I grip the staircase banister with all my might, bringing my body to a swinging halt. The metal railing slams into my ribcage, keeping me from the drop on the other side. I double over, the muscles around my scar tissue throbbing, infuriated by the sudden jolt. My vision sharpens and I finally see where I am.

I'm halfway down the staircase. I must have walked off the top. But it makes no sense. The bathroom and staircase are on completely opposite sides of the house. I would have had to turn right outside my room.

I straighten, the sweat on my scalp turning cold. Still shaking, I tread back into my room. Everything looks somehow clearer than it did just minutes before, as if I'd been walking around with a veil over my eyes.

I pull back the covers of my bed, moonlight flashing off the face of the onyx around my wrist. I pause, watching it swing back and forth in the air.

If Faolan can hurt us from inside the stone, it isn't a stretch to think he could be manipulating my thoughts. Bad energy, like Luke said, affects everything around it. It changes things. Maybe Faolan is changing me.

I catch the stone up in my palm, my finger brushing over something on its surface. My body tenses like I've jumped in freezing water. Turning my light on, I hold the stone up to eye level. The thing I've been dreading seeing since the moment I put Faolan in the onyx is staring me in the face.

There's a crack in the stone.

I rub my thumb over it, trying to clean it off, but it's there, about a fingernail's length right in the middle.

I sink onto my bed, my hands dropping. All that time trying to break it, and it just cracks on its own.

Very carefully, I place it on my nightstand, picking up my phone. It's late, but I know Luke will answer.

Maybe I hit it on the counter at some point, I try to tell myself. But I know it's not true.

Faolan is figuring out a way to escape.

CHAPTER 6

GEMMIE

Luke's hands grip the seatbelt across his chest as the SUV bounces us down the dirt road to Gemmie's house. He stares out the windshield, watching the thick wall of bony mesquite trees roll by on either side of us.

"I can't tell if you're afraid to meet Gemmie or afraid of my driving," I say, trying to lighten the mood. Luke could barely get in the car with me, knowing the state of the onyx.

He dips his head, smiling just slightly. "Little of both."

"Well, I'm a great driver, and Gemmie is an amazing person."

"You're going to tell her about the onyx, right?" he says, shifting in his seat to touch a hand to his chest. I've seen him do it enough to know he's touching the *Veri Segno*, the blood tattoos resting just beneath the thin fabric of his shirt.

"*Yes,*" I say for the fifth time, turning the car off the road and up the private drive that leads to Gemmie's cottage.

"It's just that you love to play the martyr."

I dig my fingernails into the leather seam around the steering wheel.

"I don't play anything when it comes to Faolan," I say.

I stop the car a few feet from the house. Gemmie is already

standing in the doorway, bordered by honeysuckle vines, waiting for us.

"Gemmie," I say when I reach her, falling into her arms and hugging her closely. Something about Gemmie makes me feel innocent again, like nothing is wrong and the world is safe. I cling to her for a little too long and Luke clears his throat meaningfully.

"Oh, sorry," I say, pushing back. "Gemmie, this is my boyfriend, Luke. Luke, this is my grandmother, Gemma Sayers."

"A pleasure," Gemmie says, floating over to take his hand in both of hers. Luke is so struck by the elegant gesture that for a second he looks like he might bow.

"I'm guessing you're named after the Gemma Sayers that took over the Sayers clan when she was sixteen?" Luke says, turning a pale shade of pink. It's hard not to be smitten with Gemmie.

"My Aunt Iona was a big fan of hers," he goes on. "She traded her bike for a journal that was supposed to have belonged to her. My uncle was not happy about that."

Gemmie takes a step back, tilting her chin to the side thoughtfully.

"I don't know of another Gemma Sayers, darling. I think you're speaking about me."

Luke splutters a laugh. "But it can't be you, you'd have to be almost"— his fingers twitch like he's counting in his head— "two *hundred* years old."

I scoff, waiting for Gemmie to let out her musical laugh, but she doesn't.

"Let me make you some tea, darlings," she says pointedly, moving into the house like a wisp of smoke.

Luke snaps his eyes to me. "How old is your grandma?"

I shake my head, brushing it off. "I don't know, like... she's got to be around..."

But I can't come up with a single date. I can't recall her ever talking about when she was born, or my mother even mentioning it.

Walking into her living room, with its brass picture frames and not a single modern appliance, I can almost imagine it being an eighteenth century parlor.

And knowing Gemmie, she always has a few secrets up her sleeve. I wipe the idea away. One thing at a time.

Luke and I take seats at the table in her dining room, which is little more than a nook between the windows. Luke runs his fingers over the miniature library that runs along the wall behind him. Gemmie has mounted shelves on every available surface, lining up books like silent sentries around the whole room.

He gingerly pulls out a blue cloth journal, opening it like it's made of eggshells.

"These are all handwritten," Luke murmurs, turning to me. "Have you read them? I think they're spell books."

I chew my lip, wondering why I've never bothered to open any of them. From the wonder in his face, I can tell Luke would kill to have grown up in a house like this, and I'd never fully appreciated any of it.

I pull the onyx out from under my hoodie, lifting the cord from around my neck. I hold it out to Gemmie, who's bustling around the kitchen.

"Gemmie?" I say, my voice heavy. "Could you look at this?"

She pauses, tucking her silver hair behind her ear as she walks toward me, her eyes locked on the stone. She takes it, holding it up to the light like she's examining a diamond.

"It's cracking," I say.

"Yes, I can see that."

Her finger runs across the hairline fissure.

"Ever the fighter," she says to herself.

"How do we stop it?" I ask as she places it back on the table.

She turns to the shelf behind her, plucking up a blue glass vial.

"I'm afraid I don't know. When most spirits are bound to something, they stay put." She pops the cork out of the vial. "But Faolan has never been what you would call typical."

She empties the contents, a clear liquid, into her hands and rubs them together. She clasps the onyx between her palms. After a moment, she hands it back to me.

I loop the cord back over my head, blocking out the smell of something like burned plastic trailing off it.

"I don't know how much it will help, but it's something,"

Gemmie says wearily.

I've never seen her so drawn. Even when things look their worst, she's the one person in my family who never bends under the pressure.

I shift in my seat, wishing I'd never brought up the crack.

"Does she have to wear it all the time?" Luke asks, resting his elbows on the table.

Gemmie flicks a glance at him, pulling back into the kitchen as the kettle starts to whistle.

"I wouldn't trust Stolam not to be waiting for the moment she puts it down." She sweeps the kettle off the burner, pouring water into two cups.

I sit back as Gemmie sets one in front of me. The steam drifts up to my nose in a wet cloud and I take a breath, expecting the cradling scent of chamomile. Instead, a sour, rooty smell fogs up my sinuses, and something in my brain says *skullcap*. My mother kept a small shrub of it in her garden. It always reeked in the summer. I look at Gemmie questioningly, but her face has shut down into an unmoving mask.

"Drink it, dear," she says, pushing the cup into my palm.

I tip it back, taking down a grainy swallow. Warmth spreads from the middle of my chest, tingling as it makes its way to my toes. I relax back into my chair, looking at Luke.

He's sitting on edge, his eyes fixed on the tea in front of him. He looks up to Gemmie, his expression defeated.

"It's okay," he says softly, moving the cup away. "I don't need it."

Gemmie nods, some meaning passing between them that's lost on me. She presses her hand to Luke's chest, her fingers spreading out against his shirt.

Luke goes rigid, his shoulders slamming against the back of the chair. His eyes squeeze closed and his fists clench against the table. It looks like he's on the brink of crying out, every fiber of his strength keeping him still.

A piece of my brain flutters clumsily, trying to tell me I should do something, but my limbs are so heavy it feels impossible to move. I lick my lips, trying to form words. They come out slow, sticking to my tongue.

"Gemmie, what are you doing?"

She doesn't even acknowledge me. Her eyes are set in concentration. A smell blooms in the room, something burning, and Gemmie hisses, yanking her hand away.

Luke slumps in the chair like he's just run twenty miles. Gemmie lowers her hand, but not before I spot several red, nasty welts across her palm.

"She's still protecting you," Gemmie says, moving away from Luke to take her own seat. She takes a pinch of green paste from a tiny jar on the table and massages it gently into the burns.

Still trying to shake the haze from my thoughts, I say, "Gemmie, what did you do?"

"I just needed to see what he was hiding, darling," she says wearily. "I hope you can both forgive me. There are too few members of my family left for me to be careless with any of them."

"I understand," Luke rasps. His skin is covered with goose bumps, and it almost seems like he's shaking. "I hope," he adds, then swallows. "I hope you can see how it happened. That I tried…"

The words clot in his throat. Gemmie leans over, resting her other hand on his forearm.

"I know," she says.

It's clear the visit has come to an end. I follow Luke to the door after he's recovered enough to walk and the feeling has returned to my hands and feet. Gemmie is quieter than I've ever seen her, her skin ashy and drawn. Whatever she did to Luke took a lot out of her.

"Hazel, wait," she says, turning to glide away into her bedroom. She returns with what looks like a handkerchief, but when I take it, it feels stiff, almost waxy.

"This is muslin from Inis Mór, where the Sayers clan originated. Wrap the stone in it at night. That's when he'll be strongest: when you're asleep and your mind is open."

I nod, slipping the square of fabric into my back pocket. Gemmie takes my chin in her hand, her green eyes fixing on mine.

"I just need time to find a more permanent solution, my heart," she says. "Just be strong a bit longer."

"I'll try," I say, hugging her one more time.

CHAPTER 7

OLIVIA

The ride to Luke's house is like sitting on a pane of glass. Neither Luke nor I say a word, both feeling like one move or sound might send us plummeting. I follow him down the narrow hallway to his room, my flats slapping awkwardly against the wood floor.

He closes the door after I pass through and I lower myself onto his mattress, letting my bag slide to the ground. A cluster of tiny candles on his dresser flicker, always burning for the Orishas, the deities his aunt believed watched over their family. The flames make the room warm and stuffy, like being under a thick blanket.

"What happened when Gemmie touched you?" My voice sounds far too sharp in the muffled air. "What did she see?"

Luke chews on his thumbnail, hovering by the door. He won't meet my eye even though I'm staring at him so hard I feel like I might burn a hole in his skin.

"Do you still have the onyx on?" he asks.

I pull the stone from around my neck, shoving it into my bag at my feet. Then I straighten and hold up my hands, as if I'm trying to prove I'm not armed.

Luke exhales, walking the few steps over to the bed like he's being forced at gunpoint. He sinks down next to me, so close that I catch the light scent of pool chlorine that always follows him around.

My mind chooses this moment to realize we're alone together. Alone in a house, in his room, on his bed. When you have so many siblings, being alone in itself feels like a luxury. But being alone in a setting like this, with the candles, and the linen sheets, and *him*—I can't even begin to untangle the feelings knotting themselves in my stomach.

Finally, he turns to me, his pale blue eyes catching mine. "It's not that I don't want to tell you. It's just that when I do, everything between us will change, and I'm trying to hold on to it as long as I can."

I lean forward, my hand touching his shoulder. "Nothing will change. I know you."

Doubt sticks to the words as they leave my mouth, despite how badly I want them to be true. Even after everything we've been through, I still know so little about him. I feel in my heart that I know who he is, but he refuses to give me any concept of his past. And whatever Gemmie had seen had shaken her badly. I can't gloss over a secret like that, not now, when so much is at stake.

Luke hunches forward, pressing his forehead into his hands.

"*I* don't know me," he says, echoing my thoughts. "That's the problem. I don't know if I'm good or bad, or if it's even a choice."

He sounds so fragile, so unlike his usual self. I scoot closer, wrapping my arms around his chest and pressing my cheek into his back. His breaths are short and hollow.

"You're good," I say. "I know you're good."

He turns around to look at me, so weighed down by the secret he's keeping that the beautiful blue of his eyes looks dull. My ribs close around my lungs. I can't see him like this, torturing himself.

I put my hands on either side of his face, pressing my lips to his. He almost collapses into me, pulling me closer until every inch of us is touching. I lean backward, feeling his weight shift on top of me. Heat races up my legs, melting into my muscles. My fingers drift up under the hem of his shirt, following the deep trough of his spine that cuts between the strong muscles of his back. His skin is almost burning under my fingertips. I work his shirt up, over his head, wanting to feel that warmth.

His hands cup behind my head, bringing his forehead to mine. He breaks off the kiss, his fingers curling into my hair gently, like he just needs to cling to a part of me to know I'm there.

"I can't lose you like I lost her," he says, barely more than a whisper.

If I hadn't been lying down, I might have stepped back. There's such an intense fear behind his words that for a second I white out the fact that he's referring to another girl. Then my thoughts click into place, and my body turns cold.

I disentangle my arms from his.

"Lose who?" I say. There's a harsh note in my voice. "Who did you lose?"

Luke drops his head, a slow breath winding out of his mouth.

"The *Veri Segno*. The blood my mother used. It was the blood of my...of the first person I was ever in love with. Olivia."

His words hit me like a rock in the chest. Somehow, I managed to avoid it all this time, but Luke has finally put a name to the blood tattoos etched into his chest. *Olivia.*

I turn my head away as I try to thread together what he's saying, and my gaze lands on the oval mirror in his corner. I can see the rusty-red curves and spikes of the tattoos in the reflection, how they twist like thorny vines over his bare shoulders and down his arms.

It's almost like there's a dead body on top of me. The blood that had once been in someone else, in someone that Luke had loved and touched, was now hanging over me, staring down at me. All at once, it's too hot to breathe. I squirm out from under Luke, dragging myself to the other end of the bed.

"I don't understand," I say, grasping the cold brass bedframe so hard my knuckles pop.

Luke sits up, staring at the shirt bunched in his hands. "Olivia was the first witch I met outside of Stolam. She lived in the same neighborhood in Louisiana. She didn't even know she was a witch before she met me. I taught her."

Just like me. I swallow, my throat suddenly swollen. He could have been telling my story.

"We used to do magic for each other, little stuff," Luke goes on. "Like I would make her yard bloom with lilies, or she'd send a songbird to my house at night. I knew as soon as my mother saw her, the way she looked at Olivia, that something was going to happen. I just didn't know what. On my thirteenth birthday, Stolam brought me to my ceremony, and she was..." He clears his throat. "She was already dying. There was nothing I could do."

"Stop," I say, bolting to my feet. The room is stifling, too heavy with the scent of wax and heat from the candles. I can't follow one thought through the end. All I know is that I can't hear another word. I can't be in the same room with this story. Maybe if I can get away, it won't exist outside these walls. It'll just be a ghost story I heard once. But I can't keep looking at Luke, when the evidence is still carved into his body.

I take a step, aiming my body at the door.

"Hazel?"

Luke's palm brushes my shoulder and I flinch away from it. Part of me is screaming about how cruel I'm being, that this person I care about has just shown me the darkest part of his soul, and he deserves my understanding. But the other, louder part is just begging to get away. Away from him and the dead girl trapped in his skin.

"I need to just...go home for a bit," I say. I can't look at him. I can't see how betrayed he must feel, how let down by me.

"Okay," he says softly, resting his hand on top of his head.

I almost fall over as I reach for my bag. I push past his dresser, knocking my knee into it as I stumble the last steps out the door.

My hands sweat against the steering wheel as I drive to my house. All this time, there's been another person there with us, every time I think I'm alone with Luke.

The thought of Matthew crosses my mind, how a piece of his soul had been trapped in the blood on Wyatt's back. How angry he was at my brother for stealing his life, his power. Was Olivia like that, too? She must hate me for being the one who gets to be with Luke. That I can go on living when she'll never again speak a word, or feel his touch.

I shake my head, trying to clear the image away. I can't think about this. I can't make sense of it in my mind; it's too big and horrible for one person to process. I focus on the few raindrops that dapple my windshield, how the wipers carry them away with each pass, as if they were never there. I try to imagine the memory of the last hour being whisked away too, scraped off like the rain, but it just sits inside me like a stain, spreading deeper with every passing moment.

CHAPTER 8

DEEPEST FEARS

I cough myself out of sleep. It doesn't come easily; I hang on to what's left of the comforting black of unconsciousness as long as I can until it becomes clear there's no going back. I open my eyes to the murky darkness of my room.

Frustration roils in my chest. After the stair incident last night, and the day with Luke, and school tomorrow, all I want is to escape into the folds of sleep, but my own body is betraying me.

I swallow, my throat scraping together like it's coated in sand. I sit up, reaching for the water bottle I always keep by my bed. My fingers brush over the cold glossy surface of the onyx on my night-stand and I draw my hand back. The muslin wrapping has come open and the stone sits like a present in the middle of it. Hastily, I tuck it back up, realizing I've forgotten my water tonight.

I count the steps this time, gripping the banister of the stairs the whole way down, just in case.

There's a high-pitched hum in my ears, the kind of sound that follows me around when I turn on the music in the SUV too loud, like a mosquito hovering by my ears. I shake my head lazily, padding through the kitchen. No light is draining in through the windows; the room is cloaked in a static, dark gray glow. I head for the sink, grabbing a glass from the cupboard as I go. I fill it from the faucet, the sound dull when it reaches my ears. I lift it to my lips, my throat begging for the cool touch of water.

The glass rips out of my hand, shooting forward into the sink. It shatters against the metal, sending a shock through my body.

"*Matthew*," I growl, clenching my teeth together; then the smell hits my nose, so sharp and sterile that I pause.

There's an open bottle of bleach on the counter, directly in front of my right hand, its handle pointing toward me. I lean over the sink, touching the broken lip of the glass and bringing it to my nose. The smell hits the back of my sinuses, and my blood runs cold. I turn on the faucet, washing my shaking hands.

I'd been about to drink bleach. I could have so easily poisoned myself without any thought. But I could *so clearly* see the glass in my hand, the stream of water from the faucet.

A yell splits through the quiet in the house, rattling in my bones. I jump back from the sink, all the nerves in my body bristling. Another cry tears through the darkness, echoing down the staircase.

Wyatt. I take off toward the hall, sprinting to the staircase. I take the steps two at a time, barely flinching as I stub my toes on the last one.

The door to Wyatt's is next to mine, the last one on the left. I'm going so fast that I almost run past it, sliding to a stop as I grip onto the handle. I push against the door, my shoulder connecting with the wood. It's stuck.

I pound my knee into it as Wyatt yells on the other side, finally breaking through whatever is holding it. The door crashes open and I fall through it, splaying out across the floor.

I look up for Wyatt, my eyes working to decode the shapes in the darkness. He's standing on the inward corner of his bed, bracing himself on the wall, like he's trying to get away from something. His face is twisted in fear, his eyes barely slits.

"Hazel, don't move!" He holds out his hand like he's trying to shove me back outside.

I'm pushing up onto my elbows, gathering my feet beneath me, when one of the shadows next to me moves.

Something slithers across the floor, moving toward Wyatt. I see movement at the end of the bed too, just inches from him, something writhing in the covers. Another shadow twitches, this one only inches from my hand on the ground. I spring backward, my back hitting the wall, just as the room fills with the sound of tiny bones being rattled together.

Diamondbacks. Three of them, each the length of my leg, all stalking my brother as he shakes, clinging to the wall for dear life as they close in on him.

A memory flashes through my mind of when we'd first moved to Texas. Our house was old, so many cracks and holes, and one day a Copperhead had gotten into Wyatt's room while he slept. My mother had found it just before it sank its fangs into his tiny leg, but even the infinitesimal amount of venom that had penetrated caused him to seize all the way to the hospital.

To this day, snakes remain his worst fear.

"Hazel, help!" Wyatt backs further into the corner as the snake on the bed pulls itself into a coil, its head rising above the covers.

"Dad!" I scream, pivoting toward the doorway and smashing into Abby, who's just appeared behind me.

"What is it?" she shrieks, trying to push past me, but I force her back.

"Don't go in there!"

Her eyes land on the floor behind me and she recoils, just as my dad makes it to the top of the stairs with a bat.

"What's wrong?" His eyes land on me, wide with adrenaline.

"Diamondbacks in Wyatt's room!" I'm barely able to get the words out.

I step aside as he pushes through the door, using his elbow to flip on the light. With a lightning movement, he brings the bat down on the nearest snake's head, dark liquid splattering across the wood. Its long body contracts and its tail drags along the floor, emitting one last rattle. Dad makes quick work of the other one, which has turned its course, skating toward him with surprising speed. He holds his hand out to Wyatt, who clambers off the bed just as the last snake lunges toward him, narrowly missing.

Stretching the bat out long, our dad lifts the snake off the covers, tossing him into the far corner, away from us, and finishing him off.

Lowering the bat, he turns to Wyatt, who is a shade of white I've only seen him turn when he's sick. Dad touches his head, then his shoulder, as if making sure he's all still there.

"You okay?" he asks.

Wyatt swallows and nods, lifting his arm as Abby runs toward him to hug him around the waist.

My stepdad comes toward me, his eyes calm again.

"How about you, Haze? Hanging in there?"

"Yeah," I breathe out, realizing I've been holding in a lungful of air.

"You guys stay here. I'm going to check the rest of the house. Turn on the lights and check your rooms. Be very careful."

The twins have appeared in the hallway and now head back to their room, turning on the lights in the hall as they go.

I turn back to my little brother. "Wyatt?"

"It was snakes, Haze," he says, wiping the sheen of sweat from his forehead.

"I know," I say slowly, wrapping my arms around my waist to keep from hunching under the guilt. I'd sworn to Wyatt I'd never let anything happen to him, not after Faolan had stolen his body for so long. I would watch out for him, never let danger get close to him. And I'd failed. Again.

"How'd they get up here?" Abby says, stepping away from the smashed head of the nearest one. "And three of them."

Neither Wyatt nor I have an answer. It's too big a coincidence, and as we've been saying lately, we don't get the luxury of believing in coincidences anymore.

"I'm going to sleep in the guest room next to dad." Wyatt walks past me, his steps heavy, defeated.

My sisters and I check the rest of the upstairs rooms, but not so much as a book is out of place. We split up, heading back to our rooms, though I doubt sleep is near for any of us.

Flooding every corner with light still doesn't knock off the cold lingering around my bedroom. I step carefully, bending to peer under my bed, listening for the telltale rattle of a Diamondback's tail. When I straighten, my eyes fall on my nightstand.

The onyx is out. It's sitting in the open, in the middle of the muslin square again, like I'd never touched it. I hurry to the table, looking for any sign that someone else might have moved it. The cloth around it is scorched black and peeling away from the stone, a perfect circle cut out.

Faolan burned his way through the muslin. The protective fabric made by my ancestors did nothing to stop him. The incidents of the past thirty-six hours suddenly fit together like cogs. The stairs, the bleach, the snakes. It's been him. His power has been leaking out through the crack in the onyx, reaching the people nearest to him: Wyatt and me.

I bend closer, searching out the crack. It's grown about a quarter of an inch, eating into the curved side of the onyx. Every day, he's getting stronger. And no one, not even the strongest witches I know, have any idea how to stop him from getting out.

I slam my fists on either side of the stone, fury tearing through my chest.

"*You—*"

But there's not a curse word in the world that's low and hateful enough to call him. For a man who would kill his own son with his worst fear, just because he can.

I stare into the red flicker at the center of the stone. Somehow, I know he's listening. That he's laughing at me right now.

"I will stop you," I swear to him. "You will *never* touch my family again."

As I push back from the nightstand, searching in my drawer for a bottle of salt and dumping it over him vindictively, I almost feel like I can. But I still have no clue how.

CHAPTER 9

FRIENDLY ADVICE

"**Y**ou don't look so good," Taylor says, winding up her arm to throw a softball at me. I'm on the school's athletic field, standing across from Gallagher and M.C. who are both more invested in seeing who can spit farther than catching Taylor's fastballs.

"I haven't slept much the last few days," I grunt as Taylor's toss meets my glove.

The wind blows in from the north, laced with frost. My gaze drifts over to the hill peaks in the distance, where Luke took me. Clouds cluster around them now, gray and bad tempered. There always seems to be rain hanging around these days.

Taylor purses her lips. "Why? Are you going out all night? Oh my God." She drops her hands in fake shock. "Are you the Batman?"

"I just have stuff going on," I say.

"Like PTSD?" Taylor asks, real concern underneath her tone. Despite her lighthearted nature, Taylor was one of the few people who got me through the first few weeks after the attack.

"No, like, sleepwalking issues," I say. *No, like the soul of my father is escaping into the world and trying to kill us all in our sleep,* I can't help adding in my head.

"You should ask Luke to come over," she says, catching the ball I throw back and pumping her eyebrows at me. "Bet your dad wouldn't even notice. He's gone half the time anyway."

I swallow, tugging the sleeves of my sweatshirt down. No matter how hard I try, I can't make myself address the Luke problem. I *want* to. I want to be the kind of person who can just march up to him and say, *I want to know everything because it's who you are and this is my life now.* But every time I try to pick up the phone or walk over to the senior side of the school to find him, something in me balks.

"We got in a...*thing* the other day," I say, pushing the words out like they're rocks.

"Like a fight?"

"Kind of."

"Ohmigod!" Taylor bursts out suddenly, throwing the ball down and turning on me. "Stop playing yo-yo with people who love you!"

I step back, thrown by her tone.

"It's not as easy as just 'I love him, he loves me'!" My voice rises against the wind. Even M.C. and Gallagher stop snorting with laughter and look over.

"Why not? Why do you have to make everything so dramatic and complicated?"

"It *is* complicated!" I shout. This is the closest thing we've ever had to a fight, and with my lack of sleep and the pressure of Luke's secret on me, it's more than I can handle. "I don't know what's going to happen next in my life, and maybe he just doesn't fit in it right now."

Even as the words leave my mouth, I feel how wrong they are. But I can't even begin to organize how I feel into a string of words that means something coherent. I cross my arms, trying to lock in what little heat is left in my body.

Taylor's shoulders drop, and she walks the few feet between us to wrap me in a hug. It's such a rare gesture for her that I almost don't know how to react. She steps back after a moment.

"I know you're scared, after the..." she waggles her fingers, trying to find the right word, "*unpleasantness* that went down. And I don't know Luke, not really, but I know you. And you're a different person since you met him—in a good way. If someone makes you stronger, and *gets* you, you should keep them around. Even if they mess up. We all mess up."

She punctuates her thoughts with a shrug as I bite the inside of my lip, trying to hold it together. Taylor's eyes land behind me and she leans to the left, her face hardening.

"Did you hear enough of our conversation, Alison?" she says loudly. "Or do you want to climb inside Hazel's hoodie for a better listen? Go on, scurry up in there."

I turn to see Alison Holmes a few feet behind us, trying to look like she wasn't just eavesdropping as she meanders back to her new squad of Sagestone friends.

"Don't worry, she's harmless," Taylor says, patting me on the shoulder. "Everyone knows she was royally rejected by Luke for your little self."

She goes back to her spot, picking up another softball to lob at me. I barely gather the energy to lift my hands.

CHAPTER 10

DECISIONS

It's dusk by the time I finally start my homework. Everyone is upstairs and my dad is working his weekly overnight shift at the hospital, so I spread out on the dining room table. I pull the black silk cord that holds the onyx out of my sweater, feeling the heaviness of the stone finally leave my body. At least whatever Gemmie did has kept him from burning me during the day.

I hold it up, shifting it so the light illuminates its face. I can't stop checking the crack, it's becoming a tic.

Satisfied that it hasn't changed, at least in the last ten hours, I place it on the table next to my laptop, still in my periphery, just in case.

After half an hour, the words in my textbook start to run together. The lack of sleep is pulling me down, but I still get a twitch of fear when I think about nighttime and what Faolan might have in store for us tonight. Maybe I'll walk off the roof, or he'll set the whole house on fire.

I rub my dry eyes, letting my chin rest on my fist. It's so hard to focus on school when it feels so meaningless. I'm a witch. A murder attempt survivor. Am I going to be able to go to college, get a job like normal people? It doesn't even seem possible. My mother tried, but it all blew up in her face. What kind of future is there for people like us? Assuming we can even survive the next few nights.

I reach for my computer, pulling it closer to me, and type in *spells for protection*. Most of the spells I use are from my mother's journal, but occasionally I turn to the Internet. It's astounding how many people turn to magic for help. People who couldn't possibly know what a blood witch is, or how terrible it could be to find out you are one. They just write spells or use herbs or stones without knowing the true power they're touching. Casting is about manipulating energy with intention. They can do it without any real abilities, like the kind my family was born with. The kind Stollam kills for. That's sort of the beauty of it, though. People can create their own magic.

The results suggest the typical things, sage plants by windows, rosemary over doorways, black stones hidden in strategic places. But none of them will stop Faolan, and I can't exactly search for "how to keep the spirit of your psychopathic father from killing you in your sleep."

I pick up my eraser, tapping on the tabletop anxiously as I search for something more heavy-duty.

I open a link and a full page of spells unfurls over the screen. As I scroll down, my eyes land on *banishing a ghost*.

I hover over it for a second before clicking it open. When you get down to it, I suppose what's left of Faolan must be a ghost, in the broadest sense of the word. A piece of something left behind. He's clearly stronger and more poisonous than Matthew, but they're the same kind of being.

My eraser breaks in half. I hadn't realized I'd been squeezing it so hard. The chunk left in my fingers feels smooth, slippery, almost round. I look down, opening my palm.

A black widow is squirming between my fingertips. Its thin, stick-like legs wave in the air, the red hourglass on its underside bright against its black body. I hurl it away from me, my chair falling over as I vault out of my seat, a gasp ripping down my throat.

Furiously, I rub my hand on my sweatshirt, trying to get the feeling of skittering legs off my skin. I run over to where it fell, crushing it beneath the heel of my shoe. It leaves a dark stain on the wood, its body flattened and broken.

Sweat forms on the back of my neck, like a clammy hand wiping over my skin. I have to keep my head straight. I can't let myself unravel into hysterics. That's what Faolan wants: to keep me from thinking clearly.

In a few long strides, I'm out the back door, stumbling over our black Lab, Prince, who's asleep on the stoop.

I walk into the middle of the yard, the grass cushioning my steps. I stop when I reach the edge of my mother's garden. Being out here always calms my heart, even in its current state. She kept it so clean when she was alive, but now it's dissolved into chaos. I take a deep breath of the evening air, pulling in the layers of scent and cold together.

Prince pushes against my leg, using me as his own private back-rest. I sit down beside him, trying to hold onto my sanity. I press the heels of my hands into my eyes, imagining gathering the pieces of myself back together.

The setting sun washes the backyard with a lavender-blue light. I can already hear crickets and night birds, and, in the distance, the constant roll of the river. The twisting, anxious feeling inside me starts to settle, just barely. Out here, I can almost pretend there's nothing else. There are just plants and crickets and the breeze.

A blip of light draws my eye, just near our fence. A firefly. I haven't seen any since the summer. It blinks again, moving lazily along the fence line, down into the herb garden. Another flicker, this one near the house. I hold my breath, waiting to see it again.

Another lights up, this one on my left. Then another in the garden, and another, and another. More fireflies than I've ever seen in our backyard before. One lands on my arm, walking across my skin like it knows me. Even Prince is starting to notice. He sits up and his ears perk forward, his nose following the path of the nearest one.

All around us, tiny lights are blinking. The air is filled with them, to the point that they almost look like stars. Warmth glows in my limbs, and I could almost be weightless, floating in my own galaxy. It's the most beautiful thing I've ever seen. It almost seems...

Magical. As soon as I think it, I know it's true. This is Luke's magic. Somehow, it *feels* like him. It's the kind of thing he described doing with…the girl. Olivia.

My phone buzzes in my back pocket and I take it out. It's a text from Luke.

Did you get my gift?

A smile touches my lips. I should feel uneasy about this, but with the yard full of tiny, bright lights, I can't find it in me. I write back. *I did. It's beautiful. Thank you.* After a second, his reply comes. *I just felt like you needed it. Can we talk? I need to tell you some things.*

My jaw tightens. I know I have to face this. I owe him that much. To try to understand it from his perspective.

Yes. I'll meet you at lunch tomorrow.

After a moment, he writes, *Not tonight? I can come over. Some things have happened.*

I know I can't handle more of this tonight. Whatever it is, it has to wait. I want to hang on to the glow of the fireflies for as long as I can, before I have to go back inside and face Faolan.

Let's talk tomorrow, I type. *I'm too happy to ruin it with heavy stuff. Thank you for the fireflies. Love you.*

I realize what I've written, and delete the last two words before sending it. I'm so used to signing off like that with my siblings and Taylor, it just came out. But it hadn't felt untrue.

My body suddenly feels paralyzed. *I love him.* The realization crushes my lungs with its weight. My body floods with warmth, and at the same time, my stomach turns.

Love is what destroyed my mother. Love is the one thing I can never let myself trust. It blinded her and it could blind me, too.

The fireflies are moving on, pulling back into the trees like receding waves. With the last shred of sun gone, the yard feels cold and stony. I stand up heavily, dragging my feet every step.

Prince follows me back inside. As I shut the door behind us, the picture frame on the wall next to me draws my attention. It's a family portrait, taken just a few months before my mother died. She and my stepdad stand together, arms around each other, while younger versions of Abby, Wyatt, the twins, and I smile from the foreground.

Only now, all of our eyes drip blood.

I pull the picture off the wall, holding it in the crooks of my elbows, my breath sticking in my throat. It isn't real blood, on closer inspection. It's like the ink in our eyes has melted. But the message is perfectly clear to me.

Faolan means to kill us all. Maybe even tonight.

I wheel around to the table, half expecting the onyx to have jumped, or maybe even Faolan to be standing behind me. But it's still lifeless, sitting innocently next to my computer.

Trying to use only one finger, I slide the stone further away from me, checking my chair twice before sitting down.

I look at my screen, realizing it's still on the page for banishing a ghost. I'm about to close it, but I stop.

Banishing a ghost. Banishing Faolan. It's clear that nothing is going to stop Faolan from getting out of the onyx, but if we could get rid of him, erase him forever... Everything would go away. We could go back to normal. Stolam and Isolda would never get their leader back.

Doing it feels nearly impossible. I know instantly that I could never pull this off alone; my magic is still too volatile and untrained. I would need all my siblings, and so far, our spells have been for small stuff. Helping Abby get over the flu, or making Charlotte a focus stone to help with her ADD. But sending a spirit to whatever's on the other side...I doubt *most* witches could do something like that.

But if anyone can do it, it should be us. My mother worked so hard to ensure that together, we'd be one of the strongest forces of magic possible. Powerful as he was, Faolan is still just a fraction of the caster he used to be.

And it's our only choice, I realize, the thought dragging me down. We can try, or we can wait for his next attack. If it were just aimed at me, I might not even be tempted, but he'd gone after Wyatt last night.

My fingernails dig into my palms as the image of Wyatt's terrified face flashes across my mind. How useless I'd felt, how helpless. I can't risk Faolan hurting them again.

I pull the onyx toward me by its cord, letting it drag noisily across the wood. The flickering red light is always there, deep inside it, shifting back and forth like a caged tiger. Maybe it's just me, but he seems anxious.

"This is the end of the line, *Dad*," I say aloud, all of the hate in my body pouring into the words.

I reach for my notebook with my left hand. Scanning over the site, I start to scrawl words onto the lines. I've read hundreds of spells. There's no trick to writing one. And the first spell I ever write myself is going to be the banishing of Faolan Sicario.

CHAPTER 11

MISTAKES

"So where did you find this spell?" Callie asks, lowering herself on to the floor and reaching for a black pillar candle.

All four of my siblings are sitting on the cleared-off floor with varying degrees of annoyance. Everyone's tired, especially Wyatt, who probably hadn't ever gotten back to sleep. He sits on the floor beside Abby, his head propped in his hand, his eyes half-closed.

"I wrote it," I say, popping the top of the salt container. "Based on a couple of spells I saw."

Charlotte leans forward to start lighting candles. Her eyes are gleaming. Out of all of us, I think she likes casting best. Part of her always wanted to be special, to be capable of something like what we can do.

"In Mom's journal?" Callie pushes, uncertainty trailing off her words.

I bend down to start the salt circle, but my hand stalls. A patch of darker wood sits just under my feet. After the attack, our whole living room had to be professionally cleaned. They managed to scrub up the black chalk circle and fix the scuffmarks, but they couldn't completely erase the stain from the puddle of my blood. We usually keep it covered with a rug and avoid being in here at all, but the living room is the biggest surface in the house for casting circles. And this is going to need a big circle.

"No, they were spells I found on the Internet," I state, pouring salt on the floor. I work my way behind everyone, enclosing us in a circle.

"Well, then, this seems like a great idea," Callie says, throwing her hands up. "Afterwards, let's look up how to build a car on YouTube, since the Internet knows everything."

"Yeah, what?" Wyatt says, straightening. "Why are we casting down here? What are we doing?"

I finish the salt barrier and sit cross-legged between Charlotte and Callie. From my hoodie pocket, I take out a few pieces of green aventurine—protection stones that Luke gave us for our last circle, when we released Matthew from being bound inside the walls. *Never mess with spirits unless you've protected yourself*, Luke told us. *Spirits don't act rationally. You never know what could happen.*

I hold the stones in my palm, staring at the deep green of them, and trying to settle the fear grappling in my stomach. I set them in a line between the candles and bring out my final tool: a small silver knife that belonged to my mother.

"I want to make Faolan cross over," I say. "I want to open a gate and push him through."

There's a loaded pause, then Wyatt stands up. "Well, I'm out."

"How the *hell* are you planning to do that?" Callie explodes.

"Look, spells are about intention, right?" I say, my temper rising defensively. "We just have to know what our goal is and we can do it. We five, together, are supposed to be one of the strongest teams in the history of witchcraft. Mom made sure of that. If anyone can do it, we can."

Callie reaches over and snags my notebook, her eyes moving quickly over the page.

"I combined stuff from a lot of different spells," I say anxiously, watching her face crease in disbelief. "A lot of it is things we already know."

"You want to call the Corners?" Callie says, her gaze ticking up to me.

"We have to," I say, swallowing roughly. "Otherwise we won't have enough energy to open a gate on our own."

This is the part I'm worried about. Calling the Corners means calling for help from the very force of nature itself. Witches have the power to pull in energy from the world around us, from stones and trees and the air, even from each other, to alter whatever we want to. Calling the Corners means tapping into it all, everything, at once. North, South, East, and West. It's something even Luke is hesitant to do. There's only so much energy one person can hold.

Callie drops the notebook, pinching the bridge of her nose like a teacher at her wit's end.

"You keep saying 'open a gate' like it's driving to McDonald's, but do you even know what it means? *No one* knows what's on the other side. You have no idea what you're doing, what you're opening a door into. On top of that, you think you have even a *chance* of making that demon," she points at the onyx hanging around my neck, "do anything at all?"

"I am stronger than he is." The intensity in my voice startles me almost as much as my words. I didn't realize until this moment how badly I need that to be true.

Everyone's eyes are on me, surprise reflecting across all of them.

"*We* are stronger than he is," I go on, keeping my voice steady. "We are five witches with the most ancient witch blood in our veins and the corners on our side. We are going to get rid of him tonight so he can never hurt us again."

"Totally," Abby pipes up. She's nodding emphatically. "Let's do it."

"Why can't we ask Luke what to do?" Wyatt asks, still standing uneasily at the edge of the circle. "Or Gemmie?"

"Luke is afraid to be in the same room with the onyx," I say, my throat straining to keep my voice level. "And Gemmie has no idea how to stop Faolan. Last night, he attacked me *and* Wyatt. I only survived because of Matthew, and Wyatt was lucky that dad was here. But he's not here now. What do you think Faolan is capable of doing tonight if we don't do something *now*?"

I tug the onyx over my head, freeing my neck of the ever-present weight of it. I hold it out to Callie.

"It's cracking," I say. "And the more it does, the stronger he gets. He's going to escape, unless we can get rid of him."

Callie delicately takes the stone, her face falling when she sees the hairline split. She passes it to Charlotte, and then to Abby and Wyatt.

No one says anything for a while. Callie picks at the page of my notebook. Wyatt chews his lip. I know how unnerving it must be for them to see me like this. I made so sure I was the sturdy one, the one they could depend on, ever since Mom died. I never wanted to be the one asking for help.

"I knew it was him last night," Wyatt says softly. "It just felt like him. If he gets out, do you think he'll come for me?"

I want to stand up, to go throw my arms around my little brother, but he looks so fragile, like he might shatter if I touch him.

"That will never happen, Wyatt," I promise. "I will never let him take you again."

Wyatt lifts his dark green eyes to me. "He's more powerful than us. Stolam even thought he was a god or something."

"He is *not* more powerful than us together," I shoot back. "And we're going to get rid of him tonight."

After a long moment, Wyatt sits again. Charlotte, a new soberness in her face, turns to me.

"Explain it," she says, reaching for my notebook. "What do we have to do?"

I pick up a piece of chalk, leaning over the middle of the circle. From memory, I start to draw the patterns on the floor as I speak.

"The hard part will be opening a gate to the afterlife. You're right, I don't know what's there." I look at Callie. "But there's something. Something Faolan and Stolam are afraid of. To get to it, we have to tear open a hole. Once it's open, the tear will take one soul. Then it's supposed to close."

"*Supposed* to?" Abby says, her eyebrows furrowing. "I feel like we should sort of be sure."

"I looked at almost thirty spells about this," I say, drawing the pentagram in the middle of the circle, one edge pointing at each of us. "None are exactly the same, but they've got common threads. That's what I'm going on." I draw a loop around the pillar candles in the middle. "So we'll call the corners, open the hole, then push Faolan into it. After that, the hole will close."

"How are we getting Faolan out of the onyx?" Charlotte leans over the candles, rubbing a wick between her fingers. After a moment, a tiny orange flame sprouts. It's a trick she's been working on for months now. I've never seen it come so easily to her.

"We shouldn't have to. Whatever is in that triangle mark is supposed to be the offering," I say, getting to my feet. "Everyone memorize the spell, and be ready. I'm going to call the corners."

"For the record, I think this is a bad idea," Callie says, dragging the notebook toward her again.

As they pass the spell around, I say a few words to close the circle.

"Please, let this all end up okay," I add under my breath, hoping no one can hear.

When the notebook makes it back to me, I take a shaky breath, raise my arms, and face east. I feel so tiny, like a mouse at the foot of a throne, knowing the power I'm about to address.

I open my mouth, and for a moment I can't make a sound. I swallow and try again.

"*I call upon the Guardians of the East, the power of air. Protect us in our circle.*"

CHAPTER 12

MATTHEW

"Hazel, be more respectful," Charlotte hisses at me. "Do you even know what power you're talking to?"

"Oh, my God, you do it then," I huff back.

"Fine," Charlotte says, standing up instantly.

Taken aback, I slowly lower on to the floor, reaching for Wyatt's and Callie's hands. Charlotte plants herself eastward, lifting her hands over her head and closing her eyes. When she speaks, her voice is strong and steady.

"*Hail to the Guardians of the Watchtowers of the East, power of air, wisdom, and intellect. We ask you be present in our circle as we send a spirit to the other realm.*"

I have to admit, Charlotte knows what she's doing. Watching her now, how calm and poised she looks, I can't even say I'm sure she hasn't called the corners on her own before. The thought makes a weird mistrust thread through my guts, but I push it away.

Charlotte makes a quarter turn and goes on.

"*Hail to the Guardians of the Watchtowers of the South, power of fire and strength. We ask you be present in our circle as we send a spirit to the other realm.*"

There's a tingle of static on my arms spreading down to the backs of my hands. Charlotte goes on, calling on the Watchtowers of the

West and North, and the feeling grows. It's almost like there's something hanging just over our heads, circling around us like wind.

Charlotte sits again, taking her place between Callie and me. She sends a doubtful look in my direction.

"It's all you," she says.

I place the onyx in the triangle I'd drawn for it, then pick up the knife, setting its tip on the palm of my left hand.

"Hazel!" Abby gasps.

"It's nothing, it's just a little blood, Abby!" I say, though it takes me a few tries to get the courage to actually break skin. It hurts way more than a tiny cut reasonably should. I hold my hand over the symbol for "sacrifice." It looks like a face, wearing a crown of spikes, and for a moment, I feel like pulling my hand back.

"Gotta pay the toll," I tell myself as two fat drops land on the floor. I reach back for Charlotte's hand, and she grips it considerably lighter now.

I close my eyes, trying to imagine a wall in front of me. Taking a deep breath, I start the spell.

"We rend the fabric that separates our world from what lies beyond,

We pay the cost that it demands,

We offer a soul, a being to cross from our world to yours,

We ask this in the name of the corners and of the light,

Allow us to pass unharmed and take what we give."

My siblings all take up the next chant, our voices blending together.

"Aperiesque ostius et in nobis,"

I picture touching the wall in front of me, made of something malleable. I plunge my hands into it, forcing my wrists deeper, then pulling my arms apart until I can feel it giving. It's weakening. I keep going, fighting until something tears open.

My lungs collapse. My whole body almost slams into the floor, but my muscles kick in at just the last moment. It's suddenly like I'm at the bottom of the ocean, so much pressure on top of me, crushing me down.

The first thing I see is Abby. Her eyes are huge, terrified, shining with panic as her back curves under the weight.

"What's happening?" Wyatt groans. He's almost bent in half, his chin a foot from the ground.

"I think we did it," I say, the effort of speaking exhausting.

"Well, give it Faolan!" Charlotte cries.

I look at the mark where I put the onyx, but it's empty. The stone has somehow jumped a few inches away. It's sitting just outside the triangle.

"Nice try," I growl. With my shoe, I edge the stone back, ever so slowly, across the chalk line.

As soon as it crosses, the stone lights up a furious red, and the pressure bears down on us so much, we all let out a sharp gasp. The lights overhead surge, the wires humming with the overload. The wooden boards above and below us creak as if they're being bent.

For ten painful seconds, the stone rattles back and forth like a kettle on a stove.

"I don't think it's working!" Charlotte yells at me. "You have to let him out of the stone!"

"I don't know how to do that! I don't know how I got him in there!"

"You have to *do* something! Close the portal!"

"It won't close until a soul passes through!"

A scream tears out of Abby and we both turn to her. Callie rears back, her feet scrambling. Even though I'm staring right at Abby, my mind can't make sense of what I'm seeing.

Abby is sinking into the floor. Her bottom leg, up to her knee, is gone, sucked into the ground like it's quicksand. She falls forward, off-balance, as her other leg starts to disappear too. She reaches for me, fingers splayed out, her face white with fear.

"Hazel!" she screams again.

Wyatt moves fast, hooking his arm around her elbow and pulling. She just continues to sink, almost in slow motion.

"It's taking Abby," Charlotte yells, throwing herself across the circle to grab our little sister's hand. "Do something, Hazel!"

Callie seizes the back of Abby's shirt, but nothing stops her. I clamber as best I can under the weight to grab the onyx, yelping when I touch it. I can smell my skin burning, but I hold on. I try to imagine it just like that night when I held the empty onyx and saw

Faolan in Wyatt's eyes. How I pictured sucking him out, pictured his soul compacting and flowing into the stone.

I see the opposite now. I picture the stone releasing him, and all that hateful, selfish rage breaking open like an egg.

A smoky, black mist threads out of the surface of the onyx. It drips to the floor, lazily, then rushes for Wyatt. Just before it reaches him, I manage to desperately call his name, but it doesn't warn him in time.

The smoke climbs up Wyatt's chest in an instant, shooting into his mouth and nose. Wyatt's arms drop, his head rolling back. He looks like a puppet, hanging lifelessly.

Without his added strength, Abby sinks another three inches, the whole bottom half of her body submerged. She claws at the wood, her eyes shut tight as if she can't look at herself disappearing.

I crawl to her, grabbing her outstretched hand. The force on the other end makes it feel like my tiny wisp of a sister weighs three hundred pounds. My head snaps to Wyatt, whose eyes are white, like there's a veil over them.

Faolan is trying to take back his old home.

"Fight him, Wyatt!" I yell, hot tears burning my eyes.

This is all my fault. This is my stupid attempt to control something I'm not ready for, and I'm going to lose two of my siblings because of it.

"Hazel!" Abby sobs, her hands grasping at me.

"Don't be afraid, it's going to be okay, I'm going to get you out," I lie through my ragged breathing.

The twins freeze, their faces going slack. They're both looking at something behind me.

I twist enough to see a gray-white smudge of color standing in the center of our circle. It isn't fully formed, but it has enough shape that I can tell it's a person. I blink away tears, trying to clear my vision, but the very air around it seems blurry. Then I recognize the sharp nose, the barely there details of a face.

It's Matthew.

It isn't the eye-liner-ed, dark-haired mug shot I've seen on TV for the past six months, but I know him. His round cheeks are muddled, and his sharply tipped nose is almost a smear of light, but his eyes are clear.

He's looking right at us. I almost want to beg him to help us, to throw a chair or crack a wall, anything. There's a sound, murmuring, almost like someone speaking down a hall a mile long. Then the spirit moves, drifting over the triangle mark. There's a flash, like blinking against sunlight, and he's gone.

Abby's body is released, her legs surfacing behind her so she's sprawled out on the floor. The twins and I tumble over, our counterweight suddenly gone. In fact, all the weight is gone. The pressure has lifted, and the lights have gone back to normal.

Before I can even process the change, I reach for the onyx, clasping it in my hand and turning on Wyatt. He's still just hanging there, motionless. Maybe there's time left.

I drag myself to my feet, my knees buckling. I'm so tired my body is breaking down. In desperation, I reach out my other hand to Callie.

"Help me," I say.

Without hesitation, she grips my hand in hers, and I feel a flow of heat. She's lending me all the energy she has left. I turn to Wyatt, holding the stone to his forehead and closing my eyes.

I can feel Faolan fighting me, setting the stone on fire in my hand, but I just focus on funneling him back inside.

A shriek comes from Wyatt's open mouth, like Faolan is clawing him from the inside, refusing to let go. Wyatt's shoulders twitch, but I keep pulling, pulling Faolan out, forcing him back into the onyx.

When the last piece of him is trapped, Wyatt crumples to the floor, and Callie drops behind me. I sink to my knees, gripping the burning onyx in my fist as the world spins and the side of my head connects with the floor.

In my haze, I see Charlotte rise to her knees, lifting her arms. It takes every shred of strength she has.

"*I release the corners,*" she says breathlessly, "*and close what we have opened. So it is...*"

She tilts sideways and finally collapses.

"*So it shall be,*" I finish, and my vision goes black.

CHAPTER 13

FOUND OUT

"Hazel? Hazel?"

Someone is shaking my head back and forth. I open my eyes slowly, feeling them crack with sleep.

My dad is standing over me, shaking my shoulders. The lines around his eyes sharpen in the violet morning light as my foggy mind starts to come back to reality.

"Hi, Dad," I say, my voice little more than a rasp.

He steps back, throwing his hands up. "Well, there's the last one. So can you explain what *this* is?"

He sweeps his hand over the living room. My heart skips. The *living room*. We're still in it...

I sit up too fast, making a splinter of pain shoot through my skull. The room is a mess; the furniture still pushed back, all the evidence of what we've done beneath us. Wyatt, Abby, Callie and Charlotte are all lying on the floor in various states of getting up, circles under everyone's eyes. But they're all here, and I can't help but smile at that.

The onyx. I look around wildly, my eyes landing on it at the same time as Wyatt's. Discretely, he reaches toward it, balling it in his hand before our stepfather can see it.

"What is this?" he demands again, and I wince. "Because it looks like the same thing that was here when...when that deranged cult was here."

"Different kind of chalk," Charlotte says.

Our stepdad's face flushes plum with barely controlled anger.

"I don't... That's not the point. I have *always* trusted you guys." His voice catches, and a cold wave of shame engulfs my body. I betrayed the man who has raised us as his own children. He's given us so much more than we deserved. And I'd thrown it back in his face.

"I give you the benefit of the doubt every time," he goes on. "Because you are smart kids and you make the right choices. Or so I thought. Is this the kind of thing you do when I'm at the hospital? Séances? Or some kind of satanic, drug-induced voodoo? Hazel—" He turns his disappointed expression on me. "You're supposed to look after them. You're supposed to protect them."

I look down at my knees, unable to meet anyone's gaze. "I know."

I can't even begin to explain that was what I was trying to do.

He waits a few moments before saying, "Is anyone going to explain this?"

"It was just for fun, Dad," Abby says, her voice soft and fragile. Having her, out of anyone, defend my mistake is almost too much to take.

"We were just pretending. Trying to make a joke about what happened. We were all pretending like things went differently and making it funny, so we don't have to be scared of it."

He doesn't quite look like he's buying it, but it's better than any excuse I could have made. Our stepdad sets his jaw, pointing a finger at each of us in turn.

"Your freedom is on hiatus. You're all grounded. No more after-school hangouts, no friends' houses, no seeing boyfriends. No riding around on that damn motorcycle!" He throws that in just for me. "And I'll start looking into a house sitter when I'm on call. This stuff —no more of it." He gestures at the smudged chalk marks. "If I see *anything* like this again...there will be consequences."

I can see how hard it is for him to think of punishments, even through his rage. It's so unnatural for him.

"You've got half an hour to get to school on time. I'd hurry," he finishes. "Abby, let's go. Now."

Abby shovels herself to her feet, walking out of the circle. She grabs her backpack, her thin legs shaking under its weight. Out of all of us, she should be the most shaken, but besides looking exhausted, she seems the brightest.

As she passes back through the living room, she stops, kneeling next to me and draping her arms around me.

"It's okay. It wasn't your fault," she says, low enough that only I can hear. "I wanted to do it."

She stands up, following our dad out the front door to the car. When the door closes, I realize the square of judgment I'm trapped in. Even Charlotte is glaring at me, her eye shadow smeared down the left half of her face.

Without a word, Callie stands and stomps up the stairs.

"Callie..." I call after her, but she won't even turn around.

It's the first time that her silence is worse than her words. I'm almost wishing for the tirade. I deserve it.

Charlotte stands up too, touching her matted hair.

"I know you couldn't possibly have known what you were getting into, but still."

"I know," I say.

"We only got out of that because of Matthew." Her voice drops off when she says his name.

Matthew. We lost him. The thought of him finally ending up where he belongs should be a relief, but instead it drags my heart down to the floor. He had become such a part of our lives he was almost family. In my head, I pictured him being with us for years. Maybe even forever.

But he was just gone, in an instant. To save us.

Charlotte moves to the stairs, taking them a little less aggressively than Callie. Wyatt isn't looking at me. He's staring into the black surface of the onyx as it sits on the floor in front of him. Its cord has singed off and is lying like a dead snake in the middle of the circle. I pick it up, looking at the bubbled, burned ends. Then I see my right palm.

There's a blister the size of an egg under the peeling, scarlet skin.

I can't even feel it now, just a spot of numbness, but I know that it's going to be a pain to heal, even with Gemmie's special paste.

"That was close," Wyatt says, attempting to be light but not quite managing it.

"I'm so sorry," I say, swallowing down a sob.

All of the fear and guilt is just beneath the surface. I can feel it churning; it's all I can do to keep it down.

"I don't blame you," Wyatt says, picking at the sole of his shoe. "He makes you think differently. Maybe that's one of his greatest powers. That he can make you question which thoughts are yours and which are his. Maybe that's how he controlled Stolam. But I get it. I can take the stone, if it's getting to be too much."

The words come out halted, like he's dreading the possibility that I might say yes. But I can't. I can't let Faolan near my little brother again.

"I'll handle him, Wyatt," I say, holding out my hand for the onyx. I can almost feel my back caving under the pressure of that sentence, but I know there's no other choice. "I would never ask that of you."

Wyatt leans toward me, placing it in my outstretched hand. I turn the stone over and pause. The crack has turned white. It almost looks like a scab, running along the seam, filling it up. I touch it with my fingertip, feeling a raised ridge. Looking deeply into the heart of it, I see the red light, but the fire seems to be gone from it. It's barely a glow. We hadn't beaten him, but at least we'd been able to subdue him a bit. He'd expended a lot of energy with his little show.

"We'll find a way," I promise Wyatt. "There has to be *some* way to get rid of him forever."

I tie the broken cord around the onyx. It makes a much shorter necklace now, but it's still useable. I stand up, my joints immediately complaining. There's not even time for us to change clothes, which feels like a sick joke.

"C'mon, let's go to school," I say, tucking the gem back inside my sweatshirt, where it throbs with a muted heat.

CHAPTER 14

MISSED CONNECTIONS

My body is so tired that even taking notes feels like a stretch. Midway through second period, I realize that I'm blinking for seconds at a time, just to snag a fraction of extra rest.

When lunchtime comes, I head straight for the parking lot, passing out on my patched leather backseat and sleeping right through it. I can barely shake myself awake for Pre-Calc. Once I get back into the building, I duck into the bathroom to try to fix the damage car napping has done to my hair. As I braid it in the mirror, my phone vibrates. I set it on the counter, opening my new message.

It's from Luke. Actually, there are four new messages from Luke. I must have slept through them.

Where you at? I don't see you in the Caf...

I want to slap myself. I'd completely forgotten about meeting him. He must think I stood him up. My heart twists at the thought, and I let out an exasperated hiss at my stupidity. It seems like nothing is off limits to my power of self-destruction.

Running late? :)

Are you at school? We really need to talk.

Please don't avoid me.

I wilt a bit under his obvious frustration. I'm not even sure my emotions can handle this conversation now, I'm so drained. I start to type back:

I'm so sorry, I didn't mean

The door opens and I pocket my phone. I can finish in class. Quickly, I tie off my braid with an elastic band. It's only when I turn that I notice Alison next to me, doing the same side braid as I did except with salon accuracy.

"Hey," she says easily.

"Uh, hey," I respond. Her speaking to me casually is a first.

"So have you talked to Luke yet?"

I press my lips together. She has a real talent for sticking her nose where it doesn't belong.

"Not yet," I say. "But I'm sure you'll be the first to know."

"Oh." She secures her braid, turning to me. I hate that she's so tall she can look down on me whenever she speaks. It gives me the urge to stand on my tiptoes, but I fight it.

"Well, I guess I can just tell you," she says, squaring her shoulders. "We're together now."

It suddenly feels like I'm falling, like I'm caught in that airborne moment after you miss a step. I try to remind myself that Alison is a liar; she's just so good at it that no one catches her. Like when she lied and said I put a toad in her locker in sixth grade, because my mother was a witch and wanted to curse her, and *I* got sent to detention because of it.

"You expect me to believe Luke asked you out a week after we broke up?" I ask evenly. If she wants a reaction, I won't give it to her.

"Well, you guys were never *dating*, were you? It was just kind of a..." She waves her hand like she's batting away a bad smell. That's when I spot it.

My amethyst necklace is hanging around her throat. Instinctively, I reach for my neck, feeling the indent in my collarbone where it always fits. It's gone. I never take off that necklace. It's as much a part of me as my own skin.

Alison realizes I've noticed and pats it proudly. "Oh, yeah, you left this at Luke's house so he gave it to me. It's kinda cheap, but the color is nice."

Every word of that sentence is like a pin in my gut. Iona, Luke's aunt and adopted mother, handmade that necklace, and calling it cheap is the cruelest thing I've ever heard. And the thought of Luke giving away something so important to me, so meaningful between us, is so out of character that it can't be true.

But there it sits. It must have come off when I was in his room, when we…

"Anyway, he was going to go through the whole thing at lunch, but this is probably easier for everyone," Alison says, her white teeth bright even in the dim bathroom light.

"How can you be this pointless?"

The words surprise both of us. But looking at her, all the viciousness and selfishness under such a perfectly symmetrical face, she seems almost too pointless to exist in real life.

"What are you talking about?" Alison says, giving a half-laugh.

"I hope this petty, mean-girl stuff is enough for you, because as soon as you get into the real world, no one cares if you're pretty, or if you have a hot boyfriend. People die, and horrible, terrifying things happen. And this kick you have, where you take things from people just because you want them, is the most meaningless thing of all. You are a worthless human being."

It may be the meanest thing I've ever said aloud, to anyone, but it just keeps falling out of my mouth. I can see something catch in her expression, the point where she puts on a mask to keep from showing the real stab wound. It strikes me that I may have just laid out all her fears in front of her, and yet all I can feel is grinding hate in the pit of my stomach.

I almost smile when I see her reaction. To see her look like she's cracking, finally. Ever since I moved here, had to see her five days of my week, I've never felt like I had the upper hand until just this moment.

And I want more. I want her to *fear* me. I never want her to look at me again without thinking of this moment.

Before I can stop myself, I clamp my hand around her forearm. She sucks in a breath, pulling back, but I hold her. I'm not even sure what I'm doing, I can just feel something gathering in my blood.

"All of the pain you cause people," I say, tightening my grip. "Will come back on you ten times over."

"You're hurting me," she says, trying her best to sound unaffected, but I can see the fear swelling in her eyes.

She deserves it, I think. *She deserves to be in pain.*

Suddenly, I'm appalled with myself. This is so unlike me, to wish suffering on someone else, even her. *This is something Faolan would do,* I realize with a jolt.

I drop Alison's arm, stepping back, repulsed by myself. There's a tug when I do, almost like a part of me comes away with her skin. I feel it in my chest, like a piece of me was just pulled out.

Alison scrambles backward, fumbling at the amethyst necklace. She tugs it so hard the delicate chain breaks, and she flings it on the counter.

"Fine, take it back, freak," she says, turning and colliding with the paper towel dispenser.

"You were right about my mom being a witch," I say as she's pulling open the door.

She pauses for a moment, looking like she might turn around, but she decides against it.

CHAPTER 15

INKLINGS

The drive home is as silent as it was going to school. Callie still won't look at me, Wyatt just seems so tired he might as well be brain-dead, and Charlotte wouldn't even get in the car. She just waved me on and said she'd ride home with someone else. I was too beat to argue with her, and part of me couldn't even work up the energy to care.

It's almost six by the time she gets home. I'm in the living room, still trying to wipe up chalk and salt, when I hear a car out front and stand up to look. Charlotte's in the passenger seat of a worn sedan I vaguely recognize.

When she gets out, I almost drop my rag. It's Jacob. Charlotte leans back down and gives him the kind of goodbye you definitely shouldn't give to a guy that likes your sister. She turns away, walking up the driveway to the house.

I quickly slip back down to the floor as the door opens, pretending to be in the middle of scrubbing.

"Hey," I say as she dumps her backpack in the nearest chair.

"Hey," she responds after a moment. At least some of the resentment is gone from her tone.

"Who drove you home? If Dad knew you were getting back this

late, he'd have a fit. I'm not sure he didn't rig the house with cameras."

"Jacob," she says, coming to sit next to me, her thick boots resounding on the floor.

I hadn't expected her to be so blunt, and it throws me.

"Is that not weird with Callie?" I ask slowly.

Charlotte snorts, picking up a few leftover grains of salt with her thumb. "Trust me, she's not."

"Why did you laugh like a badger?"

"I didn't, it's just—" Charlotte shrugs. "You don't really know what's going on with her lately. Since we took Mom's spell off, stuff has just been clearer for her. But not like, *totally* clear."

I shake my head in confusion. "What are you talking about?"

"Never mind. Forget it." Charlotte rubs a stray chalk mark, and a grumble of thunder overhead fills the silence.

Finally, Charlotte says, "I don't think we should keep the onyx here. I think it's too dangerous for us, and it's too dangerous for you to have to carry it everywhere."

Part of me wants to agree with her. What I'd done today to Alison is proof of what Luke has been saying all along. Stay around bad energy for long enough and it seeps into you.

"We just have to find a way to take care of Faolan for good," I say. "We can't let him escape."

"What if Stolam gets him?" Charlotte says, crossing her arms.

"Then we're all dead, I guess."

"What do you think they do?" Charlotte asks quietly. "In Stolam."

"They kill witches and steal their powers," I say.

"It has to be more than that. What do they want power for?"

"Well, who doesn't want power, Charlotte?" I toss my rag aside. "They're insane. They want to live forever and not have to work or something. They're not rational people, you can't give them rational reasons."

Charlotte sits back, her face set in thought.

"Maybe we're thinking about this wrong," she says. "Remember the spell Faolan used to get immortality? Mom said it was a Cutter Stone?"

I do remember. Mom's journal had recounted the night she found out he was making one, the realization that he meant to sacrifice one of his own children on the stone altar to gain eternal life. That was the reason she finally left him, after she saw what he'd become.

"Yeah," I say to Charlotte. "I do."

"It's meant to keep your soul bound to this realm," she goes on. "So you physically can't ever die since your soul can't cross over. That must be why our circle didn't work, because he can *never* cross over. So we should be looking for a way to bind his soul so that he can never get out and can't influence anything around him. Then he'll just live forever, harmless, in like, a jar, or something."

I touch the lump of the onyx beneath my jacket, cold threading through my veins. Faolan knew the circle wouldn't work. He probably pushed me to do it, fueled my blind fear to the point that I'd even risk letting him out of the onyx during the circle.

Every step, he's been manipulating me. Driving me to the brink of insanity with the nightly attacks and compromising my reasoning so I'd put my siblings in danger just for the chance of getting rid of him. I grip the fold of my hoodie so tightly that my joints ache. How can I possibly know what thoughts are mine and what he's planted?

He has to be stopped. I have to find a way. I can't even trust myself anymore.

"Where would we find a spell like that?" I ask Charlotte.

Charlotte shrugs. "I don't know. But we can look. And in the meantime, you need to give the stone to Gemmie."

I shake my head, opening my mouth to respond, but Charlotte cuts me off.

"No, Hazel. You can't be the only thing standing between us and Faolan. You spend so much time trying to protect us that you never even think we want to protect you too."

"I just can't ask that of Gemmie," I say.

"Gemmie has been around the block," Charlotte says, raising her eyebrows at me. "And if anyone knows where to look for a spell like the one we need, it'll be her."

I nod, stamping out the flurry of protests in my mind. It's like pulling teeth, but I know I have to admit it to myself. I can't handle the onyx. I need help.

I bend back over the floor, feeling inexplicably lighter as I go back to scrubbing.

CHAPTER 16

CONSEQUENCES

Taylor forces her hood down over her hair and glares at me. "Why are we eating out here?"

"Because you're my friend so you have to do ridiculous things when I ask you to," I respond, holding my paper bowl of soup closer to me for warmth.

It's particularly miserable today; the air is so heavy with moisture that it's work just to breathe. We're huddled together at one of the outside tables in the deserted quad, but it's better than facing what's inside.

"Why won't you just talk to Luke?" Taylor says, annoyance twanging in her voice.

"Because honestly, I can't handle him telling me he's with Alison. And I can't handle apologizing to him."

Taylor scoffs. "Whatever you did, I'm sure he forgives you. He's all about you. And Alison is a liar and a half; don't believe anything she says. Plus, she got her head split open by a falling brick yesterday, did you hear that?" Taylor laughs.

"Wait, what?" I ask, surprised.

"Yeah, yesterday, after school. She was under that old walkway from the gym and a brick fell on her and cut her from here to here."

Taylor draws a line from her hairline to below her eye. "That's what she gets for hitting you with a brick in fifth grade, right?"

My hand flies up to my own forehead, where a tiny raised scar still marks the spot where I got stitches. My breath sticks in my throat.

I did that. I know it. Luke always said I was reckless with curses, and something definitely happened in that bathroom. Guilt grows like mold in my stomach, turning my soup sour in my mouth. My only comfort is that I'll be freeing myself of the onyx tonight. Even with the strange seal on the crack, I've constantly been on edge. It seems like a miracle that nothing had happened last night, but it hasn't had its usual heat since the circle. It seems like Faolan is tired, recovering maybe. But I know it won't last.

The bell rings shrilly, and Taylor rockets to her feet.

"Thank God," she says. "I'm turning into a cave salamander out here."

I follow, trying not to picture Alison's bloodied face as I walk into the school.

———

Wyatt, Charlotte, Callie, Abby, and I all jam in the SUV after dinner, an awkward silence still hanging between us. We only got permission to leave from our stepdad because we were going to Gemmie's. And in his mind, what could be more harmless than seeing your grandmother?

When we pull up the gravel driveway to her cottage, the lights twinkle through the vine-covered windows at us. I put the car in park, and everyone trails after me up the walk.

It's only when I reach the door that it strikes me this is the first time Gemmie hasn't already been waiting for us. I knock, the wood hard on my knuckles.

"Gemmie, it's us!" I call. After a minute, I turn the knob, and the door eases open.

"Gemmie, are you here?" I say, sticking my head through. The cottage looks normal: in a state of calm chaos. There's even a squashed-face tabby staring at me from the couch. But the house doesn't *feel* occupied. It's almost like it's waiting, like Gemmie has just stepped out.

"Where would she go? She doesn't have a car," Wyatt mumbles under his breath.

"She wouldn't leave without telling us," I say, walking through the living room to the kitchen. "Gemmie!"

Everyone spreads out, Charlotte going straight for the bookshelves bordering the walls. The fat tabby jumps off his perch, saunters over to Abby, and rubs his arched back against her calf.

"Ugh, he smells like sardines," Abby says, stepping over him.

"I don't think she's here," Callie says, sitting heavily at the tiny table. "Maybe she's out casting or something. She still does that, right?"

"I just don't..." I stop, spotting a teacup in the middle of the table.

It's sitting on top of a piece of paper. I walk to it, lifting the cup, and unfolding the sheet. Gemmie's Edwardian cursive sprawls over the page.

Darlings,

 I'm out following your names. Certain things need to be protected. When you need to know, just ask—

 Non obscure osteros est latet

That's it.

I refuse to let myself buckle under the disappointment, even though my knees threaten to give. No Gemmie means no one to take the stone. He's still mine to carry.

"Great," I say, handing the paper to Callie so she can read it. "First time she's gone anywhere in twenty years and she didn't even tell us where."

"Say the spell, maybe she'll magically appear," she says halfheartedly, handing it off to Abby.

"*Non obscure osteros est latet,*" Abby reads, stumbling over the tabby, which can't seem to leave her alone.

I almost laugh at myself when I'm disappointed that she doesn't arrive in a puff of smoke.

"What does she mean, 'following our names'?" Charlotte says, turning from the bookshelf.

"Charlotte, North Carolina?" Wyatt suggests. "That's both your names right there."

"Ugh, I hate my name," Callie says, making a face. "*Carolina.*"

"What could possibly be there?" Charlotte counters.

Wyatt shrugs. "Trees."

"Maybe we can still find a spell without her," I say.

Callie raises her eyebrows at me. "You want to look through every page of these books? I've checked, they're all handwritten."

"Just try a summoning spell," Charlotte says, like it's obvious.

"How?" I ask.

Charlotte rolls her eyes, dropping the book she's holding on the table.

"Sorry I don't know *all* the spells," I say defensively as she comes up to me.

"Just try it, I'll help you," she says. She slips her right hand into my left, gingerly avoiding the crusty burn mark.

"So just say, 'Come to me, I'm searching for...' then say whatever you want and picture it coming to you. Literally as easy as that. Intent is everything, remember?"

"What happens after?" I ask.

Charlotte purses her lips. "Sometimes an idea just pops into my head, something I hadn't thought of before."

I shake out my arms, closing my eyes.

"Come to me, I'm searching for a spell to bind Faolan Sicario. Ah!" I yelp as the onyx vibrates. I yank its cord out of my sweatshirt and everyone takes a step back. But the stone isn't burning. It just hangs there, lifeless.

My eyes open and I drop Charlotte's hand. Obviously, I did it wrong. Big surprise.

But then a book falls off the shelf just above Callie, smacking her on her unsuspecting head.

"Ow?" she says, aiming a glare at me.

"I didn't do it on purpose." I turn to Charlotte, whose eyes are wide in surprise. "Is that how it goes?"

She shakes her head once before saying, "I can't make things move."

I walk over to the book, which landed open and face down on the table, and pick it up. My heart beats in my throat as I turn it over.

It's in another language. One I don't recognize. My shoulders drop a bit, and I hand the book to Callie.

"I can't read that, can you?" I ask.

She squints at it.

"I don't know if that's a real language," she says doubtfully.

The book gets passed around, each of us coming up with nothing.

"Awesome, so it could be a recipe for roasting a fish for all we know," Callie says.

"If the summoning spell chose it, it means something," Charlotte says, marking the page with a dog-ear and turning over the cover. It's bound in beautiful red leather, with symbols branded into it. I hold out my hand for it and Charlotte gives it over.

"If there's one person besides Gemmie who knows what this is, it'll be Iona," I say, tucking it under my arm.

We all traipse out of the house, the fat tabby shooting out between our legs. It jumps at Abby, who tries to lift her foot away.

"He likes you, Abby," I say, smiling. "Maybe he's your familiar."

She looks horrified. "What? No! I don't want him. He's ugly!"

Wyatt opens the car door and the cat jumps in.

"I guess we have to take him," I say, opening the driver's door. "Who knows how long Gemmie will be gone?"

"Ruby will *love* this," Callie drawls ironically, climbing in.

CHAPTER 17

APOLOGIES

Luckily, I know Luke's work schedule by heart. On the weekends, between eight and noon, he's at Gypsy, his aunt's and uncle's restaurant. And I happen to know that Iona stays home to clean Saturday mornings.

The next morning, I take the SUV over to Luke's. It still tears at my heart, walking up the grass to his house. I find myself wishing he'd open the door, even if it's to tell me he got tired of me yanking him around and moved on. Just looking at his face, at those deep-water eyes standing out from bronze skin, feels like it might knit me back together again.

I knock on the door, hugging the book to my chest. Hopefully Iona doesn't hold it against me that I panicked when I found out the truth about her nephew. That I was so selfish and concerned with how it affected me that I didn't think about how hard it must have been for Luke. He'd had to tell me that his mother murdered his first love and scarred him forever with her blood.

I'm so wrapped up in my tailspin of misery that I don't notice the door has opened.

Luke is standing in front of me, his long-sleeved swim shirt rolled up to his elbows. He looks just as surprised to see me, his mouth open slightly.

I summon my voice, about to ask for Iona and promising myself it'll come out normal, but all I say is, "I'm sorry."

I even squeak at the end. It's the most pathetic I've ever sounded, and I can't even control it. It's too much to pretend with him. Luke is the one person who has seen my worst and still is able to see good in me. I can't lie, even if it comes at the price of my dignity.

"I need your help. Everything fell apart; I nearly killed Abby, and Faolan almost took Wyatt again, and my dad thinks I'm a Satan worshipper, and I think I cursed your girlfriend."

Luke draws his eyebrows together, shaking his head. *"What?"*

I take a shaky breath, barely trusting myself to speak again. "It's just been a hard week," I measure out.

Luke steps back. "Come inside."

I do. He closes the door, walking down the hallway to his room as I follow.

"Where's Iona?" I ask, looking around for her.

"She went to help Uncle Finn at Gypsy since I had a swim meet this morning," he says, opening his door.

I walk in, planting myself in the corner. Luke peels off his swim shirt, pulling a dry T-shirt over his head. My eyes fall on the tattoos again. I freeze, my body tensing, but I force myself to keep looking.

Fear wells up inside me, but I hold it in, not letting it cloud my mind. *This is Luke,* I tell myself. He's not his past. He's not what was done to him, the same way I'm not my father.

I take a deep breath, settling the revulsion slightly. He's still Luke, under all the tattoos. That's what's important.

He sits on his bed and turns toward me, unaware of the battle taking place in my head.

"Okay, what happened?" he asks.

I keep my eyes on the floor as I go over my botched attempt at banishing Faolan, Matthew's sacrifice, and finally the incident with Alison in the bathroom. I can only imagine how it sounds, all strung together at once. He must be looking at me like I've completely lost all grip on my mental stability, like I've completely unraveled inside. He wouldn't be wrong.

When I've finished, I hear the mattress shifting under him.

"Come sit down. You look weird standing over there," he says, sounding exhausted already.

I comply, sitting on the corner of the bed and tucking my feet under me.

"So, first, why would you ever, *ever* do a circle that calls for blood sacrifice? That should be your first sign that it's not going to end well."

"I know," I say. "I just thought we could do it. We're supposed to be so strong together, I just thought..."

His face softens. "There's being strong, and then there's being smart," he says. "Secondly, *you've* told me Alison is a liar, why would you believe her?"

My ribs deflate in relief.

"So you're not together?"

"Of course not; which you would have known if you just *talked* to me."

"She had my necklace. My amethyst. She said you gave it to her."

His expression hardens. "I knew she took it. I had it out at lunch, to give back to you, and then it was gone. I even wondered if you had something to do with her getting hurt, given your history for flinging curses around. How bad do you think it was?"

"I don't know." I swallow. "This anger just kind of came over me, I wasn't even thinking. She cracked her face open. How much worse can it get?"

Worry shadows his face. "It can get bad."

He moves closer to me, taking both my elbows in his hands so I look at him.

"Why wouldn't you just tell me," he says, "at any point, what was going on?"

"Because, I—" The words clump in my throat. "I wanted to be strong on my own, for my family. And the tattoos...I still don't know how to feel about them."

Luke shifts uncomfortably, pulling his sleeve down. "You made me tell you. I knew it would change everything."

"I know," I say. "But I'm here," I say hopefully. "I came back."

He cracks a half smile, wrapping his hand around my calf. "I guess that counts for something."

I press into his touch, glad for the familiar warmth of him. The corners of his mouth dip just slightly, the most miniscule evidence of sadness in his face.

"So Matthew is gone?" he asks quietly.

My hands tighten around the book. I hadn't thought of what losing Matthew might do to Luke. Matthew was his friend when he was still alive, and Luke blamed himself solely for Stolam finding him here. Having him around, even a shred of him, seemed to give Luke comfort. But now he's gone, thanks to me.

"I'm sorry," I say again. Seems to be the only thing I say these days.

He folds his arms, his hands going a bit white.

"I have to tell you something," he says. "And it's important you don't freak out."

The muscles in my back tense as Luke takes a breath.

"Isolda finally surfaced. And she's close."

I clench my hands together, panic burning its way into my bones.

CHAPTER 18

ISOLDA

"Iona told me," Luke goes on. "She's been looking for her ever since Halloween, dowsing for her every day. She isn't in Cody, but she's around. We need to be careful. It really scared me to not be able to talk to you for a week. Don't do that again." He touches my shoulder, interrupting my spinning sense of hysteria.

"Hazel? It's going to be okay, everyone is on high alert for her anyway. Her face is on every storefront and lamppost in town. She won't get close without someone calling the police."

I clamp my mouth shut, resisting the urge to fly out of the room and back to my house, just to make sure Isolda isn't hiding in a closet.

"Hazel?"

"I'm okay," I say hollowly. But of course he doesn't buy it.

"We can cast a circle around the house, if that helps," he suggests.

"Didn't stop her last time," I say. Instinctively, I touch the onyx stone. "Why does she want Faolan? You'd think she'd like running the cult on her own."

"She wants what he has," Luke says, his face wary. "She wants immortality. Faolan is the only one who knows how to get it. He's the only witch in history to successfully make a Cutter Stone. And he can't make it for her if he isn't in his body."

"But his body is gone. It's dust, it's buried somewhere."

"There are ways to get it back. But you—and all your siblings—" Luke winces, "have to be dead."

My stomach rocks a feeling of seasickness passing through me. Everything surrounding Faolan ends up gruesome.

"Why?" I ask, not sure I want to know.

"Sacrificial magic works in balances. You are the only people now who are made of the same blood as him. Your deaths will pay for his life."

Luke lets out a breath, reaching for the book in my lap to distract himself. He traces the symbols on the cover before opening it to the middle.

"Can you read that?" I ask, peeking over the top. "What language is it?"

"This is Italian," he says, turning to a page with spiky, frenetic symbols circled around a half moon. "And this is *Stragheria*."

It's the first time I've heard the word, but still some hidden part of my brain knows it. Luke keeps turning pages, his eyes pausing over certain symbols and skipping over others.

"*Stragheria* is one of the oldest practices, it's the kind of magic The P—" he stops himself from saying "Prophet", "...Faolan came from. What makes Stolam so dangerous is that they don't use *one* type of magic; they take the most powerful from all religions. The most effective spells they use are *Stragheria*. Faolan's family makes up one of the Triad, the three oldest clans in Europe."

He gets to the marked page and stops, touching the handwritten heading.

"This looks like the book Stolam had," he says to himself.

"You can read it then?" I ask eagerly.

He gives one breathy laugh.

"The kicker is that we didn't get taught *Stragheria* until after we had the *Veri Segno*. I ran away the day after I got mine. And this isn't the kind of stuff you can put into Google Translate."

He closes the book, setting it beside us.

"Iona can't read it either?" I ask, my hopes falling.

Luke shakes his head. "She only knows pure magic."

"Don't you have another aunt?" I ask jokingly, but his expression darkens.

"You should hope you never meet Idra. I can't even joke about it; she's the most dangerous witch you will ever come across. Power and insanity aren't a good combination in witchcraft."

"What do we do, then?" I ask, resisting the urge to check the onyx again.

"We have to ask a *boschetto*, what they call a coven, and hope they tell us the truth. *Stragheria* practitioners aren't exactly open about talking to outsiders, even other witches. I'll ask Iona."

I nod. After a moment, I reach into my pocket and pull out the broken silver chain with the amethyst pendant, cradling it in my palm like an injured bird.

"Can she fix this?" I ask, handing it to him.

Luke studies it for a moment, then lifts his clear, soft eyes to my face.

"You really don't trust me, do you?" he asks, hurt carving his voice. "You think I could stand to see this on anyone else? That I'd just give it away, just like that?"

Now, after everything is behind us, I hate myself for believing the worst with so little to go on. He deserved better than that from me. He'd earned it. But I can't change that now.

"I don't trust most people," I admit quietly. "I can't even trust my family. I thought I knew Wyatt and look how that turned out."

"That was Faolan's influence," Luke says instantly.

"I know, but still. Faolan *changes* you. It's like I can't separate myself from him, he's in my head. I'm afraid of myself, I don't even know what I'll do next. I have to second-guess every decision I make. He's just so much stronger than me."

Luke stays silent, but his arms gather me in to his chest. I lean against the thin fabric of his shirt, feeling his breath moving in and out. It's not enough to settle the wiry tangle of emotions that's been scraping inside me for the last week, but it's close.

His fingers find my chin, tipping it up so he can bring our mouths together. His lips part mine, fitting between them like they've always been meant to be one. I breathe in his clean scent, my favorite smell in the world. I've missed this.

He breaks off, his hand cupping my cheek as I rest against him.

"We'll figure it out," he says.

For once, the thought of not being alone in something is just what I need.

CHAPTER 19

THE SOUL MATE SPELL

I pull the trashcans out to the curb, clenching my teeth against the freezing night air. My gaze drifts up to the tree at the end of our sidewalk. I know I can't let myself go down the rabbit hole of superstition, but the same thought comes back to me, the one I had for weeks after the attack:

That Isolda can somehow turn into a bird.

I saw an owl-like creature in our tree just before Stolam closed in on us, and weeks before that, like it was staking the place out. Or maybe somehow, she could talk to it, get information.

An old Mexican woman, a *curandera* from whom my mother had gotten her herbs and supplies, had once told me a fairy tale. A witch wants so badly to fly that she turns herself into an owl-bird, huge and contorted, to prey on people at night. A *lechuza*.

Even with magic though, there has to be limits. I've seen things that defy logic, but never a transformation like that. But it didn't mean the owl wasn't somehow connected to her.

Regardless, the tree is empty tonight, as it has been ever since Isolda escaped. I go back inside, blowing into my hands to warm them. There's a sound of dinging pots from the kitchen, and I see a dart of movement in the doorway.

Callie is standing at the counter, piles of flowers in front of her.

Huge red roses the size of oranges sit on the drainboard next to deli-cate purple lavender buds and bursting white jasmine. I can't even begin to imagine where she got it all at this time of year. The fat tabby cat Abby has named Uggo is lounging like a squashed toad on the kitchen table. He gets up when he sees me, dropping to the floor like a potato.

Callie hears him and flinches, twisting over her shoulder to look at me.

"What are you doing?" I ask.

"It's really not that interesting. I'm just trying one of Mom's spells from her teens," she says, turning back around and hunching a bit.

"Which one? I can't remember seeing one that calls for a florist."

"The one that—oh wait, it's not your business."

I step up to the counter.

"We used to be close, remember that? You used to tell me things. We shared a room for three years. Why are you like this all the time now?"

She leans her head back, closing her eyes.

"You can't even handle your own stuff these days, Hazel. Just let this one go."

"You know I'd do anything for you. Why is it so hard just to talk to me?" I push. It's been a while since big-sister Hazel reared her head, and she can't let this one go. "You're my sister. I just want to help."

"I really don't think you want to know," Callie says, tearing off a handful of rose petals.

"I do!"

"God, okay. I'm doing a spell...to tell me the name of my soul mate."

I blink. "Okay. Why is that so weird?"

Callie tosses the petals into a pot of warming water on the stove.

"I'm doing it because...I think it might not be a boy's name."

The sentence rolls around in my head before it finally catches.

"*Oh.* You think you're..."

She covers her face with her hands, massaging her forehead in frustration. "See? You don't want to know."

The dumb shock of it ebbs, and I say, "No, I do, it's just...I didn't see it coming."

She peeks through her fingers, trying to gauge my reaction. I'm not entirely sure what it is myself. It isn't something *unknown* to me, but if anyone is of a different persuasion in Cody, they certainly don't talk about it.

I realize I'm feverishly biting my nail and lower my hand.

"So you think if the spell tells you a boy's name, you'll know you're not. And if it's a girl's name, you'll know you are. Do you... like a girl now?"

Callie groans, stripping off a string of lavender buds and dropping them in the pot.

"That's the problem, I don't think I've ever liked *anyone*. It's Cody's fault, for not producing any teenagers with a face above a two."

"So how does this work?" I ask, picking up the jasmine and pulling off a tiny white star.

"I put all the flowers in the water, then I put these letters in face-down." She points to a bowl of cardboard squares with letters penciled on them. "When I say the spell, some letters will turn over that are supposed to spell my soul mate's name."

"What if there's no such thing as soul mates though?" I ask.

Callie looks like she might kick me.

"Well, then the world can just suck, I guess."

I roll my eyes, adding my flowers to the pot. Callie dumps in the cardboard letters, poking them so they all turn face down. She holds her hands over the steam, closing her eyes. After a second, she extends her left hand to me.

"If you want to lend me some energy," she sighs, "that'd be cool, I guess."

I take her hand, closing my eyes too. She pulls in a shaky breath as her palm clams up a bit. The bottom parts of my ribs start to tighten in shame. All this time, she's been carrying around this secret. And I've been too wrapped up in my own self-made suffering to catch on.

Callie clears her throat.

"*Tell me the name of the one I'm to love,*

The one who will match me and fit like a glove."

She repeats the spell three times, and when we open our eyes, the mixture is rolling with a gentle boil.

Six letters have turned over.

"J, R, O, D, N, A," she reads aloud, looking at me. Her forehead shimmers a bit with sweat. "Jarod, maybe? But there's an N."

The letters drift a bit in the pot, the N drifting into place.

"Jordan," Callie says. "It says Jordan. That could be a boy's or girl's name. What the hell, magic!"

"Maybe it's better not knowing?" I say gently.

Callie turns on me, her eyes gleaming with anger.

"You think so? So you can go back to pretending our lives aren't completely screwed up now?"

"I don't *do* that," I say. "If anything, my life is the most screwed up! I still can't bend sideways because of the scar tissue from the stab wound!"

Two tears drop out of her eyes, and more quickly take their place. She cups her nose, turning away from me.

"No, you're right. It's always about you," she says as she hurries out of the kitchen.

I throw my arms up in exasperation as if she's still here. Not even big-sister Hazel can get it right these days. I look down into the pot, where the beautiful petals have turned pallid and are being whisked around by the water. *Magic just seems to ruin things*, I can't help thinking.

CHAPTER 20

RUBY

I jolt upright in bed, my brain coming out of the sticky black of sleep a little slower than my body. My first thought is to look at the onyx, which is covered in about a cup of salt, but it hasn't moved. The room is filled with the blue half-light of dawn.

I step onto the floor slowly, pinching my arm just in case Faolan is playing tricks again. Counting my steps, I walk out of my room, listening for any sound that might have woken me. The stairs are cold under my feet, and a creeping feeling works up my calves, like the legs of spiders.

The farther down I go, the more the feeling grows, until the front door comes into view. I grip the twisted metal banister, moving slowly hand over hand. There's something behind the door. I can feel it, lurking there like a snake under a log.

I pad across the floor, not letting my heels touch the ground, as I draw even with the peephole. Rising onto my tiptoes, I look through it.

There's nothing. I turn the lock, swallowing, hoping this isn't the moment in a horror movie when people would be screaming at me not to do it.

I ease open the door just a fragment, barely enough for one eye to see through, letting in a wave of biting winter air. There's a fuzzy spot of gray on the front porch, but it seems motionless. I let the door swing wide, stepping out onto the frigid concrete.

It takes me one and a half steps to realize what it is. My back clenches, my foot halfway down. My heart pleads with me not to do it, but I have to keep walking. I have to know for sure.

It's Ruby. Callie's cat is lying on her side, her body hard. She could almost be one the taxidermy doll cats I've seen at antique stores, hollow, with glass beads for eyes. Her neck is knobby, bones out of place, and her head is twisted to an impossible position.

The memory of my first omen comes rushing back to me. I saw Ruby dead, right in front of me. And now it's real.

I know in my bones this can't be an accident. She's too perfectly positioned in the middle of our doorstep, clearly meant for us to find. I start to reach out to touch her, but my fingers won't go the rest of the way.

I look around, the porch suddenly feeling very exposed. There's no one I can see, but that doesn't mean someone can't see me. I back up, feeling for the door behind me, and step in. I turn around and jump almost a foot, barely catching the scream that shoots up into my throat.

Wyatt is standing on the stairs, rubbing his eye with the heel of his hand.

"What is it?" he asks drowsily. "I heard you walk by my room."

I point outside, and he goes to look. I turn my back away from the door, unable to stomach even a glimpse of it again. It takes him a few moments, and when he comes back inside, his eyes burn.

"Did you do that to her?"

I reel back from him, so stung by the accusation that it takes me a moment to answer.

"W—why would you think it was me?"

Wyatt grabs my shoulders in his hands, squeezing. "Hazel, tell me the truth."

"*No*," I say, prying his grip away. "How could you say that?"

He steps back, running a hand over his short hair, his eyes still searching mine like he's expecting to see something.

Eventually, he says, "Hazel, I know what Faolan is like better than anyone. He can make you do things you never thought you could do. And you've been carrying him around for so long…"

I twist my hair, realizing how right he is to suspect me.

"I know," I say. "But *this* wasn't me. I swear."

His gaze drifts back to the door. "Who, then? Someone from Stolam?"

I press my teeth together, thinking immediately of Isolda. Iona promised me she could tell if she set foot in Cody, but that doesn't hold much weight with me. Isolda has a way of bending even the few rules of magic.

"I think so," I say.

"We need to move her before Callie sees," Wyatt says, his tone sinking.

"Before I see what?"

Wyatt and I both snap toward Callie's voice. She's at the top of the stairs with Charlotte, her brow contorted with suspicion. She takes each step slowly, her misgivings visibly growing the closer she gets.

When she tries to walk between Wyatt and me, I grab her arm hard.

"Callie, don't go outside," I say.

She cuts her eyes at me, and the palm of my hand lights up with pain. It's like her skin beneath mine has turned to hot coal. I suck in a breath, releasing her, and she pulls open the door.

Her shoulders stiffen. I can only see her back, but I know her well enough to read her movements. She takes the few steps to Ruby in disbelief, her knees buckling when she gets to her. Very delicately, she scoops Ruby's body into her arms, cradling her the same way she did when she was alive.

She stares down at her for a long time, only her hair moving in the breeze. Then her head swivels, as if something has caught her eye. That's when I see the second gift the culprit left behind.

A stuffed toy witch is hanging from a twine noose on our porch, the kind of cheap thing they have at drugstores around Halloween. Her green skin and broad grin make the whole scene that much more sadistic. Callie reaches up, ripping her down.

"That's hilarious," she says, her voice trembling. She turns toward our neighborhood, shouting, *"Hilarious!"*

Flinging the doll down, she strides past us back into the house, Ruby's body tucked against her chest.

I bend down, picking up the witch doll where she landed at my feet. On her bright orange dress, someone has written us a message in marker.

WITCHES DIE LIKE WITCHES.

CHAPTER 21

ARIANNA'S BIRTHING CENTER

I sweep a pile of swim gear off the passenger seat and onto the floor of Luke's new car before climbing in. I spot a few cigarette burns in the leather, but apart from that, the car is already a steep improvement on the motorcycle. The way the clouds are darkening overhead, I'm just glad to be *inside* something.

I lean over to kiss Luke, surprising him. His fingers weave into my hair to pull me deeper.

"Well, hello," he says when I pull away.

I'm still not quite recovered from the previous day's events, but seeing Luke helps.

"You ready for this?" he asks, putting the car in gear. "Two and a half hours, just you and me."

"That's just one way," I say, clicking in my seat belt. "Then we have to turn around and come back."

"Unless we just book a hotel and stay there all night." He flashes me a mischievous grin.

I scoff. "Yeah, my dad would definitely approve of that."

As Luke turns out of my neighborhood, I pick up the burnished leather journal from the center console.

"Has Iona met this coven before? How do we know they'll tell us anything?" I ask.

"It's called a *boschetto*. Make sure you don't call them a coven. She knows the woman who owns the store we're going to, and she's the leader of the only *boschetto* Iona knows of in the whole South." Luke pulls onto the highway. "No, we don't know if she'll tell us anything about the spell, but it's the only hope we have so far."

I open to the marked page, running my fingers over the words. Gemmie's note pops into my head. Something about the words seems to match. I've read it over so many times, I've memorized the line of spell she wrote.

Holding the open book up, I say, *"Non obscure osteros est latet."*

I hold my breath, but nothing changes. Luke gives me a sideways look.

"What's that about?" he asks.

"Gemmie's gone. She left us a note with a line of spell, but we can't figure out what it's for."

I lean my head back against the seat, watching Cody unwind into rolling, rich emerald hills.

"What do you think it would be like? If we weren't witches?" I ask.

"I think you'd probably be a lot bossier," he says, a smile in his voice. "And I think I would probably be a dumb jock."

"We'd be so much happier," I say, twisting my fingers together in my lap.

Luke reaches over with his left hand, chucking me under the chin with his index. It's been so long since he's done it, it feels like finding something you've lost again.

"There's no way I'd be happier if I didn't have you. And I have you *only* because we're both witches."

I catch his hand, squeezing it in both of mine.

"If you want to tell me about Olivia...I'd like that," I say slowly.

Luke takes his eyes off the road to look at me, something both fearful and longing in his eyes.

"Are you sure about that?" he asks.

I nod, knowing in my heart it's what needs to happen. He's never run away from me, even at my worst. I'm not going to run away from him again.

"Yeah. What was she like?"

———

My back is aching by the time we pass into Fort Worth. The woman Iona told us to see, the head witch of the *boschetto*, owns a holistic birthing center just outside the city. I try not to picture her as my mother, who helped my stepdad birth babies before he joined the hospital staff.

We pull up in front of the center, which is covered in climbing vines and looks more like a plant nursery than a place for humans. I get out, my spine popping in various places. Luke walks around to meet me, handing me the leather journal.

"Ready?" he asks.

I nod, and he pulls open the entrance door for me.

I've never been to a high-end spa, but this place looks like how I always pictured them. It smells like handmade soap, and the floor and walls are all sand-colored granite. A girl sits at the front desk, her face lifting to us as we walk in. Her eyes are a dark, earthy brown, rimmed with ebony lashes that match her elbow-length hair. She stands up, breaking into a smile.

"Hi, welcome to Arianna's Birthing Center. Are you guys expecting?" Her tone is so bubbly that it takes me a moment to realize she's wearing a floor-length black dress with sleeves past her fingers. It's so bizarre that I forget to answer. I just stare at her, trying to place what century she should live in.

"*Ave di parenti*," Luke says, lifting the back of his right hand to his lips. It's the greeting Iona told him to use, the way *Strega* recognize each other.

The girl's customer-pleasing smile deflates a bit. "Oh. Well, Arianna isn't here, if that's who you want."

"We just need to speak to her quickly," Luke says. "Could you call her? It's really urgent."

The girl comes around the counter, her dress dragging along the floor. I can't help thinking it must be a pain to wash.

"No, she's like, not in the country. She's in Italy for this whole month."

I almost groan in disappointment, hugging the book closer.

"There's no way to contact her?" I ask, bordering on begging. "This is kind of a dire situation."

"Can you read Italian? You're a *Strega*, aren't you?" Luke asks her. I want to kiss him for being so brilliant.

She blinks, surprised, then grins as if it's the first time anyone's ever asked her.

"Yeah, I am and I can. What's up?"

"We need you to tell us what this spell says." I hold out the book, opening to the page. "Please be as specific as you can."

The girl takes the journal, turning it right-side up. Her skin goes a shade whiter.

"This is a book of the Fanarra," she says. "Where did you even get this? My mother would punch you if she knew someone outside a *boschetto* had this."

"Arianna's your mother?" I ask.

"Yeah." The girl rolls her eyes. "She's such a pain. Anyway."

She dips her head again, reading over the spell. Her fingers start to grip the covers, her throat contracting. She closes the book, handing it back to me, a new solemnness in her demeanor.

"I'm not sure I can help you with that."

"Please, just tell us what it says," I ask, my hand pressing over the onyx beneath my sweater. We're too close to give up now.

"Look, I don't know what you're into, but this isn't stuff to mess around with. You seem like you should know better." She starts to walk back around to the other side of the desk. "Besides, you can't even do that spell without a member from each of the Triad clans, so you're out of luck anyway."

"But she's a member of the Fanarra clan," Luke says, pushing me forward a step.

"I am?" I whisper at him, not sure if we're trying to pull some sort of trick on the girl.

"You're a Sicario," he says softly. "Half of one, anyway."

A new reverence splashes across the girl's face. "That's not exactly a thing to brag about these days," she says. "Not after that psychopath mass murderer Faolan started the Stolam. The *boschetti* aren't too fond of Sicarios anymore."

"That psychopath mass murderer is who we need the spell for," I say, dragging the silk cord out from under my sweater and holding the swinging onyx in front of me. "We need to trap what's left of Faolan Sicario so he can't ever come back."

She shrugs, the meaning missing her. "What's that?"

"This is the only thing holding Faolan's soul."

The girl almost trips on her dress trying to get over to me. She bends down, staring at the stone as it revolves on the cord.

"*What?*" she drags the words out like it has three syllables.

She straightens, narrowing her eyes at us.

"Are you messing with me? He died like seven years ago."

"Not all of him."

"How do you even have this?" She pivots to see it from a different angle. "If that really is his soul in there."

"I put him there. It's a long story. But he's my father," I finish, hoping this will be enough explanation.

Her eyebrows shoot up an inch. "Whoa. Heavy. I didn't know he had kids."

"Yep." I slip the necklace back over my head, re-wrapping it and tucking it into my sweater. "Can you help us now?"

She pauses, seeming to weigh the possibility of me lying. Then, she holds out her hand for the book. When I give it to her, she strides around the counter, pulling a clean piece of paper out of their printer. She goes to work writing an English translation of the spell, taking it line by line.

"Even if you have this," she says, not looking up. "It's not something you can go home and do tonight. *Stregas* have safeguards for spells that can do a lot of damage. They split up the knowledge between the Triad so they can only be done if a member of each clan is there. This spell is only for the Fanarra representative's part. You still need a person from the Janarra and the Tanarra clan. Lucky for you, my family is Tanarra, and I know my mother in particular would want a piece of sealing Faolan Sicario."

"But she's gone all month," I say, fidgeting with sleeves. I'm worried about waiting a few days, let alone a month.

"Well, you can't even do this spell unless it's a full moon, and the next one is tonight," the girl goes on. She holds out the finished paper to me. "And in the meantime, you have to find a Soulstone.

But you kind of lucked out, because the only people who make those are the Janarra clan and you need one of them, too."

I look over the full page of script, the words swimming in front of my eyes. My dream of putting this problem to rest today has just been shredded, and it seems like even more work lies ahead of us.

Luke's hand covers my shoulder, and I realize the disappointment is written all over my face.

"We can do it, don't worry," he says. He turns back to the girl. "Do you know anyone that's Janarra?"

She blows out a breath. "Uh, one family. But they're in the Ozarks. Long way to go."

"We can't just call them?" Luke asks. "Maybe they can help us."

"No, they're like…crazy people. The Abbascias. They live by a lake, though. You could dowse for them."

I'm about to demand to know how she thinks finding them on a map with a crystal will help us at all, but Luke slips his hand into mine, popping the bubble of annoyance rising in my throat.

"Thank you," he says to the girl. "You've helped a lot. Can you call us when Arianna gets back?"

"Yeah, totally," she says, typing Luke's number into her cell phone as he reads it off.

"Thank you," I say, my head back on straight. "I'm Hazel, by the way, and this is Luke."

"I'm Jordan," she says, her mouth widening into a smile.

I don't realize I'm crushing Luke's hand until he tries to pull it away, whispering *Oww*."

He gives me a look like I'm going crazy. "Thank you, Jordan," he says, turning to hold the door open for me.

As soon as we're outside, he turns to me. "Why'd you get all bug-eyed at the end there?"

I twist the leather book in my hands, the burden of holding in Callie's secret pressing down on my shoulders. I'm not even sure if I should tell her about Jordan. She has enough to worry about right now.

"We just have so much to do," I say, sinking down into the car seat. "And I feel like there's no time to do it."

He squeezes my knee. "Don't give up before we've started."

As he backs out of the parking lot, I pull out the onyx again, checking on the crack. It hasn't moved since the circle, and it still seems like Faolan is lying low inside it.

"Could you try to move him to a different stone?" Luke asks, watching me with clear unease. "Buy us some time?"

I shake my head, slipping it back into the pouch.

"I don't want to risk letting him out again. I don't even know why it worked the first time."

Luke chuckles to himself, that same, breathy laugh he always does.

"The funny thing is *Santería*, the religion my aunts and Isolda grew up with in Mexico, is half about superstition. I never really thought the parts about angels and keeping the Devil away were true. But now I think maybe they were on to something."

"I don't get it," I say.

"Onyx is meant to trap demons," he says. "It's meant to hold them."

An outbreak of chills races down my back. Callie called Faolan a demon by accident. I don't think I believe in spirituality and angels and demons, but every folk tale has to be inspired by truth. Maybe, after all the evil he's done, Faolan has distorted himself into something else. Something besides a human soul.

CHAPTER 22

RAIN CLOUDS

Half an hour outside of Cody, we can see the deep, sick blue storm clouds stacked over the town, thunderheads bursting out of the top. They flicker with lightning, casting an eerie gray over the sky around them.

"That doesn't look good," Luke says, biting down on his bottom lip.

"Is it just me, or has it been raining every day for the past month?"

Nervousness squirms in my chest, knowing we're driving right into the middle of that.

Expecting an answer from Luke, I turn to look at him. His eyes are fixed on the festering storm, his forehead drawn with worry.

"Yeah. It has," he says finally.

When we pull into my neighborhood, the light from the sunset is already gone, smothered by the carpet of black overhead. Rain taps constantly on the car, falling in fat drops on the windshield. In the dark, pulsing red and blue lights sting my eyes. My heart stops.

There are police at my house. I almost vault out of my seat, caught only by the belt.

"Something happened," I say, pawing at the lock on the door.

Luke pulls me back by my sweater.

"Don't jump out of the car. We're almost there," he says, calm masking the worry in his voice. "It's probably just about Callie's cat."

When he pulls into the driveway, I see Wyatt and Charlotte on the front porch, two officers standing in front of them. My siblings are both nodding, their expressions pulled tight.

I get out, Luke following behind me up the sidewalk.

"What's happening?" I ask as I draw closer to them.

The officers turn to me, and I recognize one. He was one of the responders the night Isolda attacked us.

"Oh, hi," I say to him, shoving my hands inside my pockets to keep them warm. I was only in the rain for a second, but it's already soaked my clothes.

"Another Parks," he says, giving me a tight smile. It's almost strange to hear my stepdad's name again. Ever since we'd accepted that we were witches, Sayers was the only name that felt right.

"You doing okay, sweetheart?" the officer asks, squinting at me.

"Pretty well, considering," I say. "What happened? Are you here because of Callie's cat?"

My siblings cringe. Charlotte walks up to me, grabbing onto my arm.

"They saw Isolda," she says. "She was in Cody this morning."

I look back to the officers. "What?"

"We caught her on a traffic camera. She was walking with her sister, who was reported missing from her institution two days ago."

"Idra got out of Austen Riggs?" Luke says angrily, stepping into the circle. "Why didn't anyone tell us?"

"Who are you?" the younger officer snaps.

"He's Isolda Amaro's son," his partner says, holding his hand up to quell him. He turns back to Luke. "I can't say. It was the Massachusetts police's problem until she showed up here. This doesn't need to be a situation to panic," he says, turning to me. "We're going to post a car outside your house until we find them. And we will find them. Don't you worry."

"Our dad should be home soon," Wyatt says, his arms crossed. "You should call him at the hospital so he doesn't think one of us died when he gets here."

234

"Will do," the older officer says. "We'll be just out here if you need us."

He and his partner move off, retreating to their car which is barely visible now through the sheet of rain.

Charlotte steps closer to me. "Any luck?

"Kind of," I say. "I'll tell you inside."

She and Wyatt duck back in the door, leaving Luke and me. His face reflects how serious the situation actually is.

"I may get to meet Idra after all," I say, not managing to conjure up even a little humor in my voice.

"I don't want to leave you guys alone with your dad not here," he says.

"Then don't. Stay."

He nods, pulling his hood up against the cold. "Your dad won't be mad?"

"Just move your car. He doesn't ever come in my room. You can stay up there for a while."

The faintest trace of a smile tugs at his lips.

"Okay," he says, turning to hop off the porch.

I watch him get into his car, the headlights barely cutting through the rain. As he backs down the drive, I glance at my boots, which are soaked through.

Very slowly, I lift my left foot, holding it up with my hand to steady myself.

Stuck to the sole of my shoe is a white owl feather.

CHAPTER 23

DISCOVERIES

I pull my knees in, curling up against Luke's side for warmth. Even with the heat on, the house is freezing. He's lying beside me on my bed, his long legs almost reaching the end. The *Stragheria* spell is in his hand, and his eyes track back and forth as he reads it over and over.

I put down my mother's journal, which I've been reading the last few days. I know it all well enough to know it can't help us, but it still puts me at ease to read her words, to hold something she touched so often.

Luke lets the page float down onto the covers. "She's right. It's not a complete spell. We need the other two pieces."

I chew on my sleeve. The Ozarks seem almost like an imaginary place to me. They're so far away and unknown.

"How can we possibly get to the Abbascias? Do you think maybe they could send us their part?"

Luke scratches his black hair, disheveling the soft peaks.

"It didn't sound like they were too keen on sharing. Besides, we have to find a Soulstone, and it seems like they're the only people we know who might have one."

"What *is* a Soulstone?" I wonder aloud.

"No idea. Never heard of one. But from this..." he waves the page, "...it seems like a stone that can hold a person's essence forever. No way of getting it out once it goes in."

Another roll of thunder shakes the glass of my windows. It's been constant for the last hour, which I keep telling myself is normal for this time of year. Though it hardly seems to have the kind of short-lived fury a storm like this should have.

A knock at my door startles Luke so badly that he bolts upright.

My stepdad's voice comes through the wood. "Hazel?"

"Hey, Dad," I say, trying not to laugh at Luke's panicked face.

"I thought your dad didn't come in your room," he hisses.

"He won't," I say. "Chill out."

"I'm heading to bed," my stepdad says. "Just wanted to check you were okay. Remember the police are going to be here all night. We've got nothing to worry about."

"Yeah, I know. Love you, Dad," I call.

His steps echo as he walks away, and I listen until I can hear the telltale creak of his bedroom door downstairs.

Luke leans back against the headboard, his chest deflating.

"Wow, who knew you were scared of my dad?" I tease.

He shuffles his shoulders a bit. "What? I want him to like me."

"He does," I lie, pulling my mom's journal onto my legs.

Luke looks down at it, propping his head on his arm.

"Do you think your mom would have liked me? Now, I mean. I'm sure she hated me as a baby; I mean, I was Isolda's kid. She probably thought I'd be the Antichrist."

"I think she'd really like you," I say, fitting myself against the curve of Luke's chest. "In fact, I know she would."

Another sharp crack of thunder makes the house shudder around us.

"I think I should head home before I get too tired," he says. "I'm going to have to have my wits about me driving in this."

A thought forms in my head, but it clumps in my throat when I try to say it.

"You could stay," I get out. "Here. For tonight."

Part of him instantly likes the idea. I see it in his eyes, but his mouth curves down as he thinks about it.

"What about your dad? I don't want you to be in more trouble than you already are."

"I can sneak you out in the morning. He won't know."

It's so unlike me to be doing this, devising a way to trick my loving stepdad so I can have a guy in my room, but it doesn't even feel wrong. I want him here, not just for safety. Having him next to me, jammed in the tiny space of the mattress—it's the safest I've felt in weeks, despite everything. The thought of sleep doesn't even bring the usual cold sweat I've been getting before bed.

"Stay," I say, tilting my head into his neck.

His lips brush the top of my hair. "Okay."

———

An hour later, I hear his breath deepen and I turn over to see his eyes closed. How he can sleep with the world tearing apart outside is beyond me. I settle back down, turning to the last page in my mother's journal before the blank pages start. It still pinches a nerve in me every time I see them, knowing my mother's words are written there but I can't have them.

I run my fingers over the page, trying to feel any indentation of letters. But I know I won't. The letters are there, Gemmie's spell just keeps me from seeing them.

My eyes lift to my nightstand, where Gemmie's last note is sitting open. I pick it up, wondering where in the world she could be.

"*Non obscure osteros est latet,*" I read again.

There's a twitch of black color underneath the letter, and I almost throw the journal down, thinking it's another spider. But then I see the blank page.

It's filling up with writing. It's as if my mother's hand is crossing over the page, each letter being written out in tight cursive.

I clutch the journal closer, my eyes trying to process the letters faster than possible. I can't believe I'm finally seeing these words, the things I've imagined and longed for since the day I was given the journal.

It only takes me three lines to change my mind. It isn't the entry I'd always imagined it being, something that explains why she chose

Faolan, why our lives ended up the way they did, why she joined *Stola*. All of the answers I still need.

Instead, it's a letter to Gemmie, and it tells her how to dispose of Faolan's body.

I sit up on my elbow, unable to keep reading. In six months, the idea of my mother has been whittled down from the most loving, tender person to a woman who could so meticulously tell her own mother how to dismember her husband.

Mother, the top of the page reads. *You know what I am doing and you know why it has to be done. Don't ever let yourself feel sadness for the sake of my life. You and Father were the most caring you could be. I was born differently, and I pay for my own choices.*

I've left already for Louisiana, and by the time you get here, it will be done. The pieces of Faolan must be hidden in spelled graves. I've already prepared them for you. They are in the five dearest places to me, where each of my babies were born. You will have no issue finding them.

You will need to be fast once you arrive in Louisiana. I am only two hours ahead of you. Please don't try to stop it, it's already too late for that. Faolan and I will die together, I think it's a fitting end for the crimes we've committed.

Isolda will be quick to realize what's happened and she will try to take his body. You must be there first.

When you have him, sever his head first.

I pull myself away, covering my eyes as if that could stop the images in my head. My stomach spasms; sudden nausea rolls over me. This is too much. It's too real and horrible, too dark to even hold in my mind. I want to give back the knowledge, pull it out of my memory, rub out the scratch it has just made in my brain.

I turn the page, holding it down as if the words might somehow escape. My eyes land on the next entry, written in Gemmie's meandering handwriting.

My darlings. Sometimes we must do terrible things to prevent something worse from happening. We alone, as witches, must be responsible for watching our own kind.

You must not think less of Emily. She was stronger than many will ever be, strong enough to do what had to be done. I was bound to do what she asked, to finish what she could no longer complete. Do not hate me for it, my hearts.

But now, I must secure the bones of Faolan. Stolam has determined where they are hidden; they must not find them. I have gone to get them, darlings, and then we must take care of them.

I will see you quite soon. You have all my love.

Gemma

I swallow, my mouth sticky. Isolda knows where Faolan's bones are. If she has them, maybe she can bring him back. And we'll all be dead.

"Luke," I say, twisting to look at him. "*Luke.*"

He opens his eyes, the light blue of them peeking through his eyelids.

Then a high-pitched screech bursts from my phone.

CHAPTER 24

THE WITCH-BIRD

I jump, untwisting myself to grab my phone off the nightstand. The screeching continues, splitting the air in the room, until I turn off the volume.

"Jeez, what happened?" Luke asks, sitting up.

I read the white text that's popped up against my black screen.

"It's a flash-flood warning," I say. "The dam broke."

"Are we okay here?" Luke asks, his eyebrows drawing together.

"I don't know," I answer truthfully. The only other time there was a flash flood, we lived with our mother in the house that burned down. We were fine, but the houses along the river didn't fare so well. And we're on the river now.

Voices reach us from downstairs. Through the static sound of rain beating the roof, I hear Abby's soft voice quavering over Charlotte's lower tone. I walk over to my door, cracking it so their words can reach us.

"Where do you want us to go, Abby? It's not like there's a hotel in Cody," Charlotte says, trying to soothe her.

"Do you see that?" Abby comes back, an uncharacteristic whimper in her tone. "That isn't normal."

"Want to go check?" Luke's whispers to me over my shoulder. He's gotten up, too.

"Maybe we should, just in case," I say, opening the door fully. "Just stay at the top of the staircase in case my dad comes out."

We tiptoe out and Luke slips behind the wall as I walk midway down the stairs. Charlotte is standing on the bottom step while Abby paces by the windows of the living room, only one sock on her dainty feet.

"What's wrong?" I ask, drawing their attention. "Did the cops leave?"

"Abby had an omen," Charlotte says, rubbing her tired eyes.

Abby turns on the lights in the living room, pulling aside the curtains.

"Come look at this," she says.

I take the few more steps down and reach her, peering through the window. Our lawn has been replaced by a sheet of rippling water. Our whole neighborhood looks like it's sitting on top of a lake, cars half-sunk up to their undercarriage.

"Wow," I say, unable to look away. The scene transfixes me. It's like a painting, or a dream. "What was your omen?"

"That the house sank," Abby says quietly, stepping closer to me.

"Is that Luke?" Charlotte exclaims. I wheel around to see her squinting up at the stairs. "You sneaky minx, you're shacking up?"

Luke steps out from behind the wall, his hands up in surrender.

"Please don't be mad, it's just because of Isolda and Idra being around. I didn't want to leave you guys alone."

"Does Dad know?" Charlotte asks me, far too loudly.

"No, and *shh!*" I answer.

Luke passes her on the stairs, coming to join us at the window. His face goes white when he sees the yard.

"This is Idra," he whispers to me.

"How?" I ask, bewildered.

"This is what she does," he says gravely. "Water magic."

Charlotte tramps back up the stairs, pausing at the top. "Ok, well, I'm going back to bed, you guys..."

She pauses, her mouth still halfway forming a word. Then I hear it, too. A sort of rustling sound is growing, like the sound of tissue paper being crumpled.

I look at Luke questioningly, but he's listening intently as well.

The back windows and doors explode inward, sending a shower of glass into the air. Water floods through them. It rages toward us, sweeping up chairs and tables. I see it but my brain can't make sense of it. It seems to happen in fast-forward, too quick to catch.

There's so much of it that for a millisecond I think, *I'm dreaming, I'm dreaming about the ocean*, before it hits us.

The world goes black. Dark wetness rushes down my throat and nose, scraping all the way. I cough and cough, but I can't get rid of it. It's like a hand in my mouth, shoving down and down.

I force my eyes open, but it's just a gritty dark green everywhere. Something big hits my leg, bending it back, so I get my feet on top of it and push.

My head breaks through to air, and I heave a cough so deep that a full cup of water comes up.

"Hazel!" I hear Luke yell.

I blink, trying to clear the cloudiness from my vision. My back hits something hard and flat, and I turn to grasp at it. It's the wall of the living room, I know it from the weird brown molding. I touch it, to make sure, and I see two pencil-sized splinters of wood lodged in my right hand.

Luke calls my name again, and I try to turn around. The water rushes so fiercely that it presses me into the wall. I manage to swivel to see Luke's head bobbing up across the living room near the stairs. I've been pushed to the opposite side.

Abby's arms are around his neck, and she clings to him like a drowning kitten, her blond hair almost brown with mud. Luke pulls them both along the railing to the halfway point where the water isn't reaching.

Charlotte is waiting, crouching on the stairs as the water rips by below. She reaches for Abby, pulling her over the side of the railing. Once my little sister is safe, the two of them scramble up the stairs to the first floor. Wyatt and Callie have emerged too, and are standing motionless, their mouths open.

I kick my legs, trying to touch the floor beneath me, but nothing makes contact.

"Hazel, watch out!" Callie screams, just before I see the dining room table floating toward me like a raft. I turn away, but it smashes into my shoulder, pinning me against the wall as it scrapes by.

I realize I'm screaming when I'm out of breath. My shoulder is on fire, hot pokers under the bone. Even when the table drifts out of the gaping, shattered window next to me and the pressure lifts, I can't bear to move my arm. The tiniest twitch sends a spasm of needle pricks under my skin.

I hear splashing over the constant rushing sound and look to my left to see Prince swimming toward me, his head just poking above the water. His paws send up spray in all directions. I hold out my left arm to him, catching his collar when he's close enough. His claws scrabble at my legs, trying to find purchase, and I grunt.

Setting my jaw, I push off the wall, the water tugging at my limp right arm. Prince and I work together, swimming the few feet to the staircase. Luke, his left elbow hooked around the banister, reaches out for us, grabbing Prince by the scruff of his neck and dragging us the last foot. I seize the railing with my good arm as Luke pushes the dog over the banister, away from the flow. Prince drags himself up a few steps and lies down, choking up water.

Luke and I meet eyes. His face is covered with leaves and mud, but he seems unhurt.

"My shoulder," I start to say, but then I feel something connect with my foot, something metal and clawed. It catches on my ankle, piercing through my skin like fishhooks. The weight pulls me, stretching my arm out until my fingers start to lose their hold. My face is half underwater, just deep enough to not be able to call for help, as I fight to hold on.

My fingers slip off, and my head is hauled under. It pulls me down, down to the floor—I can feel it with my elbows—and drags me along. I can hear the muted sound of clanging as my anchor knocks into the wall, caught in the surge toward the windows. It catches on the sill, rolling forward and taking my body with it. It swings me toward the surface, and I break through, sucking in a gulp of air. I'm across the room again, just barely able to see the stairs.

Callie is screaming and shaking, trying to stop Wyatt from jumping over the railing as they watch me drifting out the window into the front yard. Just as my metal anchor turns over again, taking me back down into the darkness, I see Luke push off from the stairs, his strong arms slicing through the water.

The anchor chews at my foot, twisting its hooks into me. I bend toward it, my fingers fumbling at it in the murk. I feel bars, and then three hooks, the ones pinioning my ankle. It's a grill. The fat, industrial kind our neighbor keeps on his patio.

My lungs are throbbing in my chest, begging me to fill them. I push my foot toward the grill, then ease it off the hooks, a blessed relief engulfing my leg. I kick a few times, not sure which way to go, but I pop up like a cork. The gold roof of my SUV is still sticking out of the water, like a tiny island. I kick to it, holding my arm to my chest. When I reach it, I swing my good arm up over it, but I can't pull myself up. My upper body is too shaky, too weak. I press my palm against the car, feeling my body being inched along by the current.

"Hazel," I hear beside me.

Luke grabs the roof next to me, raising himself out of the water. He turns around, grabbing under my armpits and pulling me up beside him. A cry escapes me as my shoulder contracts with pain, but it ebbs.

Luke's hand presses against the space between my shoulder blades, and a few muttered words leave his lips. Warmth explodes in my lungs and I cough—or maybe vomit—until all the water is out of me.

"Are you okay?" Luke asks, breathless.

"I think so," I say, pulling the two splinters from my hand.

The SUV shifts underneath us, bucking like it's alive. It starts to slide into the flow, revolving slowly. We lose our balance, falling onto our hands and knees. Luke pulls me in closer, wrapping his arm around my waist.

The car floats, rocking back and forth between the rows of houses. Other cars bob around us along with trashcans and branches. The rain keeps blinding me, wiping out my vision with water, but I know we're moving toward the river, pulled by the force of it.

"We need to grab something," I try to say, but it comes out as a rasp. "We need to get on top of something else."

Luke nods, swiveling his head to look. "We're going to pass that house up there, right by it. I'll grab the roof and pull you up."

We sweep toward it, the SUV listing to the right. A tree comes into our path, one of the tall bur oaks that make up the woods around my neighborhood. Its branches scrape the water, too low to pass under.

"Hold on," Luke says, realizing the same thing.

The front of the car slams into the tree, and we both slide off the front of it. Luke spins off to the left, and I catapult into a nest of branches.

They scratch at my clothes, tangling in my hair as I'm dragged through them. My body snags on one, and I gulp as my throat closes.

The onyx. The cord is stuck on a branch. I grasp at it behind my head, trying to free it as the flow pulls my body in the opposite direction. The cord is twisted, impossible to get free of. I rip down branch after branch, but nothing releases it.

The cord sears against my skin, cutting deeper. I keep swallowing, trying to get a breath down. I can hear myself gagging over the water.

Something dives from the sky, rushing at me. Sharp claws tear at my face, and I brace my arm in front of myself, feeling a flurry of feathers beat against my skin. It's here, the witch-bird. The *lechuza*.

It dives again, a shriek tearing out of it. One claw circles around my wrist, the other reaching for the stone under my jaw and slicing my chin. With my last surge of energy, I throw her off, hurling her against the branches above me.

"You can't have it!" I scream at her.

The owl-bird scrabbles for a grip, righting herself and climbing over the branch. She stares down at me, her dark eyes watching patiently.

Water rushes over my head, filling my mouth, but I spit it out.

This will not happen, I tell myself. I won't let it. Not when my mother died to keep me alive. It isn't ending like this, coated with mud and swallowing debris.

I reach for the branch over my head, my fingertips brushing it each time I bob up. If I can't get up to it, I'll make it come down to me.

I feel the strength of the current around me, so much energy to pull from. I let it sink into my body, filling my joints, racing along my limbs. I'm not even thinking, I just reach one last time for the branch, letting the energy rush out of me all at once.

As soon as my fingers touch it, the branch ignites. Flames race up the trunk, lighting up the bark like a bonfire. I shut my eyes against the brightness of it, the heat licking my face. Steam rolls off the wet bark in clouds. The owl-bird screams, so like a human scream, and plummets into the water, her wings trailing fire like a comet flying through the night.

The branch holding me collapses, dunking me back into the river. A static roar meets my ears as my body tumbles along, but I'm too spent to fight it. The pressure lessens as I float back up, and I scissor my legs a few times until my head surfaces.

There's a tug at my sweatshirt, something snagging me as I pass, but I'm already gone. My body feels detached, like I'm dragging a hundred-pound weight behind me. Even my eyelids are too heavy to lift. There's nothing to do but let myself drift into the blackness.

My good hand closes around the onyx, tucking my thumb across my fingers. I can't believe there's a time I'd be happy to feel its persistent warmth reminding me that the onyx is still mine, still my burden to carry.

CHAPTER 25

LOST THINGS

When I open my eyes, Abby, Wyatt, Dad, the twins, and Luke are all circled around me. I blink over and over just to confirm I'm really staring at a ceiling above me. My back aches. My spine is pressing into something hard, so I move the thin blanket off me, drawing everyone's attention.

"Hey, sweetie," my dad says, helping me sit up on my elbows.

My skin is tight with dried dirt, and Luke looks like he just crawled out of a street drain.

"You sure can sleep," he says. "It's midday. You slept through the rest of the night."

"You pulled me out," I say, the words raking out of my throat.

"I grabbed you when you went by. After..." He stops himself, his eyes darting to my dad.

So it did happen. It wasn't just some figment of my dying brain. I set a tree on fire.

"Where are we?" I ask.

"At the hospital," dad says. He's still in his pajamas, but they're cracking with dried gunk. "A lot more people are in worse shape than you, so they said it could be a while."

"You got out," I say, my eyes stinging like I might cry, but no tears come. "Everyone did."

"Pretty lucky, considering," he says. He climbs to his feet. "I'm going to get you a pillow, honey. The nurses here are just too swamped to do anything."

He paces off down the hall, limping just slightly.

Realizing the onyx isn't around my neck, I bolt upright, my shoulder immediately seizing up. I grunt, grasping it.

"It's here," Luke says, pulling a folded handkerchief out of his pocket and handing it to me.

I turn it over in my fingers, feeling the weight of the stone in my palm. I pull back a corner, just to make sure, and am met with the dark face of the onyx.

"All that for nothing," Luke says bitterly. "Idra is probably having a fit."

"You mean Idra caused a flood?" I ask.

"That's what she does," Luke says. "She can gather the power to summon storms, but it kills her mind. She has no sanity left, she just acts on emotions. She's easy to manipulate. That's why Isolda needs her. She'll keep coming after the onyx until she has it, and everyone is gone."

I tuck the onyx into my crusty pocket, its warmth persisting even after being in freezing water.

"Stolam knows where Faolan's body is buried. They're going to find it and bring him back. Gemmie went to stop them, but who knows if she can get there in time?"

"How do you know that?" Wyatt asks.

"Gemmie wrote us a letter. I'll show it to you when we get back to the house."

Everyone's faces fall simultaneously. It's quite an impact spread across five people.

"What?"

"We were fine up on the second story," Charlotte says. "When the water went down, we came out. That's when the house...just kind of went '*ffutt*'." She makes a gesture with her hands of something collapsing in the middle.

The blood runs out of my hands. "The house is gone?"

Charlotte nods. I lay back for a moment, my head spinning with the thought. Mom's journal. My eyes burn again, but still no tears. A hole rips into my stomach, aching with emptiness. Mom's journal is gone. It's almost as if I've lost her all over again.

"We have to do the spell." The words come out of my mouth before I realize I'm speaking. I sit back up on my elbow, meeting eyes with Luke.

"She will never get it. She will *never* get him."

Luke nods, unblinking.

Even before I was born, Stolam was taking from me. It stole my mother, my childhood, my normal life, my home. And still, it wants more. Faolan wants us dead. Isolda wants eternal life. I'm going to do everything in my power to make sure they never get what they want.

I'm going to finish what my mother started. I'm going to purge the world of Faolan Sicari

———

The Binding Stones continues in
Moonstone & Obsidian.

THANK YOU FOR READING

Did you enjoy this book?

We invite you to leave a review at the website of your choice, such as Goodreads, Amazon, Barnes & Noble, etc.

DID YOU KNOW THAT LEAVING A REVIEW...

- Helps other readers find books they may enjoy.
- Gives you a chance to let your voice be heard.
- Gives authors recognition for their hard work.
- Doesn't have to be long. A sentence or two about why you liked the book will do.

Don't miss out on your next favorite teen or new adult read!

Join the Fire & Ice mailing list at
www.fireandiceya.com

Perks include:

- First peeks at upcoming releases.
- Exclusive giveaways.
- News of book sales and freebies right in your inbox.
- And more!

ABOUT THE AUTHOR

Kate is from Austin, TX, and grew up with an insatiable desire to play make believe. She loves all things magical and fantastical, and spent a month in Mexico researching *Curanderas* and *Brujas* to add validity to *The Binding Stones*. Her aim in writing is always to blend cultures and beliefs, since she believes the future generations are meant to be a wonderful mix of the world. Now, she lives in Los Angeles with her horse, and is still playing make believe every day.

Twitter: https://twitter.com/kate_says_yall
Instagram: https://www.instagram.com/kate_says_yall/
Tumblr: https://www.tumblr.com/blog/kate-says-yall
Pinterest: https://www.pinterest.com/Zenikgirl/